KiLLiNG JACK ARMSTRONG

For Troy & Tracy,

Bob Bach

BOB BACHNER

KiLLING JACK ARMSTRONG

LIBRARY OF CONGRESS CATALOGING-IN-PUBLICATION DATA

Killing Jack Armstrong
Authored by Bob Bachner

ISBN: 9781737249146
LCCN: 2021950716

For Bob Brader
Who made our family complete.

IT WAS TIME.

I put on the Army field jacket and checked it for the third time. I had put a pair of surgical gloves in my breast pocket, a ski cap in the left side pocket, and the little pouch with the picks, mini-wrench and screwdrivers in the right. I opened the Wilson tennis bag. Galoshes, a wire hanger, the sawed-off shotgun and a box of shells. All present. I'd be in big trouble if a policeman saw the shotgun, but in just a few hours it would be at the bottom of the East River. It was a Remington side-by-side I had bought in Watertown, taken to the woods and test fired. I hadn't come close to the tree I was aiming at from fifty feet or so, but he wouldn't be that far away tonight. I had sawn off most of the barrels, following the instructions I had read in some crime novel.

I put on my rain hat, picked up the bag and went to the front door of my apartment and reached for the handle. It wouldn't turn. I hadn't even been in a fistfight since the ninth grade. It was one thing to go through the preparations, but I was never going to be able to finish it, to pull one or both triggers and blast away another human being. I tried to let go of the door handle to go back into the room, but my hand wouldn't open, and I heard a voice inside my head.

You have to do it. You swore you would.

I turned the handle, opened the door, and set off to kill Jack Armstrong.

ON A SPRING DAY IN 1982, a couple of weeks before my twelfth birthday, Ezra Gluckstein went into the ground in the Austro-Hungarian Hebrew Free Burial Association section of the Mountainview Cemetery in Liberty, New York. The Rabbi stood on one side of the open grave looking down at the plain wooden box. He spoke to twenty or twenty-five Glucksteins of various ages standing across from him and bunched several feet in front of my mother and me like a wedge of blockers keeping us from the grave. My mother held my shoulders as I squirmed, trying to peek in between the other mourners to get a better view of what was going on and maybe hear more of the Rabbi's words before the wind broke them apart.

"Keep still, Jack," she hissed. A tall Gluckstein in the back of the group turned and glared at us.

A few drops trickled from the April overcast, and the Rabbi's voice picked up speed. He was praying, now, in Hebrew, so I couldn't have followed him even if I had heard him clearly. The other Glucksteins had no such trouble and responded in places on cue, the old men *davening* in rhythm to the sing-song voice. The Rabbi stopped. The group before us stirred as one or two people broke off from the edges and moved forward.

"Can we go now, Ma?" I asked.

"Not yet, but soon."

The group melted away. People walked up to the grave, reached down to the pile of dirt beside it, picked up a clod, said a word or two, then deposited the clod into the grave. They all did it differently—some gave a gentle underhand toss, others extended their arms and dropped the clod and some pushed it away from their bodies as though it were burning their hands. The Rabbi read from a prayer book, nodding to each Gluckstein as he or she passed. Next to him, stood Ezra's parents, my *zaydie*, Morris Gluckstein, with his arm around my *bubbie*, Esther Gluckstein, who was sobbing. Past the grave, a line of mourners trod carefully down the muddy path. Some of the women in the line were also crying.

I supposed I should be crying, too. My father was gone from my life forever. But I wasn't sad. I wouldn't miss him. Not that he had been some kind of monster like Doug Swensen's father who got drunk every few weeks and knocked Doug and his mother around. As long as I could remember, my father had avoided physical contact with me. Fathers of the boys I knew hugged their sons, roughhoused with them, maybe swatted them if they misbehaved. Not Pa—most of the time it was like I wasn't even there. When he spoke to me, usually to tell me what I'd done wrong, he addressed a point just above my left shoulder, as though he couldn't bear to look at my face. If Ma was in the room he wouldn't speak to me at all; he would send messages through her, not even using my name.

"Tell the boy that, if he can't get home in time for supper, he will go to bed without it."

"How did the boy tear his new jacket? Does he think money for clothes grows in the back yard?"

"Tell the boy he has deliveries to make this morning before he can go to baseball."

The last of the group moved toward the grave.

"Come on, Jack." My mother gripped my hand and stepped forward.

"No," I resisted. I didn't know what it meant, this business with the dirt, but I didn't want to do it.

I didn't want to think about the box in the hole or what was in the box. I didn't want to walk between the stern Rabbi, his nose dripping into his speckled beard, and my grandparents, my grandfather glowering as he pointed out my mother and me to my sobbing grandmother.

"We have to." My mother yanked me after her, like she never did.

I stumbled but recovered and came along, certain she would drag me behind her if I resisted.

After a few steps she let go of my hand. "Straighten up," she ordered. She marched me up to the grave, her eyes fixed, ignoring the trio standing next to it.

Out of the corner of my eye I saw *Bubbie* Esther shake her fist at us. "He's dead because of you and your *momser*."

That wasn't right. I hadn't done anything to Pa, and I was sure that Ma hadn't either.

"Shush, Esther." *Zaydie* Morris put one hand over her mouth and waved the other at us in dismissal.

My mother gave no sign that she had heard either of them. She bent over, and, in one motion, reached for some dirt and dropped it into the grave. She turned to me. "Now, you, Jack, then we can go."

I bent down and picked up a handful of dirt, damp and slimy with the rain. I looked into the hole at the unpainted wood coffin, covered except for one spot at the end. I tossed my dirt squarely in the middle of the bare spot. "Tell me I didn't do that right," I muttered.

As soon as we were out of earshot of everyone else I asked, "Why did she say that? What did we do?" She squeezed my hand. "Don't worry, Jack. You didn't do anything. I'll tell you later."

The rain started to come down seriously, flinging handfuls over us every time a gust of wind blew the umbrella off to the side. Ma spread her raincoat over me, and we stumbled and slipped down the muddy path like some giant broken-winged bird. I climbed into the passenger seat, fastened my seat belt and turned to look at my mother. She was bent over the steering wheel, her forehead resting on the backs of her hands.

"Ma, are you OK?" I asked. No answer. "Ma?"

"Just give me a minute."

I waited a little, then began the Prayer for the Starting of the Old Car. That always got a smile out of Ma. *"Baruch atoh adonoi ..."*

"Not today, Jack, please. I need a minute of quiet before it all begins."

She sounded so desperate that, for once, I kept my big mouth shut and didn't ask her what "it" was until we had gotten home to the four rooms above the store on Ackerman Street in Saugerties where I spent the first twelve years of my life.

The store was perched near the top of Ackerman Street as it twisted its way between weed-covered curbs up from the Esopus Creek toward Locust Avenue. It had been a clean, white-frame house; you could see the original paint in places where subsequent coats of green and gray had worn away. Most of the cedar shake roof was still up, although replacement boards were nailed here and there. Patches of concrete spotted the red brick chimney, and the rusted metal cap dangled precariously, which didn't bother Pa who didn't use the fireplace because firewood was too expensive. The front porch sagged, and the front door, warped and burdened with locks, seemed designed to keep customers out rather than invite them in. The front windows were so dirty you could hardly see the piles of cans and boxes set up for display years ago and never renewed. The shutters over the windows of our apartment were warped and wouldn't shut.

After I changed from my suit into jeans and a sweater, I came into the kitchen. Ma poured a cup of cocoa from the saucepan on the stove and put it at my place at the table next to a plate with a peanut butter and jelly sandwich. I picked them up and turned toward the living room and the recently purchased TV set. I would never have done that if Pa had been there.

"Sit down, Jack, I need to talk to you."

That wasn't fair. I had behaved myself all morning. "Why can't I watch the game, Ma? You're not opening the store, are you?" I knew she wasn't, because I had taped the sign in the window myself. "CLOSED DUE TO DEATH IN THE FAMILY. WILL REOPEN MONDAY."

She pointed to my chair. "No, we're not opening the store today. But we'll have to, early tomorrow and the next day and the days after that for as long as we can."

I sat back down. "What do you mean, 'as long as we can?'"

"I can't run the store by myself, Jack. It's too much for one person."

I had never thought about that; it seemed natural that both Ma and Pa were almost always in the store with customers or stocking the shelves or something, or, if not in the store, then on the telephone ordering or at the kitchen table paying bills or just arguing about it.

"I can do lots of stuff."

"I know. You're a big help already. But you have to go to school. It needs two people, full time, and at least one of them should be a man. Too many people think they can take advantage of a woman, short her on orders, slip a can into their pockets when she's not looking, buy on credit 'Just until payday,' then never catch up. Ezra watched everyone like a hawk, thought the whole world was out to cheat him. It wasn't nice, but maybe it was necessary."

"Can't you hire someone? What about George?" George Kluzewski was a man without a regular job who worked in the store most Saturdays or Jewish holidays when Ezra's religion kept him out. I didn't learn, until later, that, if Ezra were really observant, he wouldn't let his wife or son work those days either, but that hadn't seemed to bother him.

"George won't work at anything full time. Anyway, the store doesn't make enough money to pay anybody a decent salary. We could only scrape by because we lived here and got our food from the store. I don't know what we're going to do." She slumped in her chair and ran her hands though her hair, a shawl pulled over her shoulders like a middle-aged woman, although she was barely into her thirties. She wore no makeup; lines crossed around her eyes; the corners of her mouth were drawn tight, and dull brown bangs framed her face like curtains around a stage on which a story of unremitting misery was playing out.

This was terrible. I had been thinking that with Pa no longer around being mean to both of us, Ma and I would just go on, working hard, of course, but happy. It had never occurred to me that Pa had been necessary for our continued existence.

My face must have shown my panic, because she straightened herself, smiled and was transformed back into the indomitable mother I was used to. "Don't worry about it, Jack. It'll be all right. We'll work it out, somehow. That's not what I want to talk to you about. There's something you need to know, and this is the time to tell you."

I took a bite of my sandwich. She didn't say anything at first, while I tried to figure out what she was going to tell me.

When she spoke, it was the last thing I might have expected. "That wasn't your father, who was buried today."

How could that be? I mean I hadn't looked into the coffin myself, but everybody seemed sure that the man inside was Ezra Gluckstein.

My confusion must have shown. My mother reached across the table and captured the hand that wasn't holding the sandwich. "What I'm telling you, is that Ezra Gluckstein wasn't your father."

That was less confusing, but no less incredible. For twelve years Pa had been my father. Suddenly, he wasn't,— I mean, hadn't ever been. I didn't know what to believe. "Who was?"

"It's a long story. Can you let me tell it all my way, without interrupting? Please? I don't think I can do it right, otherwise. When I'm finished you can ask questions. OK?"

I nodded and she let go of my hand and began.

"Have you ever wondered why I never talk about my family and where I grew up?"

I had been too young to give it much thought, but when she said that it did seem strange. I knew my father's family. He had taken us over to Liberty once a year at Rosh Hashonah and I had met my grandparents and various uncles, aunts and cousins. They hadn't been friendly except for *Tante* Sarah, my father's youngest sister, the same age as my mother. She had played with me when I was little, still gave me a big hug each year and had driven over to Saugerties once last year to introduce her new husband. Of my mother's family, I knew nothing.

"I don't know, maybe. You grew up in Brooklyn, didn't you?"

"That's right. My maiden name was Taub. My mother died when I was very young, and my father never remarried so I had no brothers or sisters. My father came to America from Hungary after the War, got into the diamond business and made enough money so he could hire women to take care of me while he was at work or at the *shul*, which was almost all the time. He wasn't mean to me; he was just a shy man, a widower, only comfortable in his shop or the *shul*, with no idea of how to raise a young girl. He probably should have remarried. He faithfully observed Jewish law and the pronouncements of our Rabbi, which made him very strict about what I could and couldn't do. I had little exposure to the world outside Williamsburg. Once a year, my father would bring me with him to his booth in the Jewelry Exchange on 47th Street, and I would squirm on my stool while I watched the customers. I saw no movies or television. We had a radio, but the Rabbi told us what programs we could listen to. I wasn't allowed to play it myself. As a treat for me, sometimes we would listen together to music on WQXR."

I must have been fidgeting, because she said, "Please, Jack, be patient. This isn't easy for me. Starting when I was ten, my father began to rent a bungalow near Monticello for July and August. I would stay up there with Essie, the widow of a cousin of my father, and my father would come up Friday for the weekend. During the week I went to a day camp until I was too old for it; then I just hung around the bungalow bored to death and driving Essie crazy.

"Starting when I was thirteen or so, the rules were being relaxed a little in the neighborhood. My friend, Raquel, had a television set in her house, and we sometimes sneaked looks at it when her parents were out of the house. What interested me were programs like Dobie Gillis that showed me current clothing, makeup, relations between boys and girls—all things strange to me. Current events didn't concern me. I knew that the United States was at war in a place called Vietnam. They drafted Schlomo Bernstein, who lived next door. I had only the vaguest idea what the war was about and had no notion that there was any opposition to the United States' involvement in it.

"The summer of 1969 was just before my Senior year in high school, and I wanted to work. I pestered my father until he got me a job as a waitress at a kosher hotel a half-hour bike ride from our bungalow. Essie came up, too, and spent most of the day happily gossiping by the pool in the bungalow colony and paying little attention to what I did when I was off work. Sometimes I would sleep over in the employees' dormitory and tell Essie that I had to work overtime and was too tired to bike home. I wasn't tired—we would party until three or four in the morning, sleep three or four hours and go back to work. I had more freedom than ever before and was having a very good time."

I shook my head in disbelief. My mother didn't "party" except for my birthday, when she would put candles on the evening's dessert and give me one present from her and one supposedly from Pa who had obviously never seen it before.

Her voice became bitter. "I was very different, then, from what I've become.

"Then the big Woodstock festival got shifted to Bethel which was only a few miles away from where I worked. It was going to be maybe the biggest party of all time. Most of the young employees I had gotten friendly with were trying to figure out how to go for at least part of it. With my father coming up for the weekend, it would be impossible for me to go to the festival without him knowing it; if he knew, he would never allow me to go. I was resigned to a big weekend going to *shul* with my father and having the regular Saturday night dinner with him and Essie.

"Then a miracle happened. The Monday before the festival, my father called. Someone very important to his business was coming from Europe, and my father would have to stay in New York for the weekend. He hoped I wouldn't be too disappointed. I couldn't believe my luck. I was sure I could come up with a story that would fool Essie and let me go to the festival."

My mother got up from the table and went to the stove. "A little more cocoa?" she asked. I held out my cup and she poured some in. "Another sandwich?"

"No, thanks, but can I have a cookie?"

She went to the jar and brought back two Toll House cookies, handed me one and sat down again.

"The next day I asked around at the hotel and made arrangements with a girl named Peggy who lived nearby. Her older brothers had been into camping and she got us two sleeping bags and a tent. I had plenty of money—there hadn't been anything for me to spend my pay on—and I went to the grocery store and bought boxes of Saltines and Ritz crackers, cans of tuna, sardines and peaches, six-packs of Coca-Cola and 7-Up and flashlights and candles to light the tent. We stored everything in a vacant locker in the dormitory. I called my father, that night, and told him I had been invited to spend the weekend with Helen Applebaum, whose family was also Orthodox and would take me with them to their *shul*, a different one from the one my father and I went to in Monticello. He gave permission, delighted that I wouldn't miss services. Of course, there was no girl named Helen Applebaum, but, as I expected, neither he nor Essie asked for the address and telephone number of the Applebaum family."

This was amazing. My mother was always so truthful. I couldn't imagine her capable of such deceit. And with her own father? Wasn't she constantly telling me how good Jews always respected their fathers?

"Peggy and I ended our shifts at four o'clock on Friday and managed to get all our stuff onto our bikes and in our back-packs. We had been a little worried that there might be no tickets left, but the word came back that the fences were down and it was going to be free, so we weren't surprised when we reached the Monticello-Bethel highway to find a long line of kids trudging between rows of abandoned cars. We passed them on the bikes and got to the grounds while the first performer, a singer named Richie Havens, was still on stage."

She paused and looked away for a few seconds. When she resumed, her voice was stronger. "Jack, you can't believe what it looked like. Thousands of kids covered the hillside with a huge stage far below. They ended up with like 500,000 people. We couldn't camp anywhere near the stage, but even out in the fields you could hear the music on the loudspeakers. We found room in a field where there were a lot of other tents. A family with two little children greeted and invited us to camp next to them and even offered us marijuana. Peggy took some, but I was afraid. I didn't even smoke cigarettes. A couple of guys helped us set up our tent."

This was taking too long. I wanted to hear about my father, not Woodstock. I had seen a book about it at a friend's house. It was just a lot of people sloshing around in the mud, but everybody makes a big thing about it. Why was Ma going on this way? She paid no attention to my fidgeting and yawning and, if I tried to say something, she would shush me without even slowing down.

She continued. "We decided to eat something before trying to get to the stage. The guys who had set up our tent brought over a little stove and heated their soup and coffee to eat with our tuna fish and bread. They were in their early twenties and seemed like nice guys. Terry was mostly paying attention to Peggy. That meant Jack and I paired off, which was all right with me. He was funny, and I liked his smile.

"After we ate, we decided that Jack and I would try to get over near the stage for a couple of hours, while Terry and Peggy would watch our bikes and stuff. Then we would come back and they would go. We worked our way pretty close to the stage. Standing in the middle of that huge mass of people as it grew dark with the music blasting all around us was something awesome. After a while, Jack and I returned to the tent while the others took their turn. We drank a little wine and talked. Jack told me he was active in the movement against the Vietnam War. You probably don't know much about that time, do you?"

I shook my head.

"Well there were many protests at rallies and marches, and some people even set off bombs. Jack was involved in the movement. I think he would have liked to recruit me, but I wasn't going to leave everything to set off bombs and things like that. He said that he and Terry would be doing something very important a few days after the festival, but he couldn't tell me what. He couldn't even tell me his real name. He had taken the name 'Jack Armstrong' after a character on a radio adventure series. And Terry was 'Terry Lee,' which was the full name of the hero of the comic strip 'Terry and the Pirates.' It was very exciting, and I thought he was very brave to be risking jail or worse for his beliefs."

Her voice was slowing, but she kept on. "It started raining and we went into our tent. When Peggy and Terry came back, Terry and Jack brought their sleeping bags and we all crammed into the tent together. The water was running in under the tent and the bags got soaked and nobody slept much. The next day, after breakfast, Peggy and Terry went back to the stage, and Jack and I went into the tent to take a nap."

She put her hands flat on the table, looked directly at me and said slowly, "And that's when it happened."

"What happened?" I don't know how I could have been so thick. I mean I was almost twelve and knew enough about these things, and the whole story was being told to lead up to this conclusion. Maybe I wanted to punish her by making her say it explicitly. I don't know.

She looked down at the table, then back up at me. "You happened. That's what happened. And somewhere out in the world is a man who used to call himself 'Jack Armstrong,' who has never seen you and whom you'll never see. He's your father."

How could I believe that crazy story? I think I shook my head or something. She got up from the table, saying, "Wait a minute, you might as well see what he looked like."

She went into their bedroom and came back with her little jewelry box and a tiny key. She opened the box and pulled out the tray with her few pieces of costume jewelry. Underneath was a faded Polaroid color photograph, which she handed to me. It showed two girls and two young men, their arms around each other's shoulders, standing in front of a tent. "He's the one on the right," my mother said.

He didn't look like much. He was no taller than the women. His clothes were muddy, and he had long, streaked blond hair pulled back into a ponytail. He was grinning, showing all his teeth like a dog about to be thrown a ball. His eyes were close together around a sharp nose. The other man was definitely better-looking. But where was my mother? One girl had blonde hair, almost white, so it had to be the other one. But my mother looked nothing like this laughing beauty whose light brown hair glinted in the sun, her shoulders thrown back emphasizing her breasts in a knotted man's shirt.

"Ma, is that you?"

She nodded. "Yes, I used to look like that. So, what do you think of your father?"

"I dunno. Do I look like him?"

"Not much. You have his eyes; that's all. Go look in the mirror."

I did, holding up the photograph to compare. She was right. I didn't look like him. I brought back the photograph. She put it back in the box, covered it with the tray, locked the box and took it back to the bedroom.

"What happened then, Ma?" I asked when she returned to the kitchen.

"He's gone, that's all you need to know. I don't want to talk about it anymore." She pointed to the window. "It's still pouring. You'd better go downstairs and empty the tub under the leak."

The store stocked groceries and anything else Ezra believed could be sold to the poor families unfortunate enough to be stuck in that neighborhood. His marketing judgment was terrible; as a result, a fair amount of his inventory was quite old. Needing space, he had built a one-story extension in the back and filled it with cartons of unsold cans of kippers, vichyssoise and hearts of palm, boxes of bulgur wheat, confectioner's sugar and flavored coffees, along with passed-over magazines and broken kitchen appliances put out to pasture. Intending it for storage only, he had built on the cheap and not provided heating. When the roof developed leaks, Ezra would patch them with whatever was handy. The latest leak had developed the day before he died, and Ma had put an old washtub under it pending what we all expected would be his rapid recovery. He had coughed for years, sometimes more, sometimes less. Ma, too, had coughing spells, but Ezra had never been willing to spend money on a doctor for either of them. This time, he couldn't seem to stop and had gone to bed "just for today." That night, Ma slept on the living room couch to get away from the coughing. When she came into the bedroom in the morning, she found him dead. "Pneumonia," she told me.

I picked my way along the narrow aisle between the boxes and the piles of magazines to the tub, which was located next to the family's former refrigerator. Above the refrigerator was a battered wooden sign proclaiming "Thompson's Market." Mr. Thompson had been the previous owner of the building, and it has since occurred to me that Ezra might have kept the sign as proof that he wasn't the only person stupid enough to try to do business in this unprepossessing location.

I couldn't lift the full tub, so I had to hunt for the dented cooking pot without a handle that I remembered was somewhere in the extension. It took a few trips to the back door with the pot to lighten the tub, which gave me time to consider

Ma's remarkable story. My first reaction was joy to discover that the cold, mean, stingy man who cared for nothing except money and whatever rules of Orthodox Judaism he accepted was not my father. I would not have to grow up to be like him. I could be a bold, romantic figure fighting injustice—sort of a Lone Ranger minus mask and horse. Like the man whose picture she showed me, fighting against a bad war. Even if he didn't look like much.

But, then, I realized something not so good. When *Bubbie* Esther had referred to me as a *momser*, a bastard, she was using the term literally, not just as a figure of speech. It was not a good thing to be a bastard, or else the term wouldn't be used as an insult. All the kids I knew were children of married parents, even the few whose parents had subsequently been divorced. Why hadn't mine gotten married? Did that make my mother a bad woman? She didn't even know my father's real name. It was very puzzling. I wanted to know more, but when I came back upstairs, she refused to answer any of my questions, but kept saying, "That's all you need to know."

MA WAS FIRM. SHE WOULDN'T TALK ABOUT my father anymore although I pestered her pretty often over the next few weeks. I finally learned the rest of the story—you could call it my story—a few months later. One afternoon, Ma announced that she had found a buyer for the store and building and that we were moving to New York City. That was terrific news. Ma's attempt to reassure me about our future hadn't really succeeded. I was expecting that any day we'd be out on Ackerman Street with no money and no place to go. And the alternative, staying where we were, wasn't so appealing, either. Ezra's ghost (I refused to think of him as "Pa" anymore) haunted the building. Every time a customer came in, the tinkle of the bell over the front door made me look up expecting that Ezra was coming back from a delivery that I should have made, and the screech of the door to the freezer sounded just like his whining voice calling out his latest complaint. Giving up Little League baseball was a small price to pay to escape him. Obviously, Ma felt the same way. Her voice sang as she told me the news, and she took me out to Denny's for a celebratory dinner. When we got home, she made herself a cup of coffee, opened a Dr. Pepper for me and sat me down at the kitchen table.

"We're going to have a new life, Jakey, a good one. We're going to leave this place and Ezra behind us. And the time before Ezra, too. So I'll tell the whole story to you now, this once, and we can put it away forever.

"After Woodstock, I continued working as a waitress, going back to the bungalow pretty much every night. I didn't feel like partying anymore. I had been to the party to end all parties; anything after that would have been a letdown. Jack and Terry went off on their secret mission. Before he left, Jack promised me that he would call me as soon as it was completed. Three days later, the newspapers reported that a bomb had exploded at Fort Drum, in Watertown, New York. There were no injuries, and the damage was limited to one Army truck and one jeep. A witness reported seeing two men, right after the explosion, get into a light-colored car and drive away from the place where the perimeter fence had been cut. The witness had seen their faces by the car's interior light, which had gone on when they opened the doors. The description fitted Jack and Terry. The next day, a white Chevrolet was found abandoned at a marina on the St. Lawrence River, and a missing boat suggested that the men had escaped across the border to Canada.

"The days went by with no word. Every night Essie would tell me that there were no telephone messages. She must have seen I was getting anxious but never asked me whose call I was waiting for. No news was reported that Jack and Terry had been killed or captured. At the end of August, I came back to Brooklyn and began to believe that Jack had left my life forever. I was in tears at first, but had to admit they were mixed with feelings of relief. We had no future together. He couldn't possibly fit into the Orthodox Jewish community where I'd lived my entire life, and how could I tear myself away from it to go who knew where with a mysterious fugitive? Maybe a bittersweet memory was best."

Then she discovered she was pregnant—her frightening suspicion confirmed by her doctor. That meant she had to come before her father: her rigid, moral, strictly observant father. Ma stumbled over the scene with him.

He had tottered to the edge of his desk and held on to keep from falling, while he moaned, first in Yiddish, then in English, "My daughter is dead, my poor daughter is dead." Then he straightened up, put his hands in the pockets of his suit jacket and strained until they ripped away in the mourner's tradition of rending his garments. She tried to go to him, but he backed away and wouldn't let her touch him. He insisted that she tell him the whole story, interrupting only once to curse poor Essie for her negligence. When Ma finished, he was silent for a long time, then spoke in a cold, flat voice she had never heard before, "You are no longer my daughter. But, for the sake of your poor mother's memory, I will help you. Go to your room and stay until I call you."

She went up to her room, imprisoned by her father's words, shackled by shame. A few hours later she could hear the front door begin to open and close, and the murmur of conversation, and realized friends and relatives were coming to sit *shiva*: to mourn her as dead. When the housekeeper brought her supper and told her that the last visitor had left, my mother asked if she could come down and talk to her father. The answer was "No." This was repeated throughout the next few days. In between, she read and reread the books of her childhood, brought her old toys out of the boxes in the back of her closet, did whatever she could to keep her thoughts away from the future. At times she tried to pray, but her connection with God had been broken as though He, who she had been taught was everywhere, was absent from this room.

Finally, a time came when the housekeeper told her to come downstairs, that her father wanted to speak to her. He sat at his desk, staring at a piece of paper. He still wore the jacket he had torn, which could not be changed during the period of *shiva*. A scraggly stubble had emerged around his formerly neat beard, and his hair was a tangled mess. She rushed toward him, but he held up his hand to stop her and pointed to a chair in front of the desk. The photograph of her mother, dead fifteen years, had been taken from the wall and laid face down on a corner of the desk. Ma told me that, at that moment, she wanted more than anything to turn the picture over and feel the comfort and safety that contemplation of the dimly remembered face always brought her. What stopped her, was not her father's certain disapproval, but the unreasoned fear that her mother's loving expression would have changed to one of revulsion.

She sat where she was told, head down in submission. Bereft of agency or hope, she would do whatever her father had decided.

When he spoke, it was in the same cold flat tone she had first heard a few days before. "I have consulted with Rabbi Klein, and we have found you a husband." He paused, apparently expecting my mother to react, but, in her despair, this news was no better or worse than anything else he might have said.

He continued, "We agreed that it would be impossible for you to continue to live in this community, so Rabbi Klein spoke with Rabbi Galowitz in Liberty. You have met him, haven't you?"

My mother nodded.

"He has found a young man named …" he consulted the paper in front of him, "named Ezra Gluckstein, whose family are members of Rabbi Galowitz's congregation. They are good, responsible, observant people, but have little money. Ezra has been working for several years as a clerk in a grocery store.

They would like him to have his own store, but it would take years for him to save enough money to open one. There is a store for sale in Saugerties on the Hudson not far away. I will give the young man enough money to buy and stock the store and to furnish the apartment above the store. He will marry you and acknowledge the child, when it comes, as his. The only people who will know otherwise are his immediate family. You will travel to Liberty two weeks from today and stay overnight with Rabbi Galowitz, who will perform the marriage ceremony the next day. Right after the ceremony, you and your husband will go to Saugerties, and you will begin your life as a good Jewish wife. I won't see you again."

Ma's voice broke for a moment, and she got up and walked to the window.

"Ma. Don't cry, it's over."

I started to go to her but she waved me back, then continued in a strained but even voice. "For the next two weeks, he communicated with me only through the housekeeper who went with me to buy pots, pans, dishes and other things for my new household. A man he had hired drove me in a truck to Liberty on the day before the wedding. As I left our house, my father stood at the front door, still not speaking, as though ready to bar me if I tried to turn back. I never saw him again. He died three years later."

This time I ran to her and put my arms around, crying myself. How could he have been so cruel to her? How could God have wanted such a thing?

She freed herself. "Sit down, Jack. Let me finish now so I don't ever have to tell it again.

"The next six months were a nightmare. The work in the store was endless, and got harder and harder as the child within me grew bigger and I grew tired and clumsy. Ezra never touched me, but if I didn't do exactly what he wanted, he'd call on God to witness how ungrateful I was and threaten to send me back to my father who would put me out in the street. I wanted to kill myself, but I couldn't kill the baby however much I hated it."

She looked down at the floor. "It's the truth, Jack. I hated everybody—Jack Armstrong, my father, Ezra and even you—for what you all were doing to me."

A giant fist came down on my head, but she went on before I could process it.

"Then the contractions started, and Ezra, grumbling at the inconvenience and expense, took me to the Kingston General Hospital. All my pain for the last months culminated in the delivery. You're lucky you'll never have to go through childbirth, Jack. Finally, it was over and someone gave you to me."

She paused, gathering herself to say I couldn't imagine what—certainly not what she did say.

"As soon as I looked at you, I couldn't hate you anymore. I knew that God had given you to me in forgiveness, no matter what anything my father or Ezra or anyone else might believe or might do to me. And I knew that I could survive anything as long as I had you."

Now she came to me and we hugged each other, sobbing uncontrollably, the last of my Dr. Pepper dripping from the table where I knocked it over rising to meet her.

The story ended with a ritual circumcision witnessed only by Ezra's oldest brother, who was ordered by his father to act as my godfather and to name me "Jacob" after one of Ezra's great-grandfathers, my mother couldn't remember which. There was no celebration. Then followed the grim ride back to Saugerties to the grim life she led for the next twelve years, the penance for her sin.

The rest I knew already, because I knew Ezra and the house on Ackerman Street. He was the quintessential *kvetsch*, a man destined for failure, who reveled in it, who would rather complain than engage in any other activity. In summer, it was the heat; in winter, the cold. In spring, the pollen made him sneeze, and, in autumn, dead leaves blew in whenever the door was opened. A customer would call in a big order— Ezra would put down the telephone and complain because he would have to delay his lunch to fill it, as if it mattered. Whether now or later, the soup would be too hot or too cold and the eggs too hard or too runny.

He complained to God, constantly, but respectfully, not blaming Him so much as calling His attention to his misfortunes. Blame was reserved for my mother and me. If he ran out of bread, it was my mother's fault for not ordering enough from the bakery. If he woke up early from his Sabbath nap, it must have been some noise I made and it would have been Ma's fault for not keeping me quiet. That was the worst of it—he blamed her for everything I did.

A typical episode was an occasion when I had been in a hurry to finish my chores so I could do my homework. Ezra locked up the store, came upstairs, ate his dinner and lingered over his pipe and coffee until it was my bedtime before saying, "Oh, Ruth. After you put the boy to bed, go clean up the mess he made putting out the garbage. He must want to make a party for the rats." And, of course, he wouldn't allow me to run down and clean it up myself. Throughout my childhood, I would hear that rising voice call out "Ruuuth," and my heart would sink as I tried to remember what terrible thing I had done now.

Ezra was 44 years old when he died, so he must have been over 30 when he married my mother. He was a small, thin man with a rodent-like face; he had been bald from my first memories. With his whining voice, dour personality and lack of money, he would not have been considered a catch by the young women of the Catskills. Some men in his position would consider themselves lucky to find themselves set up in business with a good-looking wife and a ready-made son and heir, but not Ezra. He often asked God in a truly incredulous tone what he had done to deserve the punishment of such a wife and son, although, I must admit, he held to his bargain and never disclaimed paternity. Also, I suppose, he gets some credit because his abuse was only verbal. He never hit me or, to the best of my knowledge, my mother.

But then, he had no need of physical threats to achieve domination of his household. My mother's coin given in consideration of the three-cornered bargain that had brought us to the damp, dark house on Ackerman Street was submission, and she didn't stint in payment. Ezra's word was her law and, reinforced by her unceasing reminders, was my law as well. After I started school and saw a little of how other men acted with their wives and children, I began to question Ezra's conduct. Ma would have none of it.

"It's none of your business what Billy Johnson's father does with Billy, and it's none of their business what your father does with you. Now, go downstairs and ask him if he wants me to make him a cup of soup."

You can be sure that I made vows and promises about the future. Someday, when I was grown, I would take Ma away with me. I would, somehow, make lots of money so she could have maids and cooks to do the housework for her. If Ezra objected, well, too bad for him. If he physically tried to stop us, I'd easily push him aside, maybe even give him a punch in the nose. But my most extravagant fantasies never included killing him. God would never forgive me if I did, and, worse, Ma would blame herself for it.

After we released each other and calmed down, I sat back in my chair while Ma got a rag and wiped up the Dr. Pepper.

I spoke first. "It's not fair. They made you marry Ezra, who was so mean to you, and you have to work so hard all the time."

"No, no, Jakey, my life hasn't been so bad; I've had you to be thankful for."

I must have felt uncomfortable at our heavy, emotional moment, because all I could think of was, "Didn't you agree not to not to call me 'Jakey' anymore?"

Her response to that was to grab me in another hug. "You'll always be my little Jakey, no matter what." She laughed.

"So now you call me 'Jack' after my real father?"

The laugh ended. "It wasn't my idea. You came home crying after the first day of kindergarten that the other kids were teasing you about your name, so we should call you 'Jack' like the Williams teenager in the next block. It was close enough to Jacob so Ezra didn't object. I didn't want to make a fuss, so it stuck."

"What do you mean, you didn't want to make a fuss? What's wrong with 'Jack?' Is it because my father never came back? He didn't know about me and you didn't know how to find him to tell him."

She shook her head. "I've told you enough. I don't want to talk about it."

"C'mon, Ma. You should tell me everything. If he's my father, don't I have the right to know?"

She thought for a while, then threw her hands into the air. "All right. It doesn't matter anymore; if you have to know I'll tell you. I did hear from him again. He called from Canada a few days before the wedding. My father was at his office, so the housekeeper answered and called me to the telephone. I couldn't believe it when I heard his voice, and I burst out with the news that we were going to have a child. He didn't say anything for such a long time that I was afraid we had been disconnected.

"I said, 'Are you there, Jack? Say something.'"

"'I don't know what to say.'"

"A knot formed in my stomach. I answered quickly, while I still could speak. 'Say you're coming to take care of me and the baby.'"

"'I can't do that, Ruth. They're looking for me all over the country. I can't possibly come back across the border for a long time, maybe even years.'"

"I tried again. 'Then tell me to come up to join you.'"

"'That wouldn't work. I have to move around a lot. Although the Canadian police aren't looking particularly hard for me, if I were too long in one place and they stumbled on me I could be extradited. I might go to Cuba in a month or two. Everything is up in the air.'"

"I made a last effort, before I choked up completely. 'I could meet you, we could get married, and I could come back here and stay by myself until it was safe for you to come back.'"

"He was sure of himself, now. 'No, Ruth. I'm in a war, wherever I am. I can't be a husband and a father for years, maybe never. It's still early on; you should get an abortion. In a big city like New York, you must be able to have it done safely. Just forget about me. What we had was beautiful, but we shouldn't let that one moment ruin the rest of our lives.'"

"'I can't,' I think I shouted into the telephone."

"'Well, you have to do what you think best.'"

"'I don't even know your real name to give to the baby.'"

"'It's probably better to keep it that way. Good luck, Ruth.' And he hung up."

She folded her hands on the table. "That's all there is, Jack. For a couple of days, I prayed that he would change his mind and call, but he didn't."

"He never called again?"

She shook her head. "No, and once I was married to Ezra there would have been no point. Maybe I was lucky; Jack might have turned out worse than Ezra. At least Ezra kept his word and gave you his name."

"That's terrible. I'm the son of a son of a bitch."

My mother got up from her chair. "Don't use that language. The past is over. We won't talk about it again. At least you have a mother who will always love you and do whatever she can to take care of you." And she went into the bathroom and closed the door to end the conversation.

I thought over what she had told me. How cruel these men, Ezra, her father, Jack Armstrong had been to the happy, laughing girl in the old Polaroid. I would have to be very good to her to make up for it. But, as I made this resolution, I remembered what Ma had said. She had hated me, as well as the others. She wouldn't have suffered so had it not been for me, for my birth. Of course, it wasn't my doing. But, there it was. Just being a good son in the accepted sense of the term wouldn't be enough to expiate that guilt. Something extraordinary was required.

And that's how I decided to kill Jack Armstrong. I refused to think of him as my father. This man was a son of a bitch or worse. He was the one who had caused my mother's problem to begin with and then smugly abandoned her, to be ground down by poverty and by Ezra. And he wouldn't even let her know his real name, probably afraid that someday one of us would come after him for money or something. It was then that I swore that I would come after him, find him and make him pay for what he did, not with his name, not with his money, but with his life.

I GOT OUT OF BED SLOWLY, trying not to awaken my mother sleeping on the other side of the blanket she had hung between our beds to give us some make-believe privacy. Exhausted by the long day's move from Saugerties, I had gone to bed early but was kept awake by the wrangling of the Pettus brothers, aged 9 and 10, who lived on the other side of the thin wall next to my bed. As soon as sleep quieted them, I became conscious of the flood of horns, sirens, squeaky brakes, and grinding gears that poured from First Avenue through our fourth-floor window left wide open to the August night. Every few minutes, a crosstown bus would reach its eastern terminus below us and sigh with relief as it came to rest. Simultaneously, like a relay racer handed the baton, another bus would utter a huge grunt and reluctantly start westward.

I tiptoed from our bedroom into the combined living-room and kitchen that constituted the rest of the apartment, closed the door, and crept along the wall fumbling for the light switch. Ugh! Something crunched under my foot and I let out a yell as I found the switch. The room was swarming with cockroaches, fleeing for shelter in the walls.

"What happened?" Ma came bursting out of the bedroom clutching at the top of her nightgown. "Oh." She looked around. "You scared me half to death, Jack. These aren't the first roaches you've ever seen."

"But so many?"

"Well, it is pretty disgusting. They're looking for all that old food we threw out. Tomorrow I'll scrub out the ice-box and get some insecticide. What are you doing up anyway?"

"I couldn't sleep with all the noise outside."

"I'm afraid that's living in the city."

It wasn't just the noise. I had my own room on Ackerman Street, and valued my privacy. The blanket between our beds didn't do much for that. And we had to share a bathroom with a stewardess who lived down the hall. My face must have shown my unhappiness, because Ma took my hands in hers and pleaded, "I'm sorry. This is a terrible apartment but it's really cheap and just around the corner from the store. We can't afford a nice place in this neighborhood just now. We weren't left with much from the sale of the building after paying Ezra's debts."

It wouldn't be easy. She had taken a job as assistant store manager in a small grocery replacing the man who had bought the Saugerties store. She would have to open the store at 6 A.M. weekdays and work until 3. On the weekends, she would have one day off and, on the other, work from noon until 9 P.M. She had to tend the cash register and keep track of deliveries of supplies, both of which she had done in Saugerties, but also had to supervise a helper, which would be new to her. It would be a tough job. I needed not to make things any tougher for her.

"Don't worry, Ma," I said as cheerfully as I could. "It'll be fine." I went back to bed and slept and woke and slept and woke as though sleep switched on and off like a traffic light.

When we woke up the next morning, my mother sent me down the hall to see if the bathroom was free, and, when

I reported that it was, she carried a bundle of clothing, towels, shampoo and soap with her and spent almost an hour doing what used to take no more than fifteen minutes in our old home. She returned, dressed in her best clothes, with lipstick and rouge on her face. I had never seen her wearing make-up; she was a different woman.

"You look terrific, Ma," I burst out.

"Thank you, Jack," she smiled, and, wow, it was almost the girl in the photograph from Woodstock. There were wrinkles the make-up couldn't completely hide. The mouth was a bit narrower, the eyes, now cautious. But it was definitely the same girl. This opportunity for a new start had brought back some of the zest shown in the photograph. Although I was too young to realize it at the time, that was my first lesson in how our faces change to reflect changes in our lives. I know I looked at faces more closely after that moment, a practice I've found quite useful at the poker table.

Ma continued. "Right after breakfast we're going to the store to talk to Mr. Baccalini, and I want to look nice. You, too. Wash up and put on your good slacks and a white shirt. People dress more carefully here, and first impressions are important."

"It's too hot for long pants, Ma."

"You can change into shorts and a t-shirt when we come back. Get into the bathroom now, while it's free."

Ma wouldn't bring food into our apartment until she had cleaned the filthy kitchen, so she took me for breakfast to a luncheonette on First Avenue. The counter and a line of tables for two along the wall filled the space. I had never eaten breakfast at a restaurant before—actually had eaten very few meals of any kind in such venues. Ezra's budget didn't include restaurants. The choices on the menu stunned me. It offered five different ways I might have my eggs prepared. I boldly ordered them "shirred" and was embarrassed when Ma asked the waitress what that was.

While we waited for our orders to be filled, I walked the length between the counter and the tables to inspect the signed photographs lining the wall. I recognized the faces of a few TV actors and actresses and the names of two baseball players, but the rest were unknown to me. Almost everybody wrote "Best wishes to Millie, from …." I guessed (correctly) that Millie was the lady with the big, bleached blonde hairdo sitting at the cash register by the door. She lived in the neighborhood and often shopped at the store where Ma worked, and they became good friends.

The shirred eggs tasted delicious along with rye toast oozing real butter, not our customary kosher margarine. As we left the luncheonette, I looked around for my next new experience in this wonderful world into which I had been miraculously transported. Just within the block where I was standing, I could see what seemed to be any kind of store one could possibly want: a Thom McAnn's Shoes, a Duane Reade drugstore, Harry's Barber Shop, Elvira's Beauty Salon, a radio and TV repair shop, and stores selling clothing, newspapers and cigarettes. Opposite me, the king of the block, a Grand Union supermarket, took up the ground floor of a shiny, white brick apartment house. How often had I heard Ezra curse the new Grand Union in Saugerties for pulling away shoppers who, by rights, belonged to him.

Ma led me across the street past the apartment house. Its 18 stories made it seem gigantic. A green canopy with the name "Mayfair House" printed in white projected across the sidewalk to the curb, where a man in a gray suit and what looked like a postman's billed hat was opening the door of a taxicab for a man and a woman to enter. Another man, similarly dressed, was holding the front door of the building open for a kid with a dog. I couldn't imagine living in a building so luxurious that they could pay people just to open doors. I thought that having a name must make it an important building like the White House or the Empire State Building but soon found lots of buildings with names.

A young man came out of the building toward us. I stopped and stared at his streaky, blond ponytail and narrow face. He was only about 5'6", too. Was it possible? Then I realized he was too young, in his early twenties. Jack Armstrong would now be in his middle or late thirties. But it was possible that he lived in this very city. How could I find him? Look, a man in his thirties, with the same color hair but cut short, came out of the Grand Union. He could be the one. It wasn't too likely that Jack Armstrong still wore a ponytail. How would I ever find my father in this huge city or in all the other cities and towns in the country? Another realization: That was the first time I had, even in my thoughts, used the word "father" for him. What did that mean? It was too difficult to comprehend. But one thing was sure—I wouldn't go back on my vow. Someday, somehow, I would find him and kill him.

Back on York Avenue we walked another block past a bank, a furniture store and a liquor store until we came to a five-story reddish stone building with "Joseph's Superette" on the ground floor storefront. The Marlborough Man, in cardboard, took up most of the window. Smaller signs advertised Coca-Cola and Cream of Wheat. A neon "Budweiser" blinked above the door.

Ma took my hand and gave it a big squeeze. "This is it, Jakey. Keep your fingers crossed."

This was the first time she had shown anxiety since the day she had announced that we were leaving Saugerties. Looking back, I wonder at her strength to leave the home and store on quiet Ackerman Street, all she had known for the past thirteen years, to come with a young boy to this rough city of trucks and cockroaches, betting everything on a job with a man named "Joseph" she had never even met. I had thought of the move as a great adventure. Everything I had experienced this first, bold morning had confirmed that. Now, I sensed a momentary shaking of her confidence that triggered the onset of panic in me, so I squeezed back as hard as I could to bolster my courage.

"Ouch," she exclaimed, and I let go. "You've gotten strong; you're not a baby anymore." We laughed together and my panic passed. And maybe hers did, too, for she took a step and firmly pulled the door open.

The interior looked a lot like our old store: two rows of shelves in the middle, the cases for meat, frozen foods and dairy along one wall and more shelving on the others. It was kept much neater, though, than Ezra had kept our store. A man sat at the counter beside the door shoving groceries into a brown paper bag with one hand while entering prices on an old cash register with the other. He looked to be in his early fifties, black losing to gray in his brush-cut hair. When he finished with the customer, he came around the counter toward us. He wore a denim apron over an open short-sleeved shirt and khaki pants. There were tattoos on both muscular arms, and his shoulders more than filled out his shirt, but he was only of medium height and seemed light on his feet. His tanned face was marred by a large nose, a twist away from being straight, and puffy scars beneath bristling eyebrows. A dangerous man, I thought; was Ma making a terrible mistake?

Ma spoke first. "Mr. Baccalini? I'm Ruth Gluckstein." She extended her hand.

The man smiled and held out both his big hands to capture hers. "Mrs. Gluckstein, welcome to Joseph's Superette. I am happy to meet you." His low, hoarse voice, with an obvious Italian accent, added to my apprehension. Years later, he sounds exactly the same, as though, in his adaptation to America, once he had brought his speech to a minimally acceptable point, he had no wish to modify it further. He turned to me and asked, "And you are …?"

"Jack Gluckstein." I held out my hand.

"I am happy to meet you too, Jack." When we shook hands, he pulled me close and looked directly into my eyes for a moment. "I hope we'll become good friends. Why don't you look around while your mother and I talk business?" I was relieved when he let me go. I felt that he had been judging me, and that, if the verdict had been a bad one, I was going to be in serious trouble. It didn't matter that his former assistant had assured Ma that Mr. Baccalini was a nice man who had been a good boss. Maybe so, but I was afraid for Ma as well as for myself.

I wandered around the store while they talked. I found strange salamis in the meat case and something called "Gelato" along with the ice cream, but the stock was generally similar to what I was used to. A couple of customers came in and brought their selections to the counter, and Ma watched while Mr. Baccalini bagged the items and put the money in the cash register. After a few minutes, a young, dark-skinned man, also wearing an apron, entered, and Mr. Baccalini called me over and introduced Ma and me to him. Luis was the helper whose job was to make deliveries, unload the groceries from the trucks, put items on the shelves and clean up.

When Ma and Mr. Baccalini finished their discussion, Ma went around the store and picked out cleaning supplies and we went back to clean out the apartment, which took most of the rest of the day. Ma seemed very pleased with what she had seen and heard, and I decided not to tell her how I felt about her new boss. It would just upset her. There wasn't anything she could do about it; she had made it clear that we pretty much depended on this job. We stopped for sandwiches back at the luncheonette and returned to the store where Ma picked out food and stuff for the apartment. There was more than even the two of us could carry, and Luis put most of it into a box on wheels, which he used for deliveries, and wheeled it back with us.

I noticed that Ma hadn't paid for any of the things from the store, and asked her about it.

"Joseph—he says everybody just calls him by his first name—didn't want any money today. He said we should start off with a full cupboard. Wasn't that nice?" She smiled comfortably. "From now on, we can take what we want from the store, but should write it down in the notebook he keeps behind the counter, and, once a month, he'll figure out what his cost was, not the price to customers, and, anything more than $100 gets charged against my salary. I think you and I can eat pretty well on $100."

To make her point, she cooked us a chicken dinner with ice cream for dessert, and we went to bed early with full stomachs and in a clean apartment. I told myself I was imagining things about Mr. Baccalini, but I wasn't convinced. I would have to be careful.

IN THE DREAM I HAD BEEN PART OF a group of men. Was it in a prison? An army camp? I didn't know where or why I was there. Suddenly we heard the menacing whine of a siren, which jolted me upright as my eyes opened. I didn't even know I was awake until the light from the street lamps and the sound of a truck came through the curtains over the open window. The whine ceased and the lamp on my mother's side of the room came on, leaking light over and around the blanket hung between our beds. I looked at my watch.

"It's 4:30, Ma. What's going on?" I called.

"It was a test. I had to find out if the alarm clock would wake me. Starting tomorrow, I'll need to be at the store by 6. Go back to sleep."

I did and slept until 7. This morning there were no roaches in the other room, and Ma had cleaned the dirt out of the corners and the stains out of the kitchen sink. A previous tenant had put up track lighting that brightened the room. We had arranged our old brown sofa and easy chairs on one side with the TV set on its cabinet against the opposite wall. The kitchen table, surrounded by four straight chairs, stood near the stove, refrigerator and sink. To complete the fiction that there were two separate rooms, the "kitchen" was covered with linoleum I had scrubbed the day before, and we had put the rugs brought down from Saugerties onto the "living room" floor. As a reminder of where we had been living, Ma had hung two reproductions of paintings of the Hudson River and a pair of bright flower prints. She had removed the photographs of Ezra's grandparents from the walls of the Ackerman Street apartment and deposited them in the trash the day we had left for the City. It was a cheerful place to sit over breakfast, and Ma was upbeat after yesterday's events.

"Lots to do, today," she chirped. "Get you registered for school, get you clothes you'll need, get me a few clothes I'll need for the store, find a temple with a *bar mitzvah* class ..."

"Wait," I interrupted. "I thought you said that I wouldn't have to be *bar mitzvahed* if I didn't want to. That it was Ezra who insisted."

She stared into her coffee cup, as though something were swimming in it. "I might have said something like that right after the funeral."

"You absolutely did, and I don't want to so that's that."

"I wasn't thinking straight, then. You're a Jew, and Jewish boys get *bar mitzvahed* to become men."

"You mean I'll stop growing if I don't, like whatshisname ... in the story?"

"Peter Pan?"

"Yeah, he's the one. Like Peter Pan. And I'll have to play with Tinker Bell? That's what'll happen to me if I don't get *bar mitzvahed*?"

Ma tried to keep her serious expression, but started laughing when I jumped up and danced around the table. After one circuit, my point made, I sat down.

"Don't be silly, Jack, you know what I mean. It's how a good, religious Jew starts off in life."

I had expected this reaction. "You mean good, religious Jews like Ezra, and his family and your father who go to temple and keep the Sabbath and eat kosher?"

She winced when I mentioned her father. I pushed on. "Do you want me to grow up like them and treat people like they've treated you and me?"

She looked back into the coffee cup, then replied, "Forget about them. There are plenty of religious Jews who are kind people. Forget about everything else. Becoming a *bar mitzvah* is something God wants you to do."

I hadn't prepared an answer to this argument, but I had thought a lot about God over the past year or so. I had prayed for things like presents and getting picked to start for the Little League team. It never worked. OK, I had been told that God wouldn't listen to that kind of prayer; I had tried it, just in case. But it didn't work any better for important things, like making Ezra go spend the weekend with his family in Monticello and leave Ma and me alone.

Ezra was a true believer. He would complain to God all week, and then, again on those Saturdays he made me walk with him the three miles to the nearest synagogue. Once there, I had seen his rapt face as he joined in fervent prayer. After the service, we weren't a hundred yards back on the road before the whine would start up again, and I'd have to listen to it all the way home. If God cared about being worshipped, He would have rewarded Ezra with something better than poverty, an unhappy marriage and death at 44. For that matter, what kind of god would have made Ezra such a cruel monster to treat Ma and me the way he did for so many years? And all the things on the news on TV? Wars and earthquakes, babies killed, people starving to death? How could Someone all-merciful do such things? Finally, if you were going to believe in God, you had to do all kinds of things that were real pains in the ass, like fasting on *Yom Kippur* and keeping Kosher and going to *bar mitzvah* classes while other kids were playing ball.

"I don't believe in God." There, it was out of my mouth. For a second came terror, but He didn't strike me on the spot, so it passed. That left Ma. I thought that she would be upset and would try to change my mind, but she didn't even sound surprised—a little sad, maybe. "That's too bad, Jack. You might be happier if you did."

"What do you mean, Ma?"

"I don't think I can explain it properly. You'll find out for yourself when you get older. I guess we'll skip the *bar mitzvah*."

I had won my objective, so it was time to change the subject. I was a just a kid, and I did what all kids do. They'll swap something of great value in the future, say a lifetime of peace of mind, just to get out of being *bar mitzvahed*. And there are no backsies. I would have liked to know whether Ma still believed, but that didn't seem to be the right time to ask. That time never came, and it's too late now.

We found Middle School 322, a big, brick building put up so long ago that the staircases at either end of the entrance hall had "Girls" and "Boys" carved in stone above the doors. We came in the back way through the concrete schoolyard by way of the gate in an eight-foot high, spiked, black iron fence. The yard was about 200 feet deep and 50 feet wide. Over the next two years I would skin and bruise my hands and knees on every square foot of it. Even though school wouldn't start for two weeks, the yard was teeming with activity. We picked our way past a bunch of boys around my age in the area nearest the fence playing some derivative of baseball using a red rubber ball. Beyond it, some girls were clustered around a big tree that looked like it was growing out of the cement. As we approached, one of them with a cigarette in her mouth ducked behind the tree. Closest to the school building, six older boys banged each other around at three-on-three basketball A number of the kids were black or Hispanic, a totally different scene than my school at Saugerties. It didn't bother me, although Ezra was voluble on the subject of the stupid, lazy *schvartzers*, who got everything handed to them by the government. As with most subjects, my mother avoided contradicting him directly, although she would grimace when he used the term and warned me never to use it myself.

The scene excited me. I could come here for the next two weeks and wouldn't have to sit in the apartment by myself while Ma was working. I loved sports and knew I could fit in. Inside, in the school office, I registered in the seventh grade, the middle of the school's three grades. After that, we walked west to Lexington Avenue, and I took my first subway ride. I knew about subways from TV shows, but actually being in the middle of the rush and the roar for the first time, knowing that I was speeding along underground, beneath big buildings and streets and hundreds of people, was a real thrill.

In just a few minutes we got off, climbed back to daylight and a department store named "Ohrbach's," which Ma had been told offered bargains. She still shook her head at some of the prices, but I guess we had no choice—we needed new clothes. We ate sandwiches at a lunch counter; then Ma treated us to a ride to the top of the Empire State Building. We could see for miles on such a clear day. Other buildings blocked off where we now lived, but I spotted a tall white building Ma said was probably Mayfair House. A plaque pointed out some other buildings and bridges and the Statue of Liberty. Way out of sight beyond the George Washington Bridge was Saugerties and my old life. My new one was at my feet.

THE SCREECH OF THE ALARM CLOCK barely woke me the next morning, and I fell back asleep well before Ma left for work. When I finally opened my eyes for good, I didn't jump out of bed as I had almost every morning that I could remember to help open the store before I could have breakfast. If I were slow in rising, Ezra's voice, more penetrating than any alarm, would pry open my eyes so that my first view of the day would be to see him bent over my bed, his face lit up with the pleasure of righteous remonstration. After his death, Ma would have let me sleep longer, but my conscience had proved even more effective than Ezra's screech, and the sound of her moving about the apartment starting her endless work day was enough to bring me out of bed.

But this morning, I had no jobs to perform, no school to attend, no obligations of any kind, except to wait for the telephone company that would be coming that morning to install our telephone. The note on the kitchen-dining room table confirmed this. Oh yes, I should also be careful about New York City traffic when I went outside. The note was weighted down with my very own house key and a dollar in change, although sandwiches for my lunch were in the refrigerator. I was free to read, watch television and, after the telephone was installed, walk about the neighborhood and, best of all, go to the schoolyard. Fortunately for my limited amount of patience, the telephone was installed by ten o'clock, and, ten minutes after that, I came through the iron gates.

My first stop was at what I learned was called punchball. The field was laid out in a forty-foot square with the playground wall serving as the line between second and third base. The batter punched a red rubber ball called a "spaldeen" and was out if it went over the second base line or hit the wall between second and third on the fly or was caught before it bounced. On a ground ball, the batter had to reach first base before a fielder threw him out. It seemed easy.

As the eighth kid to arrive, I joined one of the four-man teams. Batting fourth with two on base and one out, I had an immediate opportunity for glory. But it was not to be. I hit the ball savagely, and it shot on a line high off the left-hand wall making an automatic out. With plenty of momentum left, the ball rebounded across the field where it was caught by the first baseman before the runner on first could get back to the base. Was this a double play? If the ball had been caught before hitting the wall, the fielder could throw back to the base doubling the runner. But here, the wall had intervened. As far as any of the players knew, this had never happened before. The argument raged until someone said, "Let's ask Lloyd." At that everyone turned and flocked to the basketball court.

Lloyd proved to be a big, black kid shooting baskets. I later found out that he had lost one school year to illness and was held over in the eighth grade due to several suspensions for cutting school or various misbehaviors, which, of course, had resulted in his failing three classes. He didn't give a shit and planned to drop out the day after his sixteenth birthday, and this attitude and his size made him acknowledged king of the yard and arbiter of all disputes.

"You tellin' me the ball hit the wall an' went all the way to first base on the fly?" he asked, after listening to the back-and-forth from the two teams. "That's some big fuckin' hit. Who's the kid who did it?"

Someone gave me a shove and I stumbled in front of Lloyd. He bounced a basketball a couple of times, studied me a bit, then asked, "Wha'cha doin' here, anyway? Ya' don't go here, do ya'?"

"I will be in two weeks. Is that OK?" I still hadn't learned to watch my mouth.

Lloyd grinned. "Oh, a smart-ass. What's your name, smart-ass?"

"Jack Gluckstein."

He pretended to be chewing something tough. "Guh-luck ... uh ... Gul-luck-a-steen?"

Everybody laughed as though cued by the placards used on studio audiences for sitcoms. I managed to keep my mouth shut, this time.

Lloyd milked the laughter a few seconds, then his grin widened and his voice changed. "Sheeit. Tha's too hard a name for a po' nigger to say." He screwed up his face in an effort to think. Suddenly, the light came on. "I'm gwine call ya 'Dee Pee.'" The exaggerated accent disappeared. "Easy to say, easy to remember ... cos' you just invented a new double play. That's the official ruling." He didn't wait for the laugh this time but turned and dribbled to the basket and sunk a layup.

I knew enough not to protest, although I was burning. Nothing short of a fight would have done me any good, and the idea of fighting Lloyd was ridiculous. I also had the sense to go back to the other end of the yard with my team and stand at first base, where they put me, and pretend nothing unusual had happened. I'd be seeing these boys all school year, and being labeled a sissy who ran home because he couldn't take a little kidding would be a lot worse for me than having an embarrassing nickname. The rest of the game was a nightmare. Although I managed to keep the ball in play at bat, it was only by hitting easy bouncers right at the fielders. At first base, I missed a low throw letting in two runs and they picked me last when they chose sides for the second game, in which my performance wasn't much better. To my relief, a couple of new players showed up and I wasn't picked at all for the next game and could slip out through the gates. I had hoped that the nickname would prove to be a five-minute joke, but no, it was "Come on, DP get one hit, for Crissake," or "Can't you even catch, DP?" And I had to take it without even changing expression. At home, with nobody to see me, I collapsed onto my bed and cried with shame and frustration, and wished that Ma were there to comfort me as she had through the years. My wonderful new life had become an ordeal I would have to suffer through, mostly on my own.

Ma wouldn't be home until after three o'clock. Going back to the schoolyard was out, so I turned on the TV set. That still felt daring. In Ezra's world, daytime was devoted to work and, in my case, school and a limited amount of sports. If I were too sick for any of these functions, then I should be resting in bed, not perched in the living room watching TV. When Ezra wasn't around, with Ma's connivance, I occasionally broke the rules, but by the age of twelve, neither morning children's programming nor adult soap operas were particularly interesting. I flipped through the channels for a while until it seemed like a reasonable time for lunch, after which I went back outside to explore the neighborhood.

The most interesting thing was a big house on East End Avenue, which the policeman standing in front informed me was where the Mayor of New York City lived. I couldn't very well go inside and nothing was happening on the grounds, so I went into the park next to it and stood watching the boats on the East River until it was close enough to three o'clock for me to go to the store where Ma would be finishing. I found her and Mr. Baccalini both behind the counter, wearing identical blue aprons with "Joseph's Superette" sewn in white across the front. He saw me first.

"Look who's here," he said. "What's up, Jack?"

"Nothing."

Ma peered at me. "What's the matter?" Even from fifteen feet away she could read me. "Come here."

I shook my head. "Nothing's the matter. I just wanted to see how you were doing." I picked up a grapefruit and inspected it carefully.

"She's doing just fine," said Mr. Baccalini. "Food is food and customers are the same everywhere. Right Mrs. Gluckstein?"

"You're right about that. Excuse me." She brushed past him and walked over to me. "So, tell me what happened."

I couldn't possibly do that with that man, of all people, standing there listening. I couldn't show him weakness if I expected to protect Ma and myself from him. "Nothing, Ma. I just thought I'd walk home with you when you're done."

"Go ahead, Mrs. Gluckstein. It's ten to three. You've done more than enough for the first day. Would you like an ice cream, Jack? Or a candy bar?"

He wasn't going to get around me that easily. "No thanks. I'll wait outside, Ma." I left the store, and, in a couple of minutes, Ma came out and we started home.

"What's the matter with you, Jack? Mr. Baccalini's being very nice."

"I said 'thanks,' didn't I?"

"Yes, but your tone of voice didn't sound very friendly."

"I don't know. He makes me feel uncomfortable."

"Well, you'd better start feeling comfortable. The first thing he said when he came in at noon, was how much he liked the way I had arranged the display in the window. Then he complimented me on how neat the store looked. The lunch-time rush kept us both busy, and afterwards he said I handled the customers very well. This looks like it's going to be a really good job, so you stay on your best behavior with him."

"OK, OK, I will."

"Now, what happened to you today?"

I had some difficulty explaining the punchball game. But she got the gist of what happened well enough. "That's too bad. Maybe you should do other things during the day until school starts, and by then, those boys won't be in your class or will have forgotten about the whole thing."

I hoped she was right, but didn't feel very confident about it. Kids didn't forget things like that, and nicknames usually stuck fast. The next day, I stayed away from the schoolyard. I took my sandwiches with me and walked all the way west into Central Park and around the Reservoir. I came back to the store just before three.

Ma waved me to come over to the counter where she stood with Mr. Baccalini. He was grinning at me. I didn't like that one bit. She must have told him about what happened to me yesterday. Shit! That put him one up on me and we hadn't even started. I went over to the ice cream case and took out a popsicle before going to the counter.

"Good afternoon, Jack," he said.

"Good afternoon, Mr. Baccalini," I parroted. "Hi, Ma."

Ma frowned. I reached for the notebook where our purchases were entered. His grin broadened. "Forget it, Jack, it's OK."

Damn! I couldn't push it any more. "Thank you," I said nicely, and Ma's frown relaxed.

"Your mother tell me you have a little trouble yesterday."

Just as I thought. I had to start being careful about what I told Ma. "Nah, it wasn't anything."

"I know this neighborhood pretty well. Lots of the boys come here. Who give you the nickname?"

"Lloyd."

"Oh, I know Lloyd. He makes deliveries for me sometimes the weekend when Luis is off. Not a bad kid. Maybe I can talk to him?" He leaned forward. I had a flash of him pulling Lloyd into some alley and warning him away from me at knife point. Just what I needed.

"I can handle it myself."

He nodded. "Better that way. But, can I make a suggestion?"

"What?"

"Your mother tell you to stay out of the schoolyard until school starts. That's not so good." He reached under the counter and brought out a Spaldeen. "There's a wall at the end of 98th Street. No traffic. Go practice punching and catching. One day, maybe two. Then go back to the schoolyard."

I was stunned. He wanted to help me! And it sounded like good advice.

He continued. "Don't worry about the nickname. If they keep it, it'll mean you're in the group. I knew a boy in Italy with a big belly." He put his hands around his stomach to demonstrate. "We call him 'Grasso.' That means 'Fatty.' Everybody

51

like him. He came over here like me. Now he's tall and skinny, but everyone still call him 'Grasso' and he's proud of it, even uses it on his answering machine."

Well, I didn't know about that, but, if it meant I would fit in, I supposed I could live with "DP." I thanked Mr. Baccalini and ran out of the store up to 98th Street and practiced until my arm hurt and I had to go home for supper. I went back the next morning, and by noon, was able to hit the ball hard and low so that it would hit the ground before hitting the wall forty feet away. I went home for the bathroom and a sandwich, then went back and practiced fielding ground balls as they bounced off the wall.

The next morning, nervous but determined, I showed up at the schoolyard when it opened at nine o'clock. Nine other boys came early.

"Look, it's DP," said one in a Rolling Stones T-shirt.

"What are you doing here?" said another, a Yankee cap on backwards on his head. "You can't play punchball. Go play jacks with the girls."

I pretended I didn't hear them. They chose up for the first game and another boy and I were left out. That was no surprise. When the next game came we and two other kids who had arrived during the first game were supposed to play the winners. The kid with the Yankee cap had been on the losing team. "Hey, DP can't play," he said. "He'll stink up the game."

I might not be able to fight Lloyd, but this kid was my own size. I walked up to him. "Oh, yeah?" I said. "And just who the fuck are you?"

We stared at each other for a moment. I was just about ready to let him have it when a bigger kid, wearing cut-off jeans stepped up. "Let the kid play, Smitty. You're not so great yourself."

Now it was Smitty's turn to say "Oh yeah?" but he didn't have his heart in it and, when the other kid ignored him, he walked out of the yard. That was OK; I'd get him another time. Never let them get away with it.

I batted fourth and came up with one out and two on base. I felt as though I were batting in the World Series. I bent over, dropped the ball about a foot above the ground, aimed between the first and second basemen and swung hard and smooth as I had practiced. The ball shot away, never bouncing more than a few inches above the asphalt. The two infielders had barely started to move when the ball zipped between them and rolled all the way to the other end of the yard. By the time one of them retrieved it and threw it back I had run around the bases for a home run.

"Great hit, DP," said the kid in the cut-offs.

"My name is Jack," I answered.

He laughed and punched me lightly on the arm. "Not here," he said.

THAT ONE SWING SET ME IN PLACE for the next two years.
I had proved I could play punchball, and, although I made my
share of outs as well as hits after that particular home run, they
usually picked me early in the choose-ups. I had made a friend,
Harry Gelles, the boy in the cut-offs. Big Lloyd continued to
tease me about my name, but without malice, and, when I
took the teasing in good nature, he made me a sort of a *protégé*,
brought me into the basketball game and taught me the jump
shot. I could live with "DP" and "Guh-luck-a-steen" while I
was at Middle School 332, but I determined to do something
about those names as soon as possible.

One afternoon, Smitty started on me. We were on the
same team; he was on third base with the tying run, but I hit
the ball straight at the shortstop who threw me out at first for
the third out, ending the game.

"Way to go, DP," shouted Smitty, which I ignored. "You
really stink." Still not sufficient to start something. But when
we chose up for the next game, he refused to play on the same
team, calling me "Guh-luck-a-steen." That was permissible for
Big Lloyd, but nobody else. I got into Smitty's face. He took a
swing at me which missed. Then, I rushed him, knocked him
over and got on top and pinned back his arms.

"What's my name?" I asked.

He thought about it, so I slapped his face. "What's my name?"

He snarled at me, "Dee Pee."

I slapped him again. "What's my name, Shitty Smitty?"

He tried to get loose, but couldn't. Finally, he came out with "Jack."

"That's better. And what's your name?"

Defiantly, "Smitty."

"Not anymore. What Smitty?" I slapped him again.

He struggled for a moment then started crying, "Shitty Smitty."

I let him up and he ran out of the playground. I had no trouble from him again.

I was less worried about how I would do in the classroom than I was about the schoolyard. Ma had always made a big thing about school so I had tried my best. From the beginning, I found this school easier than in Saugerties. With more than thirty kids in most of the classrooms, even the good teachers found it hard to move the class along. I probably didn't learn as much as I should have, but getting decent grades was no problem. Ma was pleased.

I got along pretty well with the boys, particularly the ones who hung out in the schoolyard. The girls were a mystery. I hadn't had much to do with them in Saugerties and was very uncertain how to act with them, here. I just tried to be pleasant while I watched how the other guys acted with them. That way, I didn't make a fool of myself or get anybody pissed off at me.

When the weather was good, I spent most of my free time in the schoolyard, or at the ball fields and basketball courts in Central Park. Bad weather caused me a bit of a problem. I had a minimal allowance and couldn't hang out with the guys at the ice cream joint across from the school. Ice cream and candy were available at Joseph's store just by signing my name. I sometimes went up to Harry Gelles's apartment; he had his own bedroom with a big table on which we built model airplanes and played Chinese Checkers and Parcheesi, but I didn't go too often because I was embarrassed to invite him up to my own cramped place. I watched TV at home, or I'd hang around the store when Ma was there. I'd try to be helpful when Luis, the helper, was off; I'd straighten out the shelves or sweep up. Sometimes I'd hide out with a magazine in the stock room while Luis described his sexual adventures in interesting detail. He had been born in Puerto Rico, but lived in New York since he was very young and spoke unaccented English. He was a good-looking guy, and I could believe he was a great success with the girls.

One day I asked him, "Hey, Luis, how do you get the girls to do all those things you've been telling me about?"

He laughed. "You'll find out yourself, soon enough, Jack."

"Maybe, but can't you give me a tip?"

"All right, here's what's important. The girls want to do all those things, and all you have to do is give them the chance. You remember that, and you'll be a big stud." He laughed and stroked his mustache suggestively. It sounded easy, but somehow I knew it wouldn't be.

I rarely went to the store when Ma was off duty and Mr. Baccalini was there. I couldn't think of him as "Joseph," even though everybody, including Luis, called him that. He was always pleasant to me, and often waved me away when I would come to record a candy bar I had taken. But I still didn't like the frown that was so often on his rough, scarred face, like he thought "How come this kid loafs around eating candy while his mother works so hard?"

One snowy Saturday when Ma was home cleaning the apartment and I was just in her way, she asked me to go to the store for some groceries she had forgotten to bring home the day before. I was happy to put on my rubbers and winter coat and slosh the few blocks. At least it was something to do. Mr. Baccalini was busy with a customer and just nodded when I said "Hello," so I took a basket and went around the store picking up the few things. Something she wanted, mayonnaise, I think, was missing from its place on the shelf so I went to get some from the stockroom. Luis was on a break sitting on a milk crate smoking a cigarette. He jumped up as I came in.

"Oh, it's you, Jack. What's up?"

I laughed. "Why are you so nervous?"

"Joseph doesn't want me smoking in here. He's afraid I'll start a fire. I won't; I'm careful." He pointed to a coffee can next to the milk crate. "And it's snowing outside. What'cha doing?"

"You're out of mayonnaise out there," I answered.

"Look in the corner … under the pickles."

I found the mayonnaise and put it in the basket.

"You want a smoke, Jack?"

I had taken a few puffs from some of my friends, but had never smoked a whole cigarette myself. This was my chance. "Sure, Luis. Thanks."

He handed me one and I bent over so he could light it. I straightened up and took a little in my mouth and blew it out right away.

Luis laughed. "Come on, take a good drag."

I did and exploded in coughs. As though on cue, the door from the store opened and Mr. Baccalini stepped into the stock room. "Did you find … What the hell is going on, Luis?" He grabbed a fistful of Luis's shirt. "Get out!" He yanked Luis to the back door, opened it and tossed him out as easily as a bag of sugar. He turned to me. "You, too," and before I could move, he took me by the back of my mackinaw, flung me out after Luis and slammed the outer door shut.

I sprawled out in the snow. My shoulder hurt from my landing and snow melted down the back of my neck. "That son of a bitch," I raged. "He can't do that. My mother will have him put in jail. Who does he think he is, the fucking bastard?" I had been right about him all along.

"Shut up, Jack," said Luis. "He's the boss and can do what he wants."

"Oh yeah? I'll show him he can't."

Luis paid me no attention. "Shit," he exclaimed and threw a handful of snow at the closed door. "The bastard'll fire me, and I really need this job."

When I heard the word "fire," rage instantly turned to panic. What if Joseph decided to fire Ma? She had warned me to be on my best behavior with him. What would we do without this job? Lost in New York without family or friends? How could I have been so stupid?

We pulled ourselves up and shook off the snow. When we went to the back door, we found it locked against us.

"I guess that's it," said Luis. "I was thinking of getting married, too." He crossed himself and said something in Spanish. He looked so miserable that I forgot my own troubles for a moment.

"I'm sorry, Luis. I didn't want to get you in trouble."

He shook his head. "It's my own fault, Jack, not yours. I'm just a stupid asshole. I guess we have to go around the front. My coat's in there."

"Yeah, and my groceries."

We walked around and came in the front door. I hoped there would be customers so Mr. Baccalini would have to restrain himself, but the store was empty. Luis walked slowly to the counter; I made myself follow him. However bad it was going to be, I had to face it. As we approached, Mr. Baccalini stood up from his stool, scowling, and leaned toward us. His big hands gripped the edge of the counter.

"I'm sorry, Jo … Mr. Baccalini," said Luis looking down at the counter.

"Me too," I said. I tried to look straight at Joseph, but couldn't pull my eyes away from his hands. I rubbed my shoulder and rotated my arm a couple of times. It had already stopped hurting.

"You give Jack the cigarette?" Joseph asked Luis.

I interrupted, before Luis could answer. "No, I got a couple at school and this one was the last."

"Luis?" No answer. "All right, then. Go back to work. One more time you smoke back there with or without Jack, I throw you out for good. *Capisce*?"

"Yes sir." And Luis, moving faster than I had ever seen him, raced to the other side of the store and began to rearrange the vegetables.

My fear lessened—Ma's job was safe, but I was still in trouble. There was a long pause.

"Look at me, Jack." I pulled my gaze away from his hands to his face. It was still menacing. "Your mother know you smoke?"

"No, sir."

"Who's going to tell her?"

"I will, when I get home."

"You do that. And if I catch you back there again, I'll throw you out too. You hear me?"

"Yes, sir." I recovered the groceries and fled the store, before something worse happened.

My relief lasted until I reached our building. Then it struck me—I had to tell Ma. The snow had stopped, so I brushed off the top two steps and sat down to prepare what I would say. After a couple of false starts, it was clear that I should just tell her what happened, without explanation. After all, what explanation could I give? I would be contrite, but not overly so, since, after all, the big bully had physically thrown me out of the store. I had no idea how she might punish me. Whatever it might be couldn't be as bad as that moment I believed I had caused the loss of her job. With that settled, I got up and pressed our intercom button. Ma buzzed me in immediately and I climbed up to our apartment with confidence. My mother was standing at the open door. She wore an apron and held a wet mop that dripped soapy water on her shoes. Her face was grim.

"How could you, Jack?"

My confidence evaporated in the heat of her indignation. "You know?" I stumbled through the door and skidded on the wet floor, almost dropping the groceries before I could put them on the kitchen table.

"You took so long that I got worried and called the store. Joseph told me the whole story. How could you do such a stupid thing? It's just the two of us, and I have to trust you, and now I can't. What are we going to do?" She dropped the mop, pulled the apron up over her face, and began to cry.

This was worse than I had imagined—even worse than that moment in the store. I burst out crying, myself. What had I done to her, the source of everything good in my life? I had done things I shouldn't have, and she had scolded me or punished me lightly, but she had said, more than once, "You did a bad thing, Jakey, but you're a good boy."

I cried as though my world had ended, which, in a way it had. You remember the first time you discovered that your actions could cause pain to someone you love? That's when you lose your innocence—not when you fumble your way into some girl's pants. Ma let her apron drop while I was still sobbing my regrets, my promises and my pleas for forgiveness.

"That's enough, Jack," she said, and I slowly ceased my caterwauling. "You're still my son and I still love you. We'll have to start over and see how much I can trust you in the future."

"Oh, you can Ma, I promise. I'll never smoke again or do anything …"

"Stop it, Jack. I don't want to hear promises. We'll just have to see what happens. And you'd better be respectful to Mr. Baccalini, who's behaved better to you than you have to him."

That set me back a bit. "But, Ma, he threw me out into the snow."

"So what? You don't look hurt. He told me not to be too hard on you."

"Really?"

"Yes, apparently you said something to help Luis, even though you were afraid for yourself. He thought that made up for a lot. I'm not so sure he's right, but if you can come out of this with any credit at all, I won't try to take it away from you. Now put away the groceries, and I'll make supper."

We never referred to the incident again. I don't remember all the vows I made that day except the one I kept. I've never smoked a cigarette since.

I thought a lot about Joseph. That's right, he had become "Joseph" in my mind, I didn't know why. He had proved himself rough and tough with a quick temper, but had now done a couple of nice things for me. More importantly, he was treating Ma well and she was very happy in the job.

I didn't forget my earlier vow, either, although I couldn't do anything about it yet. From time to time, when Ma was at the store, I would go into her jewel box and look at the faded photograph, so I would remember exactly what he looked like. After many failed attempts, I drew a copy of his face that was a pretty good likeness and then made several copies of the copy with changes, like a beard or a moustache or changing the length and color of his hair. Some days, when I thought of it, I watched out for men in their late thirties who looked like what he probably would now, and once I stared so closely at a man that he got angry.

"I'm sorry," I stumbled. "Uh, I thought you were my father's friend, Jack."

"It's OK, kid. No, I've never been called 'Jack.' Sorry."

When I thought about it later, I realized it was crazy. First of all, I had a better chance of being hit by lightning than finding him that way. And what would I do if a miracle happened and I found the bastard? I could hardly beat him to death with my bookbag. Anything I might say would tip him off or do something else to ruin my plans. I would have to wait until I was old enough to make a good plan and carry it out. In the meantime, I would just keep the vow alive and hope that, when I was capable of acting, I'd somehow be able to locate him. I did, however, start reading about the anti-Vietnam war movement at the 96th Street branch of the Public Library and I cut out and kept any articles I came across in the unsold newspapers and magazines from the store. I kept them in an envelope marked "Personal" under a pile of my school papers in a box at the back of my closet. Ma respected my privacy, and I was sure she wouldn't open the envelope without asking me. None of the articles mentioned anyone named "Jack Armstrong" or "Terry Lee," and none of the pictures matched Ma's polaroid.

As I read these articles, I wondered, at first, why so many people had been so violently against our government over the war. I had learned a little in history classes about World War I, World War II and the Korean War, and it seemed like everybody had joined in to support our country fighting for world freedom. As I read more, I found that many people accepted that the Viet Cong and North Vietnamese were aggressors—we were fighting to stop Communism from taking over the world, and those against the war were traitors. But many others believed that the United States had no business interfering in a fight among the Vietnamese and were opposed to the killing and destruction that we brought, much of it to civilians. I wasn't able to work through the complexities of the arguments, but one thing made me feel that the government position might be the right one. Nobody who behaved like Jack Armstrong had could be a hero.

THE SMOKING INCIDENT changed the relationship between
Ma and me. Well, maybe it didn't as much cause the change
as signal that it was taking place. I had been an obedient boy,
done what I was told to do and refrained from doing what I
was told not to do. I had obeyed Ezra because he would have
punished me, or worse, punished Ma if I hadn't. I had obeyed
Ma to obtain her love and approval.

Obeying Ezra and Ma hadn't made me a good young citizen in all respects, however. Along with my friends, I stole
apples from the Carlsens' trees, threw chestnuts at the windows of the empty Glendenning house, and hammered nails
into Mr. Hiltz's tires because he wouldn't let us cut through
his backyard to get to the creek. I was more careful than most,
though, so rarely got caught.

I lived a double life at school, also. I was always current in
my homework—Ma would have known if I wasn't—and got
good grades. Being studious bought enough good will among my
teachers to earn no more than a mild rebuke for my occasional
misconduct. Although I was highly competitive at sports, I generally avoided the fights that tended to boil up out of competition.

As a result of my planning, I rarely saw my conduct distress
Ma. It came as a shock to both of us to realize that without
disobeying any express command (the possibility of smoking
had never come up), my conduct could adversely impact her

life. Obedience was not enough; she couldn't possibly warn against all the dangers I might encounter. As she had said, she needed to trust me, and to become trustworthy I had to cease being a little boy. And so, shortly before my thirteenth birthday, without benefit of a *bar mitzvah* or other ceremonial acknowledgment, I became a man.

I doubt if Ma went through that analysis—I know I didn't. But it was obvious. There were no more daily reminders to brush my teeth and change my underwear. She began to consult me about family plans and allowed me to pick out my own clothes. All good things, but there were no more occasions when she would come upon me without warning, grab me in a bear hug and attack me with kisses. And although I had been asking for it, I was a little sad that "Jakey" had been retired.

I grew more private and tried to solve my problems without her help. I made it clear that she didn't need to come straight home after her shift at the store but could stop at Millie's for a cup of tea or run some errands. I paid more attention to what she said so she wouldn't have to repeat everything and tried to anticipate what she might need or want.

But I never could have anticipated the next thing she asked me to do. One spring Sunday morning right after breakfast, she retired to her "room" on the other side of the curtain and a half-hour later came out dressed in the plain black dress she had used to wear on the rare occasions Ezra took us to functions with his family. I knew she hated that dress; she hadn't taken it out of the clothing bag since we had moved to New York. She never wore much makeup, but today wore none at all nor any jewelry, except—I couldn't believe it—her thin, silver wedding band. I had thought she had thrown it away after Ezra died, but there it was.

"What's going on, Ma? You going back to Saugerties?"

She didn't even smile. "Go put on your navy pants and a clean white shirt and find your old *yarmulke*. I'm taking you back to the neighborhood I grew up in and don't want us to look too different from everybody else there."

That didn't sound like much fun. "Why do you want to go back there after the way they treated you?"

Six months ago, she would have brushed the question aside but now took it seriously. "I've one aunt, *Tante* Leah Goldfarb, my mother's older sister, who didn't break with me. We've written to each other two or three times a year, and in her last letter she wrote she was sick and would like to see her sister's grandson before she dies. Besides, one time you should see where you came from. So, go change."

I did as Ma asked, although she had to help find the *yarmulke* in a pouch in the big suitcase. She put it into a ropy bag she sometimes used as a pocketbook when she went shopping, took our winter coats out of the closet and handed me mine.

"Ma, winter's over. Let me take my windbreaker."

"You won't melt and it will look better. Come, let's get it over with."

As we came out of the subway car, Ma opened the bag, handed me the *yarmulke*, and pulled her gray *baboushka* over her head and tied it under her chin. "That's the best we can do, Jack. Let's go." She marched to the stairs and went up them slowly, banging her feet down on each step, as though afraid of missing one.

Out on the street, I saw why Ma had made such a production of how we dressed. All the women wore dark dresses falling within inches of their shoes, their hair covered with shawls or *baboushkas*. Most of the young ones pushed carriages or strollers with babies and were accompanied by older children. Even young boys wore *yarmulkes*, and some, my age or even younger, had *payes*, strings of hair dangling down the sides of their heads in front of their ears, like the men, who were mostly bearded and wore long black coats over black pants and white shirts. A variety of *yarmulkes*, brimmed black hats and even a few big, round hats made of fur topped their heads. They often paused to talk to each other as did the women with other women, but the sexes paid each other no more attention than they did the street lamps and the fire hydrants.

Ma set off along a broad street between two story brick buildings, signs in Hebrew identifying the downstairs stores, wares often set out on tables on the sidewalk in front of them. Here and there, men tended pushcarts between the parked cars. They occasionally called out in Yiddish to people passing on the sidewalk and waved some piece of merchandise to attract customers. Nobody paid us attention except one woman, Ma's age, accompanied by three small children, who stopped and smiled at us we approached. I thought she was going to say something, but Ma looked past her without slowing. When we came to the next corner and waited for the light to change, Ma turned to me.

"That was Rivke Lookstein. We went through school together."

"So why didn't you say hello? She was going to speak to you, but you ignored her."

"They threw me out as though I were a criminal. Not Rivke, personally, but they're all together on these things. For a minute, here in the street, she was happy to see me again, but she'd never invite me into her home. I don't want any part of them."

There was nothing I could reply to this. I didn't know then how important it is to have a place and people from your childhood that you feel connected to. I will always be a kid from Saugerties and could walk down Ackerman Street today as though I owned it. I'd be happy to see the kids from school again and even cranky old Mr. Hiltz.

We turned off onto a side street of four-story brownstone buildings. I saw bursts of white and pink all the way down the block from flowering trees growing from square plots in the sidewalk. Women sat on the stoops and *schmoozed* while they kept watch on children playing on the sidewalk. At one house, two boys in the street tried to catch a ball that a third bounced off the steps. Ma stopped at the next house, climbed the steps and pressed a button on a plate next to the door.

A buzzer sounded. Ma pushed open the door and we went inside. Down a hallway, a middle-aged woman came toward us saying something in Yiddish that I couldn't understand. Ma and Ezra had mostly spoken English at home, and I only knew a few words. When Ma replied I heard her say "Yakov," my Hebrew name. Assuming it was an introduction, I stepped forward with my hand outstretched. The woman shrunk away. Stupid of me; I knew I was old enough so that physical contact with me would be forbidden.

"I'm sorry," I said. "I forgot."

She smiled. "I understand. I'm Mrs. Gutman. I come to your *Tante* during the afternoons. Come in."

We followed her to a door at the end of the hall and through it into a shadowy room lit only by a small lamp on a table and by fragments of sunlight that leaked between the window blinds. There was a musty smell like from opening a closet closed for a long time. My shoes thumped on the floor, bare except for a few scatter rugs. Cushions and throws covered heavy, dark furniture. A tiny, white-haired lady sat in a wheelchair next to the table with the lamp. She started to rise from the wheelchair, and Mrs. Gutman sprung to help her, but the old woman sank back into her chair and held out her arms.

"Ruth?" she called in a voice as weak as a song on the radio heard through the walls of our apartment.

Ma rushed to her and they hugged each other amid a storm of Yiddish. Ma freed herself, pointed at me, and I heard my name again. I was careful this time, stepped forward, but just smiled and nodded.

"No, no," said the old woman and held out her arms. I came to her and she put her arms around my neck ever so lightly and feathered my cheek with her lips before releasing me. "Such a big boy, Ruth. Sit, sit, both of you." Then she said something in Yiddish to Mrs. Gutman, who pushed the wheelchair up to a bigger table covered with a lace bordered cloth then left the room.

Ma and I sat at the table in chairs covered in faded rose-col-ored fabric. *Tante* Leah spoke to Ma in animated Yiddish and to me in slower English. After a few minutes, Mrs. Gutman brought in a tray with a teapot, cups, sugar, lemon, milk and a plate of *rugulach*, small pastries filled with chocolate. They were delicious. When we finished them, *Tante* Leah reached for a manila envelope sitting on the side of the table and took out an old photograph, which she handed to Ma. After one glance, Ma burst into tears.

I jumped from my chair and ran around the table to her. "Ma, Ma, what's the matter?"

"It's all right, Yakov," said *Tante* Leah. "It's a picture of me and my sister, your grandmother."

Ma, still crying, handed me the photograph. It showed two young, dark-haired women in black dresses, each holding a hand of a plump baby who was trying to stand. I could see the older one in *Tante* Leah's faded features, and the younger one was the very image of my mother.

"And the baby?" I asked.

Tante Leah's laugh brought strength into her voice. "That's your Mama, *boychik*."

Ma spoke in pain. "That's the first time I've looked at a picture of my mother in almost fourteen years. My father wouldn't let me take any of the few he had in the house."

"It's for you, *Liebling*. Keep it. Look, Yakov, see how much your Mama looks like her. How beautiful she was. No Rabbi could keep the men from staring at her." She laughed again, and the years fled her face.

I turned to my mother. "What happened to her, Ma?"

"She died in childbirth when I was four. She was only twenty-three years old. I have vivid memories of her." Ma shook her head. "But, I don't know which are real and which I only imagine. *Tante*, did she have a white dress with a collar that glittered?"

"No, never. You must have seen a picture of some movie actress. Your Mama dressed like in the photo, like we all dressed."

"That's what I mean. I couldn't even remember exactly what she looked like until I saw this photograph. How did she come to marry my father?"

It sounded to me like he was someone so awful as to be unmarriageable. Like Ezra. I supposed she had reason to feel that way after the way he treated her. The question was answered with a long response in Yiddish. I asked *Tante* Leah to repeat it in English.

"Your grandfather was not a bad man, Yakov. He loved your grandmother very much. Your mother, too. When your grandmother died he became very ... *biter*. What's the English word, Ruth?"

"The same, 'bitter.'"

"Yes, bitter and cold. He couldn't love anymore. He only thought of business and the *Torah* and our laws. And when ... *it* ... happened, he couldn't listen to his heart. And all the *balebatim* ... What, Ruth?"

"Big shots."

"Yes, big shots, told him to do what he did to your mother. He listened to them and not to me and a few others who told him not to."

"And he never regretted it?" asked Ma.

"He could never admit it. It killed him, maybe. His heart got sick six months later and he died, what, two years after that? And look at you. You have a good job and a beautiful son. You wouldn't have been happy living here with all the laws. They'd have made you marry some man who might have been even worse than the one you did marry."

Ma shrugged. *"Ver vaist?"* Who knows? That I understood.

Ma put the photograph back in the envelope and the envelope in her bag. We said our good-byes and made our way back to the subway. Ma said nothing the whole time until we were down on the platform and the train was pulling in. She put her hands on my shoulders and looked into my face. *"Tante* Leah is right. It turned out for the best." I think she was going to kiss me, but the doors opened and saved me.

THE REST OF THAT SCHOOL YEAR passed without incident. My grades were OK; none of the boys in my class gave me any grief, and, if they still called me "DP," it was without mockery. I had become friendly with several boys, but with none as much as with Harry. Unfortunately, he, as well as most of the others, would be going to sleep-away camp for most of July and August. That expense was beyond the Gluckstein budget, which was dedicated to moving us into a small two-bedroom apartment in the fall. I was happy to stay in the city for the summer in exchange for once again having the privacy of my own room. As the school year ended, we received the bonus news that I had gotten off the waiting list and into a Fresh Air Fund camp for the last two weeks in August. I felt bad that Ma wouldn't have a vacation, but she assured me that her one day off each weekend was enough vacation for her.

We made the most of that one day. A couple of times we went to Coney Island and once to Orchard Beach in the Bronx. We visited the live animals in the Bronx Zoo and, one rainy day, the stuffed ones in the Museum of Natural History. There were boat rides to the Statue of Liberty and to Bear Mountain. I was astonished at how Ma changed during these excursions. My serious, careful mother, worried about work, placating Ezra or satisfying Mr. Baccalini, taking care of me and the apartment, stayed at home and sent a cheerful laughing companion ready for fun.

With my friends away much of the summer, I started to hang around the store while Ma was working. Luis and I had no more bull sessions in the stockroom. I made myself useful filling the shelves and picking trash off the floor. Occasionally I would carry groceries for one of the older women and make a quarter or fifty cents. Luis delivered the big orders in his wagon and was touchy about letting me do it because he counted on the bigger tips.

One morning, Ma called me from the store while I was eating my breakfast. Luis was out sick and the produce supplier was going to make a big delivery. Could I come and help her? I was happy to be useful and spent the day bringing fruit and vegetables in from the truck into the stockroom, taking blotched bananas and wilted lettuce out of the bins, throwing them into the big garbage cans and replacing them with fresh merchandise and, finally, making pyramids of the tomatoes, apples and oranges. It was hard work, but I didn't mind and enjoyed the ten minutes I sat on the stool behind the cash register while Ma went to Millie's to bring us back sandwiches for lunch.

When Mr. Baccalini came in, Ma told him what had happened. He gave me one of his long looks, then opened the cash register and held out a ten-dollar bill. "This is for helping out, Jack."

I hadn't expected to be paid and Ma said, "You don't have to pay him, Joseph. He was just helping his mother."

"No, no," he said. "Someone does good work he should be paid." He pressed the bill into my hand.

Well, all right. I took it. "Thank you, Mr. Baccalini. Let me finish cleaning up the stockroom and throwing out the empty boxes."

"That's good. And call me Joseph." He smiled. Maybe I had been wrong about Joseph. He had given me advice, been generous and, most important, provided Ma with a good life for the first time since she was a child.

"OK, Joseph." I smiled back at him.

I liked having money in my pocket. Ma wanted me to take it to the bank and open a savings account, but I refused. For the first time I could buy a comic book or even go to a movie without asking Ma to take the money from the little we had. The first ten dollars didn't last long and I was alert for the opportunity to earn more. In August, when Luis took a week off to go to Puerto Rico with his new wife, I pushed to replace him instead of the temporary worker Joseph would have hired. I didn't mind the work and, this time, let Ma take me to the bank where I deposited most of my earnings.

I had a good time at the Fresh Air Fund Camp, starred at baseball, stumbled around a tennis court and got my advanced swimmer's certificate. I was glad to get home, though, looking forward to eighth grade, my last year at MS 332, where I would be one of the lords of the playground. Even better, we would soon move and I would get away from that fucking blanket that hung between our beds.

Ma picked me up at the bus station. She acted a little funny on the way home, firing questions at me non-stop, like she wanted a play-by-play account of every baseball game and the biographies of all six boys in my cabin. When we got home, she started cooking supper right away and was too busy to talk to me. That had never been a problem before; she could carry on a conversation while doing three other things at the same time. When we sat down to eat, she started the questions again. Finally, there was a pause and I asked "Have you found us an apartment yet?"

She took a long time answering, chewing and rechewing a little piece of chicken as though it were a big chunk of gristle. Finally, she swallowed, looked at me, took a drink of water, then looked down at her plate. What was going on? Did we not have enough money to move? Or maybe she had already signed a lease and was going to take me to see the apartment right after supper. Yes, that had to be it.

"Not exactly," she said. That was all?

"What, what do you mean?" I couldn't stand it.

"Something happened while you were away at camp." I must have looked frightened because she leaned forward and raised her hands. "Something good, Jack. Something very good."

I was totally puzzled. If it was so good, why did she take so long to tell me about it? "What, Ma, for Christ's sake. Tell me."

Now, the blow came quickly. "Joseph and I are getting married."

"What?" I jumped up from the table knocking my chair over backwards. That son of a bitch. That sneaky son of a bitch …

"He knew that with you gone I'd be alone …"

Got me to let my guard down …

"So, he asked me out to dinner …"

When I wasn't there to protect her …

"And we had such a nice time …"

How could I have been so fucking stupid as …

"That we did it again and then …"

To believe him …

"He made a wonderful Italian dinner at his apartment, and …"

I was totally right about him from the beginning.

"He asked me …"

"NO!" I howled. "NO. NO. NO!" It was over. One short year of freedom, and now we would be back under the heel of another man, who was much stronger than Ezra ever dreamed of being.

"Jack, control yourself. Sit down."

I couldn't sit down. I couldn't even stand still but stamped back and forth across the room. "You can't do this, Ma. You might as well kill us both."

"Stop acting crazy. You're not five years old anymore, throwing a tantrum. I'm not saying another word until you sit down and finish your supper."

"I don't want any more food." My appetite was gone. "I want you to take us somewhere away from that gangster."

Ma got up from the table and pointed to my chair. "For the last time, SIT DOWN!"

I had never heard that voice before, and, crazed as I was, I went to my chair and sat down.

"Now be quiet," she said almost as strongly, "and listen to me."

"But, Ma ..."

"I said BE QUIET!" She continued in a more familiar voice—the one she sometimes used when she didn't want to hear any argument. "Joseph is no gangster and never was. He can't help how he looks. He's a kind and generous man. His wife and child died years ago in a fire, and he's kept himself alone ever since, afraid to let anybody else into his life. Maybe that makes him seem a little rough. And after what happened to me ... It's a miracle we've gotten together, and I won't let you spoil it."

She looked as though she would throw her plate in my face if I said anything, so I kept my mouth shut. But I wasn't finished by any means. I wasn't going to let this happen. No way.

She continued. "I know you didn't like him at first, but I thought you'd gotten over that. You've been much friendlier to him lately. I don't understand why you're so upset. Are you afraid I'll stop paying attention to you? I won't. You're my son and I'll always love you. That won't change."

She paused, which I took for permission to speak. I kept under control, with difficulty. "Don't you know he just wants to get control of us so we'll work like slaves and he won't have to pay you? He'll be just like Ezra, only worse. He'll beat us up like Mr. Swenson used to do to his wife and Jimmy. Can't you see that, Ma? You can get another job. I can work. Let's get away from him before it's too late." I had never made such a strong argument, had never wanted anything so much as to make her believe me. I prayed to God that she would —to get that I would believe in Him.

Ma tilted her head and looked at me as though I were some strange creature standing in her living room. When she spoke, her voice was soft. "My poor Jakey. You're really afraid of Joseph. Don't be. Trust me. He's a wonderful man. He'll never hurt either of us. Maybe he won't be your father, but, if you give him a chance, someday he'll be your friend."

It couldn't be. "No," I said again, but quietly. "No, no, no."

"I'm sorry, Jack. I'm going to marry him. You'll have to get used to it." She picked up her plate and took it to the sink, ending the discussion. She didn't hear me mutter to myself. "I never will."

It was just too much for me. I couldn't kill Joseph. It wasn't like killing Jack Armstrong sometime in the future when I would be grown up and could plan the whole thing out and nobody would suspect me. I couldn't possibly pull it off now, and, if I could, I'd probably get caught, and, if I didn't, Ma would know somehow and never forgive me. At least I was over thirteen and getting bigger and stronger while Joseph was at least fifty and getting older and weaker. If we could get through the first year or two, maybe I could protect her and we'd be safe. Talking to him would get me nothing but trouble, so I kept away from the store for the next few days. Then, one morning after Ma had gone to the store, the phone rang.

"Hello?"

"Good morning, Jack. This is Joseph Baccalini."

"Oh."

"I think we should talk. Have you had breakfast yet?"

"No."

"You know Millie's restaurant?"

"Yes."

"Will you come now at eight o'clock?"

I thought a moment. He wouldn't do anything at Millie's, and I couldn't avoid him forever. "OK."

As I followed Joseph behind the backs of the customers sitting at the counter, the celebrities in the photos lining the wall on my right seemed to smile at me in sympathy. "Poor Jack, you're in for it now," they were saying.

I ordered the same shirred eggs I had eaten my first day in the City, but had no appetite today. I couldn't even finish the bacon, the only food kept off our table by Ma's Kosher upbringing, so particularly desirable when available. There was nothing wrong with Joseph's appetite. He finished off a big plate of corned beef hash topped with a poached egg and accompanied by home fried potatoes before the waitress even got back to the table to refill his coffee cup. He wiped his mouth, put down his napkin and stared at me until I gave up and laid my fork on the plate.

"Your mother say you don't want us to marry. Why, Jack?"

I shifted in my seat as though my back itched, but didn't say anything.

"You think I won't be a good husband, won't be kind to her? Or maybe I won't be kind to you?"

His voice was quiet, reasonable, but again I didn't answer. He sighed.

"Well, I tell you a little about me. I was born in Italy, in Verona. My father was soldier, killed in the war. My mother, too—a bomb a few months before the end. My mother's brother had come over to Brooklyn, so they sent me here. I was sixteen, old enough to go to work in the fish market. All the time, I smell of fish." He smiled at that. "They make jokes about me in the neighborhood so I fight the jokers. I win and the jokes stop. One day, a man take me to the gym and put boxing gloves on and teach me to box. Soon I see I can get paid to box and I quit the fish. I do good for four, five years. They call me 'Joe Bacco' and the Italians come to see me fight the Irish boys and the Puerto Ricans. I meet a beautiful girl and we get married. We buy a little house and have a little baby boy.

"'Now,' my wife say, 'you quit boxing.'

"But we need money, and I can't make so much back at the fish or any place else. I have to keep boxing for two, maybe three, more years while we save the money. My wife don't like that I leave her with the baby and go to Philadelphia or Boston or Cleveland to box and come back with my face messed up like this." He pointed to his nose and the scars over his eyes. "I have a big fight in Chicago. If I win, maybe I get to fight the champion, Carmen Basilio. Italians would love that. Even if I lose, the money is very good."

He stopped and signaled the waitress for more coffee, poured some cream in it and stirred it slowly for a long time, saying nothing. He put the spoon down and held up the cup with both hands, but didn't drink. "In the middle of the night

before the fight, they wake me up at the hotel and tell me …
my house has a big fire and my wife and son are gone."

He drank some coffee, put the cup down and shrugged.
"I should have been home, but I wasn't. They say they get
someone else to fight, but what difference does it make? So,
I fight. No good. They stop it in the third round or he might
have killed me like I hoped he would. When I get out of the
hospital I go back to New York. I don't spend the money. I
work here, I work there, finally at this store. The owner retire
fifteen years ago and sell me cheap."

The waitress came to the table, Joseph nodded and she put
the check down. He continued. "I never want to marry again,
have more children. Maybe I let something terrible happen to
them too. But now I meet your mother. Terrible things happen
to her, but she stand up. You understand?"

I nodded. That was Ma.

"She make me believe that I can make good things happen,
not bad. I can't forget what I did, but I don't have to do it again.
Together we can make a good life. For you, too, Jack. I promise."

He was very persuasive, but then he gave me that long,
searching look of his. I couldn't let my guard down until I knew
what that meant. "Excuse me, Joseph," I said. "I have to go to
the bathroom." When I came out, I saw he had left money next
to the check. He nodded toward the front door and I walked
out ahead of him. "Thank you for breakfast," I said

"You're welcome," he answered.

And that was all. It was wrong, but I could do nothing to
stop them. I threw no more tantrums, let Ma buy me a blue suit
and, a month later, came with them to the Municipal Building
for the wedding. During their brief honeymoon in Atlantic City,
I spent the weekend with Harry's family, then helped Ma pack

for the move to Joseph's apartment: five comfortable rooms in a prewar apartment house on 89th Street. She consulted me on the furnishings for the second bedroom which became my room, and Joseph gave me a radio of my own. I thanked him politely. All conversations between Joseph and me were polite, but they only took place when necessary. Once or twice Ma started in on my attitude, but when I responded, "Was I rude or something?" she closed her mouth and turned away.

The weeks passed, and I had to admit, closely as I watched, I never saw or heard Joseph make any gesture or say anything that might be interpreted as a threat to either of us. Ma certainly seemed happy doing little things for him and chattering on about the customers or Luis or what she and Joseph would be doing together on a Sunday afternoon when the store would now be closed. She would kiss him on the cheek when he came home and would sometimes put her hand on his shoulder when she walked past his chair. I kept myself from thinking about what might be happening behind their bedroom door, but, judging by her cheerful face, there was nothing going on she objected to.

I had excluded myself from this happy relationship. Ma would invite me to join their excursions. I would politely decline. They would each pause from time to time during the dinner table conversations to give me an opportunity to speak. At most I would take advantage of the opportunity to ask one of them to pass the salt. I didn't scorn the pleasures of ordinary family life. I would have loved to be a part of the warmth and camaraderie I saw when I was on some outing with the Gelles family, but the price would have been too high. I would have had to let down my guard, and I was resolved never to do so again. On those terms, I could do what Ma had ordered—I got used to it.

A BIG DISAPPOINTMENT THAT FALL was Harry Gelles's move to Westchester. Coming right after what amounted to losing Ma, I was hit pretty bad. It wasn't just Harry; I felt like I was losing a family, after all the time I had spent in his apartment or on trips with his parents and younger brother. Scarsdale might as well have been the moon, as far as travel was concerned. I needed to find some activity in bad weather other than closing myself off in my room with daytime television. I started hanging out in the 96th Street Library, the Metropolitan Museum of Art and even the Museum of Natural History across the Park. It wasn't that I was that into acquiring culture, but those places were warm, dry and, best of all, free. I was still on my old allowance of a dollar a week, didn't feel like approaching Ma for an increase and didn't want to touch the twenty dollars or so rolled up in a sweat sock in my drawer that I had persuaded Ma not to put in the bank from my earnings for work in the store.

I was friendly with a number of the boys at school, but our interactions almost all took place in the classroom or the schoolyard or the Park. With a room of my own, I could now invite someone up to our apartment, and I started to think over possibilities. One Friday in October, with rain predicted for Saturday, I decided to ask a boy named Tony Schloss what he liked to do on the weekends. I hoped the answer wouldn't be the movies, but was a little disappointed to hear that he liked to play cards. I don't have to tell you what place cards held in Ezra's home—right next to the statue of the Virgin Mary. But, I had seen Joseph teaching Ma how to play gin and they seemed to enjoy it, so I asked Tony if he would play with me Saturday.

"Let me ask Leonard," he answered.

That was not so good. Leonard MacInnes was new to our class and something of a bully, although I had not so far had a problem with him. But, declining to play with him would have been an insult triggering trouble, so I promptly welcomed the idea, and, a few minutes later, Leonard approved and it was set. After dinner, I asked Ma for a gin lesson, so I would be prepared.

"Why don't you ask Joseph?" She spoke casually, but I didn't have to be a genius to know that she was looking for any opportunity to reconcile me to him. My present course of polite coexistence would have been spoiled if I refused to ask him. Besides, I didn't want to show up at Tony's tomorrow totally ignorant of the game. Joseph seemed pleased to be asked and gave me a half-hour grounding in the game, which seemed enough to get me started.

"After all, it's not like you're playing for money," he concluded the lesson. I agreed and thanked him nicely. I had to admit to myself that he had been perfectly pleasant.

Tony's family was out of the apartment when I arrived, so we could play at a card table in the living room. Immediately there was a problem.

"You can't play three handed gin," Leonard pointed out, obviously correctly. "And nobody wants to sit out. We should play poker. Right, Tony?"

"OK. My father has chips somewhere. I'll go find them."
He got up and left the table.

"Uh, uh I don't know how to play poker," I told Leonard.

"Don't worry," he said. "It's simple and lots of fun. We'll teach you. We don't usually play it because it's not so good with only two players. We'll play five card stud. You get one card down and one up, the first round, then three more rounds so you have four up and one down. You bet after each round."

Then he explained to me the order of winning hands. It certainly seemed simple.

Tony returned with the chips and divided them up. "The white chips are a penny; the red chips are a nickel and the blue chips are a dime. You can only bet a penny the first round, two the second, three the third and a nickel the last round."

I was surprised. "We're playing for money?"

Leonard laughed. "That's what makes poker fun. But it's only pennies. Is that OK?"

They both looked at me with puzzled expressions as though to say "What kind of a wimp are you?"

"Yeah, sure," I replied with much more confidence than I felt.

"Ante up," said Leonard, and he and Tony put a white chip in the center of the table. "Put a penny in the pot, Jack." I did.

The first hand I had a three face down and a jack face up. Leonard's up card was a ten and Tony's was a nine.

"You're high," said Tony. "Do you want to bet?"

I put a white chip in the center of the table. "I call," said Leonard." Me too," said Tony, and they each put a white chip in too.

My next up card was a two, Leonard's was an ace and Tony's a king. "Two cents," said Leonard. "Call," said Tony and they each put two white chips in. I did the same.

My fourth card was a six, Leonard and Tony each got sevens. We all put three chips in the center.

My fifth card was a queen, Leonard's a five and Tony a four. "A nickel," said Leonard. "Call," said Tony.

I paused and peeked at my down card and looked around the table. I only had a queen high and both Leonard and Tony beat that. "No bet," I said. "You mean, you fold?" Leonard asked shaking his head.

"Yeah, I guess so."

Leonard turned over his down card. "Two tens, back to back."

"Beats ace-king," and Tony turned over his down card as Leonard pulled all the chips to him.

You might question how I could remember every card in that hand played so many years ago. But it's true. I can remember a lot of hands I've played over the years, and that one, the first, was very important. When we quit at five o'clock and counted out our chips, I found I had lost $4.31, most of which was won by Leonard. I only had a little over two dollars in my pocket. When I told them, they smiled and said I could pay them Monday in school or, if I wanted to, let it ride until next week when we could play again and maybe I would get even. That sounded good.

Of course, I didn't tell Ma and Joseph what happened. I said we had played a little gin and watched a football game on TV and that I had had a good time. I took some money out of my sock and paid my debt on Monday and waited impatiently all week for Saturday when we met again at Tony's house. It went a little better, because I didn't call them every time on the last round. But I still lost over two dollars. The following Saturday, I got good cards and won over a dollar, but the next week, my luck disappeared and I lost almost six dollars.

The next Saturday, Leonard suggested I might do better at draw poker. It didn't help. I didn't like not being able to see any of the cards they were holding and lost again. I was furious and determined to get even. But at a dollar or two, the best I had done so far, that was going to take too long. So, the next week, I asked if they ever played for a little more money and they agreed to double the stakes. It was a disaster. I lost ten dollars which used up all the rest of my savings plus a little. They let me owe them the deficiency, but I had to quit playing while I gradually paid them off out of my allowance. That meant no money for anything else, not even the cross-town bus, for the next few weeks. And Christmas was coming up, when I would be expected to give some kind of present to Ma and to Joseph.

I had two problems. The first was what to do on weekends without any money. All right, back to the 96th Street Library. To my surprise, my half-hearted search for a book on poker found Herbert Yardley's *The Education of a Poker Player*. Although I was no longer strictly limited to books from the children's section, I knew better than to try to pass a book with that sort of title under the grim scrutiny of Miss Childs, the warden at the checkout desk. I put Yardley under my coat while *Captains Courageous* was duly logged out with as close to a smile as Miss Childs could muster. Then, would you believe it, I found *Oswald Jacoby On Poker* on the table in front of the thrift shop on Third Avenue priced down to twenty-five cents.

I kept the books together with my Vietnam War material. It was a humbling experience discovering how stupid I had been. I spent several weeks studying the odds and learning when to drop out, when to call a bet and when to bet or raise someone else's bet. Next came strategy and the psychology of the game, facial expressions and other "tells" that could help to figure out what the other players held.

I was impatient to try out my new skills and win back some of the money I had lost, but I no longer had any savings in my sock drawer. While I thought I now knew enough to win from Tony and Leonard, I also knew that on any one occasion, anything could happen. So, while I was studying my books, I gritted my teeth, walked any place I couldn't use my bus pass, and stayed out of movies. And I still had Christmas to deal with.

At the local hardware store, I had seen a multipurpose instrument with knife and screwdriver blades and a couple of other functions that would be perfect for Joseph, but it cost $12, which I didn't have. For Ma, the drug store had all kinds of fancy soaps and stuff that would be fine for another $10 or so. I decided to tackle the hardware store first. I stood over the tool, looking around to see if anyone might see me. It would only take an instant to slip it into my jacket pocket where nobody would notice it when I walked out. But my arm wouldn't reach for the shelf. I left the store cursing under my breath.

Back home, I calmed down. I wasn't a thief. Was that such a bad thing? I had to admit it wasn't. It got me thinking and I realized that I probably could earn some money helping out at the store during the holiday season, if I weren't so set against Joseph. Could I be wrong about Joseph, too? It was time to open my mind a little and evaluate the situation as it actually was. Whether an epiphany or mere rationalization, I don't know, but that evening I asked politely whether I might be of use at the store and was rewarded with an offer from Joseph and a happy smile from Ma.

I felt good at earning the money to purchase the items I had contemplated stealing. Ma and Joseph gave me a small

TV set for Christmas, and I spent most evenings, after my homework was done, with the two books and a deck of cards while the TV covered the sounds of shuffling and dealing. Soon I had a stake of twenty dollars, enough of a cushion for at least one game. Tony was delighted when I asked if there was a game Saturday, and, I set off in the morning, armed with a peanut butter and jelly sandwich, to meet an imaginary couple of friends amid the dinosaurs at the Museum of Natural History.

My first hand was at five-card stud. Tony was high with a king and bet a nickel. Leonard called with a queen and, holding a three and an eight, I folded. And so it went for the first four hands; I folded one weak hand after another. I knew I was doing the right thing, but started to worry. I mean I couldn't win if I didn't play, and I had to ante each hand. But the next hand gave me a pair of nines which won the pot.

At one point, Tony, annoyed that I was dropping out of most hands, asked, "What's the matter, Jack? Are you chicken or something?"

I just gave him a dumb look and shrugged. "I don't know. I thought maybe if I sit out a few hands I won't lose so much."

Leonard chipped in, "But you can't have any fun if you don't play."

He was right about that. There was no fun in sitting after I folded watching Tony and Leonard play out the hands. That was my first exposure to something every winning gambler knows. You don't play for fun: You play to win. It's hard work. I threw away a lot of bad starts and won with enough of the good ones so that I ended the day ahead four dollars. Not much for six hours of work; less than I made working at the store. But I had proved my point. Money could be won, and I could win it.

The following Saturday, we met again. Since they realized I wouldn't stay in without a good hand to start, they became more cautious when I was in, particularly if I bet or raised. It was time to go to the second stage. Then, I bluffed Tony out of a winning hand. Finding out that I might bluff confused them, and, for a while, anyway, they returned to calling my bets which I made on good hands. This continued for another three Saturdays, by which time I had won back all the money I had previously lost.

Tony owed me five dollars from the last game. I came up to him before our first class on Monday. "You got my money?"

He made a face and tried to go into the classroom, but I stepped between him and the door. "What's the matter?" I asked him. "You were happy enough to take my money when I lost."

He looked at the ground. "Leonard says you were cheating."

"WHAT? That cocksucker. What did he say I was doing?"

"He didn't know, but said you must have been to win so often."

I was furious, but kept under control. "Well, did you see me cheat? They were your cards, not mine. Did I do any fancy dealing? You were on my left and cut the cards before I dealt."

He shook his head, slowly. "No, I didn't see anything wrong. Maybe it's because you used to lose all the time and then you came back and started winning all the time. How did that happen, anyway?"

I didn't really want to tell him, but we weren't going have any more games, that was for sure. "I got two books on poker and learned about all the mistakes I'd been making. You and Leonard make enough of the same mistakes, so, when I stopped making them, I started winning."

"Oh, I see. Like what, for instance?"

That was too much. "What am I, a fucking teacher? Go look yourself. Yardley is one; Jacoby the other. Now are you going to pay me or not?"

He made a face, but reached into his pocket and pulled out a five-dollar bill. "All right, I believe you. Leonard can really be an asshole."

Tony was right about Leonard, and I knew it wasn't going to be as easy getting the ten dollars he owed me. I waited until gym, the last period, so he would have heard from Tony about our conversation. As we came off the basketball court, I caught up to him.

"You have my ten bucks?"

He stopped and grinned at me. "Nope."

"How come? We always settle on Monday."

"I don't pay cheaters." He paused, as if a new idea had come to him. "In fact, you should pay me back the money you cheated from me over the last month. I'll figure it out and let you know how much." He snickered and continued toward the locker room.

I grabbed the back of his T-shirt to hold him. "I didn't cheat, you fuck, and you know it. Haven't you talked to Tony?"

He turned and knocked my hand away. "Keep your hands off me. If Tony is dumb enough to pay you, that's his problem."

"So, I should tell everybody that you're a welsher?"

Now he grabbed me by the shirt. "You do, and I'll kick the shit out of you and tell everybody you're a cheat like all kikes. Got that, Guh-luck-a-steen?'

He gave me a big push and down I went. I had to make an instant decision. Although Leonard was bigger and stronger, I wasn't really afraid of a fight with him. I mean, he wasn't going to kill me, and there were two or three kids coming out of the gym who must have seen him push me. Backing down would not be good for my image. The problem was that Mr. Novak, the gym teacher, was still in the gym collecting the basketballs and would see the fight, demand to know what it was about, probably report it to the principal, and Ma and Joseph would find out what I had been doing. I couldn't chance it. I'd have to get him another time. I sat up slowly.

"Go fuck yourself, you cocksucker," I said. It was only token defiance. Leonard knew it and went on into the locker room without looking back at me.

I got up as the other kids arrived. "What was that about?" asked one of them.

"Nothing. Some bullshit that I fouled him." And that was the end of it. I knew Leonard wasn't going to be too anxious to talk about the incident either. My career as a hustler had to go on hold. But at least the incident taught me to make sure that the losers pay up at the end of the game.

Sure enough, I got my chance at Leonard. We had a big arithmetic test—five questions printed on three sheets with spaces below to show the work. Time was up and everybody turned in their papers and left the classroom. Leonard wasn't very good in arithmetic and was the last to finish. I was long done but waited for him without particularly knowing why. He finally got up and walked out after depositing his three sheets on the pile on Miss Curry's desk. As I followed him, Miss Curry got up from behind the desk and went to the coat rack in the corner where her coat was hanging. I was leaning over the desk with my papers in my hand when I saw that the pile of papers was face down. I snatched up Leonard's third page and hid it in one of my books, then dropped my papers on the pile. There was quite a scene the next arithmetic class when

Leonard got his paper back. It took the principal, Mr. Colton, to accept Leonard's protestations that he had completed the test and that maybe Miss Curry had lost the sheet, so Leonard was graded on the first four questions. I would rather they gave him a zero on the fifth, but you can't get everything.

The experience with Leonard clinched it. I had to change my name. I wasn't going to deny that I was Jewish, but Jacob Guh-luck-a-steen had to go. I chose "Jack Stone." As I expected, Ma raised no objection to the change. I could have taken as a last name "Taub," her maiden name, but that side of the family had behaved as badly as my stepfather's side. It wasn't a complete break from the past, as "Stone," of course, is the translation of "Stein." Joseph's lawyers filed the papers and my new name went on my application to the Cabot Academy, in Cabot, Massachusetts.

HOW, YOU MIGHT ASK, did a middle-class Jewish boy from New York City, happen to go to Cabot Academy, traditionally an elite incubator for the sons of rich New England Wasps? Well, change has a way of trickling into the most assault-proof castles through cracks in the stone walls, gaps in the barred windows and between the spikes of the heavy portcullis. Of course, money was the principal factor. With the movement of the New England textile mills to the Carolinas and Puerto Rico, their owners often moved their homes to more salubrious climes and ceased to send their offspring or their money to Cabot, and exclusive Protestantism became a luxury the school could no longer afford.

As might be expected, the few Jewish boys admitted came from rich families, active in charities and politics, whose clean-shaven fathers belonged to Reform synagogues, if any. One of the earliest Jewish graduates of Cabot was a boy named Paul Horowitz, whose father had made a fortune in real estate in New York. On Paul's untimely death from Lou Gehrig's disease, his grieving parents established a full scholarship at Cabot in Paul's name to be awarded to "A young man of the Jewish faith residing in New York City, who exhibits the same outstanding character and intelligence as the late Paul Horowitz, as demonstrated by an essay on a topic significant to those of his faith."

One of my teachers persuaded me to apply for the scholarship "just for fun," although my grades were only good, not great. I chose "Assimilation" as the topic of my essay and took the old schoolyard for my example. The essay related how I modified my speech and mannerisms to help me fit in with my schoolmates. It was total bullshit. I said I made a great effort to lose the Yiddish accent (which I never had) and persuaded my mother to let me go to school without my *yarmulke*, when the only time I wore one after Ezra's funeral was the day at Williamsburg. The message went over big at Cabot and I won the scholarship.

Ma was ambivalent. It was a wonderful educational opportunity, guaranteeing later admission to an Ivy League college, but her mother's heart resisted the separation from her *boychik*. I wasn't anxious to leave her so soon, and my relationship with Joseph was improving, but I still felt an unnecessary third in their connubial household. I hadn't formed any new close friendships since Harry Gelles had moved, and was piqued by the challenge of the competition of brighter kids and, yes, by the challenge of assimilation in this schoolyard away from home.

So, one September day, Joseph drove a rented Ford Ltd. to Cabot Academy with Ma in the front and me crammed in the back next to a trunk, duffel bag, suitcase and a box with emergency food and whatever a worried mother might think of to make the rigorous prep school life bearable for her denested bird. When we got there, someone took a picture with my box Brownie of the three of us, stiff and straight, under the big oak in front of Baldwin House. Ma insisted I wear a suit to make a good impression.

They had told me I'd be wearing jackets and ties for the next four years. What they hadn't told me was that I would also be wearing a suit of armor all that time to protect me from emotions. At all costs, I would keep mine inside me and keep others' away from me. Mustn't show anger, mustn't cry— these things could cause trouble. And so, after my first night, I resolved not to cry again. I left my bed at the bell the next morning, washed, put on my new sport jacket and followed the crowd down to breakfast determined to stick it out. And I did. Cabot gave me a great academic education, but at the cost of a shriveled selfhood, deprived of the spontaneity, the honesty, the openness I feared, but that could have enriched my life.

I was fortunate in the assignment of my roommate. Bobby Miller was from Western Massachusetts. His Episcopalian father, I later discovered, had been born Jewish, but had been so thorough in his conversion that he hadn't even had Bobby circumcised. I had to make do with half a Jew since the only two other full-blooded ones in our class roomed together down the end of the hall from me on the second floor of Baldwin House. More important than his ancestry, Bobby was a perfectly nice kid, and, although he now lives in Seattle, we try to get together every year or so.

Bobby was invaluable to my project of assimilation at Cabot. I borrowed his blazers, cable-knit sweaters and narrow ties until I could afford to buy my own. I mimicked his insouciant speech, adding a touch of sarcasm, lacked by the good-natured Bobby, but common to many other classmates. As a result, after a few weeks, the poor, Jewish boy from First Avenue morphed into a quintessential Preppy.

The school thoroughly organized our lives. It sent us from class to sports to meals to study hours and back to our dorms. We were restricted to the bounds of the School property, except that on Wednesday and Saturday afternoons, we were given freedom to go to the Village of Cabot. Saturday night, we had our choice of the movie in Founders Hall or pool, ping pong and other games in the basement of Baldwin House. I was ready to work my newly acquired poker skills on my classmates, but gambling was strictly prohibited and I had no opportunity to win anything other than an occasional cheeseburger over a ping pong match.

The second Saturday night of my stay at Cabot featured the British movie *Lucky Jim*, starring Ian Carmichael and Terry Thomas. I had no idea that it would become significant in my life. As Bobby and I drifted back to Baldwin House, we fell in with our neighbors, Clayton Anderson III and Ted Kimball. Clayton, star tackle on the Freshman football team, already sprouted the black hairs that would eventually cover his chest and, with his size and strength, cause him to be known as "Bobo, the Gorilla." Fortunately, except on the football field, Bobo was a most amiable and generous gorilla.

"Have they refilled the machines, yet?" asked Bobby, referring to the vending machines in the basement of Baldwin House that dispensed potato chips and pretzels. "I'm starved."

I shrugged. My tight budget didn't provide for regular visits to the machines.

"They promised next week," replied Bobo, a big consumer. "But …" he looked at Ted, who nodded permission. "My mother sent me brownies and you guys can come and have some."

Homemade brownies! A treasure beyond price. I tried not to show too much eagerness. "That would be great, Clayton."

Then Bobby hit the right note. "I'll go down to the basement and bring back Cokes."

We piled into their room for our feast. Baldwin House was a large old structure assembled in stages over the years, with a wing added here, an extra floor there, walls torn out or added to accommodate a growing number of inhabitants as it changed from a family home to an inn to its present use as a dormitory. Bobo and Ted's room showed the age of the original structure in the sagging ceiling and the uneven floor. On two walls were sealed fixtures that had once held gas mantels, and the outline of a filled-in fireplace was on another. There was a big hook above a window with a coil of rope around it. I walked over to look at it carefully and saw that one end of the rope was attached to the hook and that there was a leather sling and a pulley attached to the other end.

"What the fuck is this thing?" I asked.

"That's in case of fire," answered Ted. "You let the thing out the window, put your foot in the sling and lower yourself with the pulley. The next guy pulls it up and repeats. All the rooms had them before they built your wing with the fire escape which is just a few steps away."

I looked at it and then at Bobo, who might have already reached two hundred pounds. "Have you tried it, Clayton?"

"No thanks. I'll get to the fire escape if I can't use the stairs."

Bobby arrived with the Cokes and Bobo went into the closet and brought out the brownies, which were delicious. I was still curious about the thingummy. "How about you, Ted. Have you tried it?"

"No, it's not supposed to be here anymore, but someone missed it when they took them out of the other rooms. If you want to try it, be my guest."

"Try what," asked Bobby.

"That fire thing." Ted pointed to it.

Bobby walked over to it. "Not me," he said. "But Jack will try anything, won't you, Jack?"

"I don't know about that," I said. But I was a little flattered at the thought.

"How about it?" asked Ted. "Or are you just as chicken as the rest of us?"

How could I accept being called chicken, even though everyone else in the room did? I was working hard trying to fit in. Maybe this stunt would help. I went to the window, pulled it up and looked down. The light from the basement window showed grass maybe fifteen feet below me. People must have thought the thing was safe or they wouldn't have put it up in the first place.

"OK." I took the rope off the hook. "Someone help me get over the sill."

"You don't have to do this, Jack," said Bobo.

"It's no big deal. Give me a hand." I put one foot in the sling and awkwardly climbed onto the sill, holding the pulley brake with one hand. Bobo gave me a little shove and I went over, the brake keeping me dangling. I gradually loosened the brake. Kaboom! I shot downward and slammed into the ground. Pain exploded all over me for a moment, then concentrated in my right knee, my hands, which had tried to cushion the fall and my left temple where my head had struck the ground when I pitched forward after landing. I didn't dare move for a few moments while mentally checking to see where else might hurt.

"Jack," yelled Bobby. "Are you all right?"

I gradually lifted my head. Yes, the neck was sore, but not too bad. I put a hand up to my temple. Tender, but no blood. I rotated that hand. It hurt but not the sharp pain of a broken wrist. Same for the other, so I sat up slowly. A twinge or two elsewhere, but nothing too bad.

"I'm OK," I called, but when I looked up there was nobody at that window, although a number of other windows opened and boys looked out to see what happened. A few moments later all three of my companions came running around the building from the front door and stood over me.

"Stop staring and help me up," I said shakily.

"Should we get an ambulance?" asked Bobby.

"No, just let me try to get up."

Bobo slowly pulled me to my feet. I could stand! I tried a couple of steps. The right knee hurt but didn't give way. I wanted to go back to my room and go to bed, but the others insisted on taking me to the infirmary, my right arm around Bobo, my left around Ted, with Bobby in advance to open doors and clear the way. The nurse bandaged my cuts and scrapes, poked and pulled various parts of me, declared that there didn't seem to be serious damage, but insisted I stay overnight to see the school doctor in the morning.

"Go back to Baldwin House, boys," she told my friends. "This boy may not be smart, but he's obviously very lucky."

Ted laughed. "So tonight, we saw both Lucky Jim and our own Lucky Jack."

And that's who I'll be forever. Born "Lucky Stone" in Yiddish, "Lucky Jack Stone" was a neat change. The nickname, itself, proved my good luck. Others, such as "Bubbles" Moness or "Squeaky" Kent (whose high voice didn't break until Thanksgiving) were not so fortunate. And, I discovered, as Joseph had said, the nickname cemented my acceptance.

The schoolwork was tougher than I had been used to, but there weren't a lot of distractions, and I put in the necessary time to keep up. I couldn't see the point of studying Latin, but the school insisted on it so I memorized and still remember all the silly rules such as "Verbs such as believe, persuade, command, obey, serve, resist, envy, threaten, pardon and spare govern the dative." Who the fuck except a Preppy even knows what the dative is?

ALTHOUGH IT APPEARED ENDLESS AT THE TIME, that first year at Cabot seems, in retrospect, to have lasted no more than a month or so. That's probably the result of countless repetition, each week filled with the same activities as the week before, imperceptibly advancing the year just as we turned the pages in the textbooks.

The low point of a week might be a loss in one sport or another by the Greeks, the gray-jerseyed crew I was assigned to for my four-year sojourn, to the crimson-clad Romans, my roommate Bobby's designated clan. The high point could be a good Saturday night movie like *The Terminator*. Even the Village of Cabot, where we were allowed on Wednesday and Saturday afternoons, became, after the first few weeks, a routine, pleasant, but unexciting. A cheeseburger and a chocolate frappe at Doc's, a stop at the dry cleaner or the barbershop, a peek at a Playboy at the stationery store: That was about it. Juniors and Seniors were occasionally permitted to attend evening events at Cabot High School at which real live girls could be present, and, once each semester, the two upper grades held a supper dance. The School apparently felt that contact with the fair sex was not beneficial to Freshmen and Sophomores.

Of course, we talked about sex constantly. My roommate made the mistake of putting a picture of his eighth-grade girlfriend on his dresser. By the end of the first week, he couldn't go anywhere without hearing "How's Roz, Bobby?" or "When's Roz going to give you the two bare boobs?" The latter was about as far as our thirteen-year old imaginations would take us with any female we actually were on social terms with.

Pornography, however, was right up there in popularity with homemade brownies. Freddy Thomas, the masturbation guru, had managed to acquire a Marilyn Monroe "Golden Dreams" calendar picture, that he rented out at fifty cents a night.

As most of my classmates, I had learned the basics before I came to Cabot. Freddy was way ahead of us, though, and would cheerfully demonstrate various grips or introduce us to the use of enhancing substances such as Vaseline. In line with my established reputation as one who would try anything, I failed to check with Freddy before I tried Vicks Vaporub. A very big mistake.

Our publicly stated sexual preference was uniformly heterosexual. I don't think any of us were yet actively engaged with either girls or other boys, so we never questioned those statements, and terms like "homo," "fairy" and "queer" were still used freely as insults without being meant seriously. Cabot was hardly in the forefront of social change. By my senior year, however, the school was reluctantly reexamining its official antipathy to homosexuality, and, a few years later, allowed several of its well-regarded faculty to emerge from the closet.

One of them, Professor French, was the housemaster of Baldwin House. He frequently joined us in the hour after dinner when we were permitted to use the Rec Room. A slender man, nearing sixty, with wavy white hair and a lined face, he would walk around the room, an unlit pipe in his mouth, applauding a good shot at the ping pong table, putting an unused pool cue in the rack and making casual conversation with the students. Sometimes he would kibitz a boy playing gin or hearts, stand behind him and put his hands on the boy's shoulders for a few seconds.

The first time Professor French put his hands on Bobby, I could see Bobby squirm. Professor French immediately removed his hands and walked away. When we got back to our room, as soon as the door was closed, Bobby turned to me. "Did you see what French did?"

"Yes."

"He must be a fag."

I knew very little about homosexuals, but I liked Professor French who made Freshman Math understandable and was patient with the rowdies of Baldwin House. "I don't know, Bobby. Maybe he's just being friendly, like some kind of uncle."

"You think so, Jack?"

"Yeah. My friend Harry Gelles's father sometimes put his arm around me when he played touch football with me against Harry and his brother. He was as macho as they come."

"OK, I wouldn't like to think French was queer. He's a good guy."

Professor French continued his habit and I had conversations with other boys like the one with Bobby. We all got used to it and didn't wriggle too much so Professor French wouldn't be embarrassed, because he remained a good guy all year. Whatever he may have done away from Cabot, he never touched a classmate of mine except in the middle of the rec room with all of us present.

I thought about the possibility that I might be a queer myself. I checked out my classmates in the shower. A couple of them still had smooth, hairless, soft bodies that might feel good. But they had no tits! How could you have sex without tits to play with like those of the babes in the magazines? And even the most babe-like of these kids was soon going to grow body hair and muscles and angles instead of curves. Could I ever have sex with Bobo, the Gorilla? Impossible. And the things I had heard that queers did to each other? No, it wasn't for me. That was a relief.

The day before Thanksgiving, I took the bus into Boston and Amtrak back to New York, a ride I came to know well, with its white New England churches and Gorton's Ready-to-Fry Codfish Cakes signs. Ma insisted on coming to Grand Central, which violated the spirit of independence I had been cultivating, but it did feel good to see her face on the platform where she met me. For three days, I slept late, ate like a pig and was babied unmercifully. Ma stayed home from the store to make me big breakfasts and take me shopping for winter clothes. She was bright and cheerful and her face was somehow different from the one I had always known.

"What are you staring at, Jack?" she asked me Thursday morning at breakfast. "Do I have food on my face?"

She frowned for a moment and wiped her mouth. That was what was different. The muscles over her eyes were no longer drawn in the slight frown I had known as long as I could remember.

"No, Ma. You look good. You look happy."

She sat back in her chair and smiled. "I am happy. I have my health, I have Joseph and my Jakey is home. What more could I ask for?"

I looked down at my plate. Joseph had given me a big hello when he had gotten home from the store the night before. It looked as though he had been about to hug me but my hand was already outstretched, so he took it and shook it vigorously.

At dinner, conversation was more comfortable than it had been in the past, and it was impossible not to see the affection between Ma and Joseph. I had to admit I had been mistaken in what I feared and the way I had acted when she had first announced their plans. Just to top it off, after dinner when Ma was in the kitchen, Joseph paused as he came back to finish clearing the table, and pushed two twenty-dollar bills into my shirt pocket.

"Don't tell your mother," he whispered. "Get something special."

I was still thinking what to say when he snatched the last plates and disappeared into the kitchen as Ma came out of it. I knew what I had to do. "I'm sorry. I was wrong. Terribly wrong."

She nodded three times slowly. "Yes, you were terribly wrong and nearly ruined my life. I had a big argument with Joseph. He was going to back out because he didn't want to come between you and me. I had to have faith enough in him that he would prove to be the man I believed he was and that you would become man enough to see it. OK, you've admitted your mistake to me. Now you have to tell him."

I must have made a face, because she stood up from her chair, leaned over the table and shook her finger. "Today. You thought you were enough of a *mensch* to protect me? You should only become as much of a *mensch* as that man you insulted. You don't sit down for Thanksgiving dinner until you've done it."

I've always hated to admit when I'm wrong, maybe because Ezra found fault with everything I did or didn't do. I'd sort of hoped that telling Ma would be enough. Joseph could see from the way I talked and acted that I had gotten over my fit without an explicit confession of wrongdoing. But, I wasn't going to get off that easily; I went to my room and tried out a few approaches, so I wouldn't look like a jabbering idiot. Regretful, but retaining some shreds of dignity. That would do it.

On Thanksgiving Day, Joseph kept the store open until noon for people who forgot the cranberry sauce or needed more vegetables because Uncle Charlie, Aunt Martha and their kids came after they had said they weren't. Our dinner wasn't until four so I had plenty of time. Joseph came home at one, took a shower, dressed and was headed for the living room and the football game when I intercepted him.

"Do you have a minute, Joseph?"

"Sure, Jack. What's up?"

He leaned against the doorjamb and cocked his head attentively. He had put on a clean white shirt with a red and blue striped tie and navy slacks. I could hear Ma open the oven door in the kitchen. WQXR was playing a string quartet, and the first delicious smells of the roasting turkey spread through the apartment. It was a comfortable, homey scene like nothing I had ever experienced before, and it drove my rehearsed speech right out of my head.

"Yes, Jack?"

"I'm sorry, Joseph," I blurted. "I'm so sorry."

He looked puzzled for a moment, then straitened up, put his hands on my shoulders and looked into my face with a serious expression. "You love your mother, Jack. For that I can forgive anything. We never speak of this again, *capisce*?"

I nodded and it was done.

I went back to Cabot and the darkened month of December. As I trudged through the first snowfalls to four o'clock class in the fading twilight, I would remind myself that Christmas was not far away. But when it came, it didn't seem to

Over the course of my stay, in addition to James, the chauffeur and occasional butler, and Cal, the man on the tractor who took care of gardening and maintenance, I met Tina, housekeeper and wife to James, Mary, her assistant (the Millers thought "housemaid" was demeaning), Cook, whose actual name I never learned, and Grace, kitchen "assistant" (same reasoning as above). I thought it was right out of *Lifestyles of the Rich and Famous*, although I was to see more extravagance later in my visit. And I must say that the Millers didn't seem to be trying to impress anybody, least of all me. They didn't ring bells. If Mrs. Miller wanted to speak to one of the servants she would go and look for her, and, twice I saw Mr. Miller go into the kitchen to raid the fridge for a snack.

I hit tennis balls with Bobby and improved my game sufficiently to partner him against Mrs. Miller and Danny, the brother. We putted golf balls on the putting green on the other side of the house and spent a lot of time in the pool alternately racing each other and threatening to drown Danny, who would put up with anything to be with his older brother. The Millers kept extra bikes in the garage, so we rode together all over the neighborhood as far as Dean Dairy, which had the best ice cream I had ever tasted. Occasionally we would drop in on one of Bobby's friends, all of whom seemed to live in houses no less opulent than his.

The last evening, Bobby and I, without a desolate Danny, were invited to a pool party by a girl named Janet Hoving, a close friend of Rosalind Graham, Bobby's girlfriend. This establishment put Bobby's to shame. It was an enormous sprawling Tudor structure with several associated buildings: a guest house, a servant's house and a large structure with an indoor salt-water pool (the Hovings had made their fortune in

last any longer than the Thanksgiving weekend. Then came the long winter slog when the day was taken up with putting on and taking off overcoats and galoshes. Walking to the Village was an Arctic expedition and the best thing that could happen to you was a couple of days in the infirmary with one of the many childhood diseases that ran through the House like wildfire.

Winter eventually turned into spring and then one day the school year ended and I went home for the summer. While my Horowitz scholarship would continue to cover tuition and room and board, my life at Cabot incurred plenty of other expenses, and I insisted on doing my share to contribute. The married Luis had shed his mustache and his stories of sexual conquests for pictures of his wife and new baby, and had taken on more responsibilities in the store, allowing Joseph and Ma more time off, sometimes together. A part-time helper had been hired to perform some of Luis's former duties, and, conveniently had quit when his night school year ended. So, I fitted right in for the summer.

MA INSISTED, HOWEVER, that I have some vacation
Miller's parents had invited me to spend a week v
their home in the suburbs of Springfield. It prov
eye-opener in many respects. I was picked up at the
by Bobby in a station wagon driven by a man in a
introduced to me as "James." When we arrived at
home, James took my suitcase from the trunk and d
up a staircase while I was greeted by Mrs. Miller and
old brother of Bobby in a living room as big as our e
York apartment. Mr. Miller came home from his of
time for dinner. An older brother of Bobby was spe
summer touring Europe before starting law school.

The Millers' New England style house was almos
Baldwin House, similarly assembled over many gen
but with the parts fitted together more evenly, staircas
gically situated and an HVAC system that allowed me
the temperature for my room. I had my own bathro
cable television and a telephone with a card telling
to reach different parts of the house, local, long dist
emergency services. Out the window, I could see a sw
pool with a small low building at the far end, a tenni
beyond it and after a fair-sized stretch of green lawn, cu
being mowed by a man on a tractor, a long line of thic
spruce, which I correctly guessed to be the property li

salt), changing rooms and a huge trophy room. This room was decorated with the heads of African animals jutting from the walls and skins covering a half-dozen couches and scattered over the floor between them.

Bobby introduced me to the famous Roz, a quiet brunette who stuck close to Bobby throughout the evening, and to the others, including Artie Doran, Bobby's closest friend, and Janet Hoving, our hostess, a lively blonde with a face like Molly Ringwald's, curly hair and an already well-developed body. There were maybe ten of us altogether, about evenly divided between boys and girls. As far as I could tell, Bobby and Roz and one other couple were the only ones paired off.

We all changed into our bathing suits and went into the pool. It was even saltier than the ocean at Coney Island and floating was easy. After a while an informal water polo game started, which mostly served as an excuse to grab someone of the opposite sex who held the ball and dunk him or her until the ball came loose. Janet and the two other girls in bikinis were particular targets. When the opportunity came, as Janet held the ball in the air away from me, I grabbed her to me in a bear hug and pulled her underwater with me, so her whole body pressed against me. I had an instant erection and let go of her. As we surfaced, she no longer held the ball and was grinning at me.

"Is that part of the game, Jack?" she asked and swam away before I could answer.

Shortly after that, the game ended and we changed out of our suits and moved into the trophy room. Sandwiches and soda and cake were laid out on a couple of tables. As we finished eating, Janet turned on the most amazing stereo system. It sounded as though we were right in the middle of the orchestra.

"Make some room," she said and we pulled the couches and skins away from the center of the room for dancing.

Bobby and Roz were the first on the floor. I started for Janet, but Artie Doran got there first and for the next hour I couldn't seem to get near her. I danced with a couple of the other girls, trying not to be conspicuous although I was a terrible dancer. Finally, my chance came as she took a break at the soda table.

"Would you dance with me, after your drink?" I was trying hard not to appear too eager.

She took a long look at me. "Actually, Jack, I'm exhausted, but come with me and we'll sit one out together."

She led me back around the pool and into one of the changing rooms, snapped the lock on the door and lay down on one of the rolling *chaises* that get placed around pools. She moved to one side and patted the other. "Come and sit here."

I was there in a flash and called upon my memory from the movies of how to proceed without looking like a fucking idiot. I bent over slowly and put my hands on either side of her head. No resistance; excellent. I continued until our lips made contact and, hooray, she responded and put her hands behind my head. How long to hold it, though, I worried. No problem; when she took her hands away, that was the signal. She smiled in a sleepy way that made me kiss her again, lest she should actually fall asleep. This time, her mouth opened and her tongue slipped between my lips and wriggled about searching for mine. Very nice.

I would have liked to use my hands more actively. I didn't really need to hold her head, did I? She wasn't going anywhere. But before I could try anything, she gently pushed me up and away, sat up, pulled her cashmere sweater over her head, removed her bra and lay back down. And there they were! The two bare boobs every boy my age dreamed of. I didn't have to try to remember any movies now; I had played this scene in my head a hundred times or more. I stroked those perfect fifteen-year-old tits, squeezed them, bent and kissed them, nibbled the nipples, while Janet closed her eyes and made purring sounds punctuated by "yes," "not that," "again" and other directions, which I followed assiduously.

Suddenly she sat up again. Oh no, it was over? She reached over to me, loosened my belt, worked her hand under my shorts and began to fondle my erection. It was heavenly, but nature soon took its course.

"Ooh, what a pig you are," she said. She bent over and picked up a damp towel from the swimming party, wiped her hand at one end and gave it to me. "Clean up time."

It was over. Two towels later the *chaise* was clean, my pants just a little damp and only my shorts still a mess. Her bra and sweater were back on and her hair combed, so we made our way back to the trophy room, where nobody seemed to have noticed we had gone except the head of a rhinoceros who looked at me reproachfully. However, when we returned to the Miller house, Bobby held me back at the door to my room.

"So where did you and Janet go?"

"Uh, to one of the changing rooms."

"Did you make out with her? Tell me the truth." This was evidently a big piece of news.

I was torn between the desire to boast and the fear of embarrassment. "Well, sort of."

"How far did you get?"

I paused, trying to remember whether what had happened fit the definition of third base or was only second base, but then had a good idea. "I don't ask you how far you get with Roz, do I?"

That stumped him. Roz, as a serious girlfriend, was off-limits to that sort of kiss and tell.

"Oh, well OK, then." By implication, Janet was now my girlfriend. I didn't mind and hoped that she wouldn't either. After I got back to New York, I persuaded a telephone information operator to give me the address of the Hovings in Longmeadow, Mass. and sent her a brief non-committal letter thanking her for inviting me to her party, which I enjoyed greatly, and hoping I would have the opportunity to see her again sometime. It took twelve drafts to get what I felt was the exactly right tone, basically Emily Post with just the tiniest hint of Robert Browning.

AFTER ANOTHER TWO WEEKS AT HOME, I returned to Cabot considerably changed from the boy I had been in Saugerties, or New York City or even the previous year at Cabot. Jacob Gluckstein, mired in poverty and constantly belittled by his presumptive father, had grown into DP and Guh-luck-a-steen, struggling in the schoolyard and out of synch with his home-life. Next came Jack Stone, a token Jew surrounded by wealthier, better educated boys and facing, without family support, the strict rules and codes of a new school.

Now I was Lucky Jack, a comfortable sophomore, familiar with all the rules and the customs, hardly distinguishable from my classmates. I had passed all my classes and had been the second baseman for the Freshman baseball team. I had several friends and no enemies. And I kind'a, sort'a had a girlfriend who, as Bobby told our friends, was "really hot" and "built like a brick shithouse."

Ma's life had become a good one, too. Joseph seemed to be just as kind and generous as Ma said he was, and she wasn't working nearly as hard as she had when we first moved to New York, not to mention when we lived in Saugerties. While their life was nowhere close to the luxury in which the Millers lived, the apartment was comfortable, they ate well and there seemed to be enough money for decent clothes, movies and other modest entertainment.

Jack Armstrong and the damage he had caused was fading out of Ma's life and my vow was fading too. I would probably never find him, anyway, and it occurred to me that maybe I should just forget about him and not burden my life with the weight of such a vow.

My second year at Cabot passed much the same as the first, but with much less anxiety. My grades were OK: excellent in Algebra, not so hot in Latin and French, surprisingly good in English. With the encouragement of Mr. Chase, the English teacher, I discovered that I liked writing and turned out a couple of pretty good essays and one short story that was accepted by the School's literary magazine. In the spring, I made the junior varsity baseball team. My visits home at holiday times were pleasant. Ma expressed pride and Joseph, approval. Not a bad year, at all.

Janet attended the Emma Willard School in Troy, New York, and our homes were two hundred miles apart, so there was no question of getting together during the academic year. I had given up on her after three weeks passed with no response to my first letter, when I received a pale blue envelope addressed in a feminine hand and with a Troy postmark. The letter inside was brief, acknowledging my letter, with a few words describing her roommates and admitting that it might be nice to see me again someday. I reread it several times when Bobby was not in the room. The tone was totally casual and the closing just "Your friend," as mine had been.

But, she addressed me as "Dear Piggy." How about that?

I spent the next week crafting another letter, no more personal than the first. My guess was that writing any sooner might put her off. Three weeks later came a similar response. And so, we corresponded like pen pals for nine months. Several times I drafted letters reminding her of our encounter in the changing room and extolled the delights of her kiss, the beauty of her breasts and the softness of her hand. I would take each letter into a stall in the bathroom and, making sure I was alone, pretend it was happening all over. Afterwards, I would tear up the letter and flush it down the toilet. Given the limitations imposed by geography, that was the best I could do.

When the summer came, I returned to work at the store, first making sure I had another invitation to visit the Millers at a time when I knew Janet would be home. The weeks passed agonizingly slowly. I had little in common anymore with my few friends from earlier school days, and my principal recreation was watching TV and playing in pick-up baseball and basketball games in Central Park. A couple of times I went to movies and dinner with Ma and Joseph. They were pleasant, but my past attitude toward Joseph was a cloud over our relationship, and the emotional armor I had adopted at Cabot now prevented me from going beyond the superficial with my own mother. I guess that's the price of growing up.

As soon as I was settled in the back seat of the Miller's station wagon, as diffidently as possible, I inquired about Roz and his other friends—oh yes, including Janet.

He laughed. "Why do you ask? Do you have some sort of idea of seeing her while you're here? You think I don't know that you made out like a bandit last summer and have been writing her all year?"

I was nonplused; no other word describes it. "Oh, did Roz say something?"

"Of course. She's Janet's best friend. And I'm yours, you asshole. You shouldn't try to keep secrets from me."

"Sorry, you're right." I didn't tell him I kept secrets from everybody. "What did she say about me?"

He laughed again. "I was sworn not to tell you, but you'll have a chance to find out tomorrow night. We're double dating. Say, 'Thank you, Bobby.'"

I punched him in the arm, and we wrestled around in the back seat until James turned and said, "Cut it out, you two. I can't see the rearview mirror."

After an early dinner, we went up to our rooms to shower. I didn't want to repeat last summer's accident, and, with the stimulus of anticipation, had no trouble releasing some of the buildup in my tank. When I was ready, I went into Bobby's room.

"Where are we taking them?"

"It's a home date. Janet's parents are away and Roz is sleeping over. We're going to watch TV and then, who knows?" He leered and with his sleeked-down brown hair and narrow face, looked like an otter about to seize a fish.

That sounded very interesting. "What do you mean?"

"It's a big house with lots of bedrooms. It's up to you what you do in them. But, from what Roz told me, it sounds like Janet is hot to trot. Do you have protection, just in case?"

This was all a lot to process, and I just stared at him stupidly.

"Here you go." He opened a bureau drawer, rummaged under some sweaters, pulled out a box and handed me a little foil envelope. "My brother, Frank, gave these to me for my sixteenth birthday." Then, sarcastically, "You know how to use it, don't you?"

I came out of my trance. "Yeah, yeah. Thanks, I forgot to bring some," as if I had the balls to walk into my neighborhood drug store and ask Mrs. Goldschmidt for condoms.

He grinned at me, but didn't say more. He was always a smart kid.

Janet gave me a chaste kiss on the cheek when we arrived. She looked terrific dressed in a purple blouse and a pleated miniskirt, and I immediately surveyed them to locate the buttons for later. We went through an enormous living room into an entertainment room with a huge TV opposite couches arranged in three sides of a square around a big coffee table. A variety of cookies and sodas were on the table. A tall rack held a veritable tower of videos. Bobby and Roz took one couch and Janet and I the other.

"What would you like to watch?" asked Janet, and started reading off the titles. I didn't care. I hadn't come for the movie.

When she got to *The Hunger*, Roz stopped her. "Who's in that?"

"Catherine Deneuve and David Bowie. They're vampires. It's wild."

"Sounds good," chimed Bobby, and that was it.

Janet put on the movie and dimmed down the lights, so I could barely see which cookie was which. As far as what was happening on the other couch? Forget it.

Almost immediately, Janet snuggled up and we started making out. I followed the movie out of the corner of my eye. It was great, the movie, I mean. The rest was nice enough, but when I went after her buttons, she pushed my hand away. "Not now," she whispered.

Finally, in frustration, I pulled away and poured myself a Coke and took a couple of cookies. "All right," Janet whispered, and announced to the room, "Intermission." She got up and stopped the movie and turned the lights back up a bit. "Jack's never seen the house, so I'm going to show him around."

She took me from room to room, each one perfectly decorated and maintained. The family were art collectors. On one wall was a Renoir, on another a group of Rembrandt drawings and in her bedroom, a painting of a young dancer was over her bed.

"Who's that by?" I asked.

"Degas," she answered and flung herself on the bed below the painting. "My parents made me take ballet lessons, but I hated them. Dancers have to work all the time and have no fun." She moved to one side on the bed as she spoke, and took off her shoes.

You can believe I accepted the invitation, shed my shoes and lay down next to her and pulled her to me. After one long kiss, I went for the buttons on her blouse with no resistance. When it came off, she unhooked her bra and dropped it on the floor. Her tits were even bigger than last summer, and her nipples jutted out as soon as I touched them.

It took me a few minutes to work up the courage to put my hand on her leg, but there was no resistance, so I moved it up toward the Promised Land.

"Did you bring something?" she whispered.

What? I blanked out for a second, then, of course, I reached into my pocket and put the foil envelope on her night table.

"It's such a clever pig, all prepared." She laughed as she unbuttoned and pulled off her skirt and then, I could hardly believe it, her panties. "Well, come on then."

I tore off my clothes, lay back on the bed and grabbed the condom.

"Don't be in a rush," she said. "Let me have a look first." She raised up on her elbow and trailed her fingers down my chest, pinched a nipple and continued down. When she touched my erect cock, I congratulated myself on my precautions. It quivered but didn't disgrace me.

"The tip is so smooth," she said. "How come you're circumcised? None of the boys around here are." She suddenly blushed. "That's what I've been told, anyway."

"Of course, I'm circumcised. All Jewish boys are."

A volcano erupted. "What?" She rolled away and jumped off the other side of the bed. "You're Jewish? Lucky Jack Stone?"

"It used to be Jacob Gluckstein."

"I don't give a shit what your name was. Get out! Now!" She pulled off the sheet to cover herself. "My father would kill me if I fucked a Jew."

What could I say? "Calm down, I'm going." I got up and dressed as fast as I could.

"Hurry up. That son of a bitch Bobby should have told Roz. I can't believe she knew. I'll never speak to him again. Turn around, so I can get my clothes."

She ranted on while we both got dressed and she hustled me back downstairs. I grabbed the foil envelope on the way out the door. It was a good thing I hadn't opened it.

When we got back to the recreation room, Bobby and Roz weren't there. Janet made me leave the house while she stormed back upstairs to roust Bobby out of Roz's guest room, where they had more successfully finished what I had so eagerly started just a few minutes before. When we got home, I told Bobby the whole story. I didn't know whether I was angrier because of the anti-Semitism or because I had been deprived of what I had so long been anticipating.

"Maybe the worst thing was she never shut her mouth so I couldn't get a word in to tell her to go fuck herself."

Bobby tried, but he couldn't stop the laughter that burst out. "I'm really sorry," he said, but started laughing again. "I can just imagine the look on her face when she found out she was stroking a Jewish cock." And he started laughing again. "I guess you could call that *coitus interruptus hebraicus*."

More laughter and, angry as I was, I began to see the humor in it.

Finally, Bobby got serious. "It's my fault. Sometimes I forget you're Jewish. It certainly doesn't make any difference to me." He then told me about his father. "I didn't say anything originally to Roz or anyone because ... well, because it shouldn't matter, and, if I said something, it would make it matter. And then, it would make it worse later that I hadn't originally. And finally, it was going to be so great that you were getting to boff the princess, that I just hoped it wouldn't come out or wouldn't matter if it did."

"It's OK, Bobby. There'll be other princesses, and I'll be ready." I showed him the foil envelope and put it back in my wallet.

XIV

MY JUNIOR YEAR STARTED much like the first two but with the
benefit of some relaxation of the rules. We were free to go anywhere on campus until nine in the evening. On the weekends,
after Saturday morning classes we could apply for passes to
go beyond the Village, although that required approval of the
destination such as a written invitation to somebody's home
from an adult.

The Juniors shared a large recreational facility with the
Seniors in the same building as the Main Dining Hall. It
opened every day at four after classes and P.T. were over and
featured a bowling alley with two lanes of candle-pins, an ice-
cream bar and two small meeting rooms in addition to pool
and ping-pong tables. Bobo Anderson, his roommate, Ted
Kimball, Jim Ingersoll, already known as "Mighty Mouth" and
I would arrange for one of us to get there early on Saturday
evenings when we didn't care for the movie and grab one of
the rooms, set up a bridge table and chairs, and we would
play cards.

We tried crazy eights, which was too childish, and gin,
which required selecting who was playing together, which
became a pain. Then Hearts, which was fun mostly when the
three of us ganged up on Mouth, and he invented a whole new
vocabulary of curses for us. Then, one Saturday, Ted found a
box of chips in the game closet and we turned to poker. The

other three were not very good, but, since we weren't playing for money, I went along with them throwing my chips into the pot with any junky hand. Since they were all bright guys, they gradually learned what they should and shouldn't be doing and occasionally asked me things like the odds on hitting a full house holding two pairs.

The second Saturday we were playing, Professor Follansbee came into the room and stood watching for a moment. He was the youngest teacher and in his first year, which was why he was the one who had to give up his Saturday nights to supervise the Rec Room.

"Poker, boys?" he asked, a puzzled expression on his boyish face.

Everyone answered, "It's not for money, sir."

He looked relieved, took off his glasses and polished them. "Uh, whose chips are they?"

I guessed that he was stalling while he decided whether to stop the game.

Bobo answered, "They were in the games closet, so we assumed it was OK to use them."

That settled it. Bobo, besides having been elected Captain of the football team for next year, was our class President with a sterling reputation for integrity.

Follansbee smiled. "All right boys, have fun. But, remember, no gambling is allowed, for good reason. I have a cousin who's ruined his life, lost everything he earned and stole from his parents, because he got hooked on poker, horses, sports betting and anything else he could gamble on."

"That's a terrible story," I said gravely, and everyone agreed.

There was dead silence while Follansbee left and closed the door until Mouth asked, "Whose deal?" and we all broke up.

Although he intended the opposite, I think Follansbee got us started thinking about playing for money. The thought was not new to me, but I had no intention of hustling boys who had become my close friends. Being reminded that it was forbidden, however, seemed to make the idea more attractive to the other three. That set the stage nicely for the introduction of Al Washburn to our game.

Al lived in the Village of Cabot. He had dropped out of Cabot High, the local public high school, after his junior year, for reasons I never learned, joined the Army and participated in the invasion of Grenada. By finishing high school at Cabot Academy, he could be assured of getting into a top college. As a reward for his patriotism, he was given a scholarship for his tuition as a day student. He was a sub on the football team and became friendly with Bobo. I had a French class with him.

He occasionally came to our facility on a Saturday night and bowled or shot pool. The Saturday after Follansbee's visit to our game, Al came into our card room and stood watching for a while.

"How much are the chips?" he asked.

"The whites are one, the reds five and the blues ten," I answered.

"Dollars?"

"Actually," said Mouth, drawing it out, "they're *rasbucknicks*."

"What the fuck are those?"

Bobo spoke up, "He's kidding you, Al. That's money in *Mad Magazine*. We don't play for money. They throw you out for gambling here; it's not the Army."

"That's no fun. You've got to play poker for money."

Mouth, again, "No, it's lots of fun. The losers have to clean up the room and put away the chairs. It gets real exciting some nights." And we all laughed.

"Well, in that case, can I sit in?" Al asked, so we made room for him and gave him chips and thought nothing of it. He played with us the next couple of Saturdays, but usually managed to make some remark about how dull it was. At the end of one evening, he asked, "Well, would you guys like to play for money if you could do it without getting into trouble?"

"How would we do that?" asked Ted. "Follansbee might walk in at any minute."

"We could play at my house Saturday afternoon. We're big boys. Nobody is going to say anything to get us in trouble."

"What do you say, Jack?" asked Ted. It was common knowledge that my budget was not as generous as most other boys, and he was being considerate.

I had been about to demur, when Mouth came out with "Lucky Jack? This is his big chance."

So, of course I answered, "OK by me, but don't say you weren't warned."

The following Saturday afternoon was the final football game and Bobo and Al were unavailable, but the Saturday after that we assembled around a circular table in the Washburn's basement. I wasn't worried. I had reread my two books and knew I was a better player than all of them except maybe Al. I was still relieved when it was agreed that the maximum bet for the first couple of cards would be a nickel and thereafter only a dime. This was supposed to be for fun, not the business that poker has since become for me.

It went the way I had expected. Mouth stayed in on anything. Bobo and Ted were a little more cautious. Al was also in the pot for the first cards, but frequently dropped out after that, and, if he was still in at the end, was usually the winner. I played the way I had learned and dropped early if I didn't have good cards. Al brought us cookies and sodas from the kitchen. At the end of the afternoon, Mouth was the big loser of about fifteen dollars, which Al and I split up. The other two came out about even. Everybody had a good time.

We started to play every Saturday. The results were usually similar. Either or both Al and I usually won. Mouth usually lost, except one Saturday he hit winner after winner and walked out with twenty-one dollars. Late the following Saturday, we heard a knock of the door from the stairway to the basement. For a moment, I froze. The School had found us out? Al looked at me and started laughing.

"They gotcha, Jack." He went to the door and ushered in a slim, dark-haired girl of fifteen or sixteen. "Guys, this is my sister, Faith. You caught us, kid." He laughed again.

The girl flashed a smile in our general direction and looked quickly away. "Mom said to remind you that we're leaving at 5:30 to go to Grandma's for supper and it's 5 now."

"Oops! I had forgotten. Thanks, Faith. OK, guys, settle up. Sorry, but duty calls."

On the way out the door, as you might expect, Mouth asked, "How did an ugly mug like you get a nice-looking sister like Faith?"

"Never you mind," said Al. "She's top in her sophomore class at Cabot High and hasn't got time for a bunch of poker-playing bums."

She looked nice enough, but was no Janet. Why did I have to be Jewish, anyway?

The varsity baseball squad was invited to a high school tournament in Florida over Easter vacation. Since I had been on the junior varsity as a sophomore, I automatically was included. We took the long train ride down on the weekend before Easter and came back to Cabot on Good Friday, which didn't leave enough time for me to go home for Easter. When I told Al, he invited me to spend the weekend at his house instead of staying in the near-empty dorm. His mother wrote an invitation and I had no difficulty in obtaining approval from the School.

Cabot had no chance against the schools from Florida that had been playing all winter, but we did win a consolation game against an Ohio school. I played second base most of the time and did pretty well.

That Good Friday afternoon, Al picked me up at the station in the family car so I wouldn't have to lug my suitcase, and drove me to their house for dinner. Mr. Washburn was a jolly, rugged man in his late 40s, a former athlete whose appetite for food and beer had already put him out of condition. He taught P.T. and coached teams at Cabot High. Mrs. Washburn was more abstemious and could be mistaken, in dim lighting, for Al's sister rather than his mother. She had been a teacher at the High School, but had stopped to raise her children, and now was selling cosmetics at the Cabot Emporium. Both parents were pleasant.

Growing up among three extroverts, it was not surprising that Faith was less a talker than a listener. Her plain, regular features, devoid of makeup. wouldn't attract a second look, but I gave her one anyway. When she caught me, she demurely dropped her eyes to her plate.

After dinner, Mrs. Washburn and Faith began to clear the table while the men headed to the basement to watch the Boston Celtics play the New York Knicks. With the Celtics down eighteen points at the half, Mr. Washburn yawned and excused himself.

"You want to watch the rest of this disaster?" asked Al.

"Not particularly. What else is on?"

Al thumbed through a copy of TV Guide. "A couple of stupid sitcoms and some old movies that are halfway through. You don't play chess, do you?"

"No. My stepfather tried to teach me, but it was too much like work."

"We could play a little head-to-head poker?"

There was a challenge. I thought I was the better player, but it was hard to tell in our Saturday games. He probably had won a little more than I did. "OK, let's do that."

Al got out the cards and the chips, and we started. It went much the same as in our regular game. Al was undisciplined and frequently stayed in the pot for a round or two with inferior hands and gave up a lot of nickels and dimes in doing so. But when it got to the last card and the quarter bets, his judgment was better than mine. I couldn't bluff him and when I had the goods he usually folded. I began to wonder if he had picked up some mannerism of mine, a "tell" which would indicate strength or weakness.

We had been playing a little more than an hour when Mrs. Washburn and Faith came in.

"What have you boys been up to?" Mrs. Washburn looked at the table, but of course there were only chips and no money. "Can't you find anything better to do than this, Alan?"

Al laughed. "C'mon, Mom. You and your friends play once a month."

"That's different. We spend more time gossiping than playing. And it's only pennies. You're not playing for money, are you Jack?" She probably suspected she wouldn't get the truth from her son.

"No, Mrs. Washburn, it's just for chips."

"All right, but stop and come down with Faith and me to Carvels for ice cream."

That broke up the game and probably saved me money, particularly since Mrs. Washburn insisted on paying for my ice cream cone.

Saturday morning, Al and I slept late. Mr. and Mrs. Washburn had gone to work and after a pot luck brunch, we went with Faith to a Cabot High basketball game, where Al and I speculated on how badly the Cabot Academy team would have beaten either of these two. After the game, Faith went off with her friends, and, as though it had been discussed and agreed to, Al and I went back to the basement and continued our game. Things went the same as the night before, except that I got upset with losing and played too loosely which was worse. By the time we put away the cards and chips, I owed Al almost forty dollars. I only had twenty with me, but he said I could pay him next time.

Sunday morning after breakfast, the family went to Easter services at Cabot's Methodist church. I accepted the casual invitation to join them. The subject of my religious persuasion didn't come up. At the services, we were joined by Al's uncle, aunt and their daughter who then came to the Washburn house.

We played some three-on-three touch football followed by a big Easter dinner. Everybody had fun, except that I couldn't get over losing all that money to Al. In retrospect, it was a good thing that the day was filled with other activities so we couldn't play, or I would have lost more.

Classes resumed the following day. I dug out my stash of winnings from the group game and paid Al the twenty when I saw him at French class. We had an exam scheduled for Thursday, and it seemed like a good idea to study for it together Wednesday afternoon when we had no classes or sports. He came up to my room after lunch while Bobby went to the Village and we drilled each other conscientiously for an hour, then decided to take a break. Al grinned sheepishly and drew a deck of cards from his pocket.

"OK," I said, "but we have no chips."

"We can keep track on a pad. That's better than having chips lying around if anybody comes in."

I knew it was stupid. Unlikely as it was that we would be caught by one of the teachers, the result, if we were, would probably be expulsion. But, fuck it, I was determined to get even and, to do so, suggested we raise the stakes from nickel-dime-quarter to ten-twenty-fifty cents. As anyone with any sense would have predicted, I lost another thirty-five dollars by the time Bobby returned. And I flunked the French test.

By Saturday, I had calmed down. My savings had been sadly depleted, and I wasn't a masochist. Losing was no fun for me. I hesitated but ended up going with the gang to Al's on Saturday afternoon. It went as usual; Al and I each won a few dollars from the other three. It wasn't enough to get excited about, but I enjoyed winning again. I decided that the group game was OK, but no more head to head with Al. Actually, I didn't play much at all that semester. My success at the Florida tournament put me on the varsity baseball team which took up the remaining Saturdays.

Our first game was at Cabot High School, and I was excited when the coach put me in the starting lineup at second base. When we came out onto the field before the game, I went to say hello to Mr. Washburn who was coaching the High School team.

"Good to see you, Jack. What position do you play?"

"Second base. This is my first game on the team."

"Well, good luck to you. Al is visiting Michigan this weekend, but Faith is over there." He pointed to a spot in the stands. I waved to her and she waved back, and I went to the Academy bench.

It was a close game. I hit two singles and scored the winning run with a slide under the High School catcher's tag. After the last out the two teams lined up to shake hands with each other. As I walked away, Faith came up to me and held out her hand.

"Congratulations, Jack. You were very good."

I shook hands. She had a nice firm grip. "I'm sorry your team lost." Yes, a firm grip but a soft hand. "Would you like to go to Doc's for something?" Now, where did that come from?

"Don't you have to go back to the Academy?"

"No, let me shower and change and one of the guys will take my stuff back on the bus and I can walk back later."

She hesitated a moment, then, "All right, I'll meet you at the front door of the gym."

At Doc's, hungry after the game, I ordered a cheeseburger; Faith ordered a fruit cup.

"Fruit cup?" I asked.

She shrugged. "I'm on the track team and the coach doesn't want us eating ice cream or cake or stuff like that."

At that, I couldn't help looking at her legs. From what I could see between her skirt and socks they were perfectly nice legs suitable for running and anything else you might think of. She caught me and gave me that demure look down.

I quickly recovered. "What's your event?"

"Quarter-mile and the mile relay."

I summoned my limited knowledge of track. "Isn't that the toughest event? Don't you have to go full speed the whole time?"

"That's for the Olympics or major men's track. High school girl's quarter miles are much slower. Some try to run in front all the way. I follow and hope I can sprint at the end."

"Does it work?"

She smiled modestly, "Sometimes yes, sometimes, no."

"Well, I have to come see you run."

"That would be nice."

The waitress brought our food, which relieved me of the necessity of promising to come to the next meet. We had a pleasant conversation. Without her voluble family around her, Faith easily held up her end. As expected, she was interested in sports, but also played the guitar. She idolized Al and spoke glowingly of his patriotism and his successes at football and his early acceptance at a couple of colleges. When asked, I confirmed that he was a good poker player—I didn't go into detail.

She was also a good listener and was interested in my home and family, of which I gave her the Readers' Digest version. Her reaction when I told her I was Jewish was one of curiosity as to how I came to Cabot, but with no negative implication. Apparently, her father had not threatened to kill her if she slept with a Jew, but it didn't matter since I had no such inclination and I sincerely doubt she had either. When we finished, she insisted on paying for her fruit cup, and we split the tip and set off in our separate directions with a casual good-bye.

XV

THE SCHOOL YEAR FINISHED. My batting average was .345 and I led the baseball team in runs scored. Even so, I was surprised when they elected me co-captain for the next year. My grades were just OK. The competition was tough and baseball took up a lot of my weekend time. Besides, I have never enjoyed studying, just considered it a necessary means to an end, and I knew that merely graduating would get me into a good college.

My summer was split up. For most of it I stayed in New York and worked in the store while first Luis and then Joseph and Ma took vacations. The month of August, I spent as a junior baseball counselor at a camp in Maine owned by the Cabot baseball coach. It was a pleasant change, and I found that I enjoyed teaching the kids. Bobby Miller took a summer course in France, so I missed the annual visit to his home. Considering what had happened the previous summer, I probably was better off not coming within ten miles of Janet.

It seemed like only a couple of weeks before I was back at Cabot, a senior, one of the big men on campus. We had no time for poker. Most of us had increases in our extra-curricular activities. Bobo was co-captain of the football team and class president. His roommate, Ted, was on the soccer team and even Mouth achieved success as the lead in the fall dramatic club production of *Macbeth*. I led Sunday morning batting practice for baseball hopefuls in the Field House. But the biggest demand on our attention was our futures. Where would we go to college? Between campus visits, wrestling with applications and the endless discussions we had with each other, we were lucky that our teachers were inclined to be charitable toward seniors who skimped on their studies.

The generous Horowitz scholarship had covered tuition, room and board at Cabot for four years. The college placement officer told me that, with a reasonable SAT score, I had a good chance of getting in to any college I wanted. But my grades weren't likely to win me much scholarship aid at the top schools. I had discussed the subject with Ma over the summer. I decided to apply to Yale and Princeton, expecting to get in and hoping for substantial financial aid, to Tufts and Oberlin, where I had a better chance at such aid, and to Columbia, where I could cut costs by living at home. This meant a lot of applications and several campus visits which made for a busy fall.

When Bobby first approached me about the Fall Dance, I thought he was nuts. Fine for him. Roz was scheduling a trip to the area to visit Harvard and Wellesley and could stay at the Cabot Inn and come to the dance, the closest thing Cabot had to a prom.

It wasn't for me, though. "One, I don't want to spend the money, two, I can't dance, and three, I don't have a girlfriend to invite."

Bobby was prepared for my answer. "All it will cost you is cleaning your suit. I'll teach you a couple of steps; most of the music they'll play you can do whatever you feel like. And you can go stag. They always bring over a carload of girls from Sara Mitchell. Or Bobo's girlfriend, Inge, can get you a date from there. She's bringing one for Ted, already."

"I can only imagine what the number two girl Inge gets will look like. Or, worse, anyone desperate enough to come in that cattle car."

Bobby had an answer to that, too. "I don't know; Sara Mitchell locks them up pretty good. Even a good-looking girl might be looking for some action."

"What a dreamer. Why do you want me to go? Roz must be pissed at me over that thing with Janet."

"Actually, she's not. She liked you. She told Janet off for being an anti-Semite, and they didn't speak to each other for months. She'd like to apologize to you."

Well, how about that? "Thank Roz for me, but I think I'll pass."

Bobby frowned, but then brightened. "How about Al Washburn's sister? You told me she was very nice. She's still at the High School, isn't she?"

"Forget it, Bobby. The world is full of nice girls whom I don't need to take to a dance."

He dropped the subject, but a day or so later Bobo raised it. He wanted the four of us, with dates, to take up one of the eight-person tables at which we'd have a buffet supper to break up the dancing. I had thought a little more and admitted to myself that Faith had been very pleasant company. True, she wasn't the sex-bomb Janet had been. But, after my monastic life at Cabot, spending a few hours in close physical contact with a perfectly nice girl didn't seem such a bad idea.

I called her, first inquiring about Al, away at Michigan, and the health of Coach and Mrs. Washburn. Then, awkwardly, "Uh, I wonder if, uh, you might like to, uh, come to our Fall Supper Dance."

A long pause. "When is it?" Tone, surprised, unsure. Well, why not? I was unsure about asking her.

"Saturday, November 10." Now I'm sounding too eager. Shit.

A short pause, suitable for looking in a date book. How full could it be three weeks in advance?

"That would be very nice." Not like her prince had brought the glass slipper, but not exactly forced at gunpoint, either.

"Great, I'll call you with the details." Or possibly mail her the printed set of do's and don'ts with the date and time filled in in ink.

"I'll look forward to it. Thank you, Jack."

When she said my name, I knew it was all right.

"Bye, Faith."

"Bye, Jack."

The arrangements were easily made, particularly since several of her friends at the High School had been to such dances and told her the drill. On the day, I walked to her house arriving at 6:45 with her mother ready to drive us back to the dance and to pick her up at 10:15 a few minutes after the official end. Her mother greeted me at the door, fetched Faith's coat and her own as Faith came down the stairs.

I should say "flowed down the stairs"—she was so graceful. I was knocked out. Her ponytail had been replaced with a cascade of deep black hair falling to the top of a pale blue sweater above a full navy skirt. Her regular features, now accented by a little make-up, were perfectly proportioned, her eyes black holes that overcame my gravity. She stopped a few feet in front of me, while I stood like a dummy, staring at her. This time she didn't drop her eyes demurely, but gave me a big smile.

"Hi, Jack."

I broke out of my catatonia, "Hi, Faith. You look terrific." She sure did. I shot a glance at Mrs. Washburn, who had put on her coat and was holding Faith's out to me, a smug smile on her face. That's right, she worked in cosmetics. Great work, Momma.

Bobo and Ted were standing guard by the front door of the gym waiting for the arrival of their dates from Sara Mitchell. As they greeted Faith, a small yellow school bus arrived and seven or eight girls piled out trying to ignore the indignity of their transportation. Bobo rescued his girlfriend, a six-foot Nordic goddess, and Ted's date, a contrasting tiny brunette.

The dance committee had decorated the gym with fall foliage, pumpkins and red and yellow crepe paper. Bobby and Roz had commandeered one of the supper tables and we all sat down for introductions and inspection. I was reminded of the time I stopped to look at the dogs off the leash at Cherry Hill in Central Park. A professional dog walker arrived with a pack of six or seven dogs and all the rest gathered round for a grand session of sniffing and tail wagging with a couple of warning growls as they sorted out the new standings in the community. Now, we all looked around and rated each other, although the boys had already established their own ranking, from Bobo, the Alpha, through me and Ted to Bobby. Among the girls, I was pleased to see Faith holding her own against Roz and Alison, Ted's date. No one was going to challenge Inge, The Valkyrie, who could have stepped from the cover of Strength and Beauty Magazine.

"Good evening, everybody," the P.A. system blasted. "Welcome to Autumn Dreams at Cabot Academy." A little platform had been constructed for the DJ under one of the basketball backboards, and a guy in a Cabot High letter sweater waved to everybody before turning to his equipment to play Nat (King) Cole singing "Autumn Leaves." Couples started out on the dance floor. I turned my attention to an inspection of the nearest pumpkin, while the other three couples at our table went onto the floor. When I finally looked back at Faith, she justifiably seemed puzzled.

"Yes Jack?"

I spread my hands. "I really don't know how to dance. Bobby tried to teach me, but it didn't work."

"Oh. That's all right. Come, let me try."

That was the first time I learned the great truth that nothing attracts a woman as much as stumbling at some act that a proper macho man would perform smoothly. It tells her she has nothing to fear from the poor sap so she can let herself go with him.

Faith took my hand and led me out to an open portion of the floor. She tucked my right hand around her waist, held up my left hand and started to turn slowly to her right. "Small step with the left," and I stepped. "Now slide the right," and I slid. "And again," and I docilely followed. Once we got it in time to King Cole, it wasn't that bad. Fortunately, the next number was "I Want to Dance with Somebody," and, as Bobby had said, for that song and the next few you could move your feet pretty nearly any way you wanted as long as they were in time with the music. I clomped up and down in one place while Faith moved gracefully back and forth, somehow resisting the reasonable urge to dance away from me to the other side of the gym.

After a while, I gave her a break and we got glasses of fruit punch from a large pumpkin and went back to the table. I told her about my college applications. She was sympathetic to my financial concerns as she would have similar ones next year. She hoped to become a doctor, but, knew it wouldn't be easy to get there. When the conversation became serious, she jumped up and pulled me back to the floor.

The DJ was playing a stretch of slow numbers. I gradually lost my fear of tripping or stepping on Faith's feet, and just enjoyed the sensation. It came to me that I was holding something precious in my arms. Without thinking, I pulled my right hand against her back and without resistance her body came up against mine. I don't remember what I had been saying, but I stopped in mid-sentence. Faith said nothing either and we moved slowly together, until the music stopped and supper was announced. I took her hand and we went back to the table.

On our way we passed near the DJ's platform. "Hi, Faith," he called, and I slowed.

"Hi, Billy," she responded unenthusiastically.

"How's Gordo?" he asked.

She didn't answer but pulled me toward our table where we sat down next to each other.

"You know the DJ?" I asked her.

"He's in my class." She sighed. "I suppose you'd like to know who Gordo is, too."

"I guess so."

"He's a Senior I've been going out with. Does it matter?" Now she dropped her eyes.

It was none of my business, I thought, but heard myself say, "Yes."

"Then I won't anymore."

She raised her head and smiled so beautifully that I rose from my chair, bent over her upturned face and kissed her with everything I had. My chair clattered on the floor and a chorus of cheers and applause echoed around us. When I released her, I lost my balance and would have fallen over if Bobo hadn't shown up to catch me.

"Go, you tiger, go!" Bobo clapped me on the back and picked up my chair. I quickly looked at Faith. Her eyes were wide open and her fingers were at her lips as though checking for damage, but when I caught her glance the corners of her mouth turned up and she nodded once.

We had our supper and danced some more and barely spoke the rest of the evening. When we had our coats on and came out of the gym, Mrs. Washburn was waiting in the car. Couples were ducking around the corners of the gym or partly hiding their embraces behind the Grecian columns holding up the portico, but we walked straight to the car and I opened the door for Faith.

"Thank you, Jack, for a lovely evening," she said formally, and got into the car.

"You're very welcome, Faith. I'll call you tomorrow." As I closed the door I could see her laughing, and I laughed, too, all the way to the dorm, jumping to touch every tree branch along the way.

THAT WAS THE BEGINNING of the happiest time of my life. I couldn't believe how my heart, or whatever it was, lifted with joy to see Faith walk in the door at Doc's or wave at me as she emerged from the High School building. Every Wednesday and Saturday afternoon I didn't have a baseball game, I headed off to the Village. I went to her track meets and she came to my baseball games. If one of Faith's parents was home, we would usually meet elsewhere so they wouldn't become alarmed at how much time we spent together. But the basement at her home was the only place we could reliably go to physically demonstrate our affection, and we did dearly love to do that.

Faith was a marvelous kisser—her lips now a butterfly, now a luscious tropical fruit, sometimes a wedge to open a path for her tongue. Her body would react correspondingly, barely touching me or melting into mine or grinding against me like someone in the throes of lust. I loved making out with her, except for one problem. She did all these marvelous things with her clothes on.

I was totally in love with Faith. That meant that, although I desired her, I also cherished her, admired her and respected her. She wasn't Janet; I didn't expect to hop into bed right away. I certainly wouldn't want to unless she did also. But she told me she never had and wasn't ready to do so now, although she was sure that doing so with me would be immensely pleasurable.

When would the time for this immense pleasure arrive? If she had only given me a date, six months say. But I knew enough not to ask her. We were years away from marriage, even assuming our love lasted that long, which I hoped would be the case. Her resistance was too strong to be overcome by argument or ultimatum—that would result in my losing her which was unthinkable. Would I have to settle for as much of Faith as she could give me and, for the rest, go to Mademoiselle Hand? Possibly, but I didn't have to decide that yet.

I resorted to attrition: the age-old process that has converted the resistance of untold numbers of virgins into cooperation. The first time that, during a particularly soulful kiss, my hand settled on her breast, it was gently removed. Ditto, the second and third times that day and on the succeeding two or three days. I was encouraged to note, however, that it took slightly longer each time. I went home for Thanksgiving. The following Wednesday, after we acknowledged how much we had missed each other during the brief hiatus, whether or not that was the cause, the hand was permitted, although sweater and bra continued in place.

The next objective was skin, which might be reached by unbuttoning tops or by reaching beneath those without buttons. That was achieved when I returned from the Christmas vacation. From there, matters progressed fairly easily to where, if we were assured against interruption, I was allowed to caress and then kiss her small but perfectly formed breasts. Below her waist, however, was strictly forbidden territory.

If this reads in some measure disrespectful or cynical, know that I was as tender and reverent to Faith's body as a committed priest might be to the cross around his neck. Love is strengthened, not weakened, by its physical manifestation.

The physical was not everything, either. We spent hours talking and laughing and encouraging each other, celebrating our triumphs and consoling our defeats. For all the time and attention I gave to Faith, I found my grades improved. She said the same.

My college results were almost exactly as predicted. Lacking sufficient financial aid elsewhere, I decided to go to Columbia. Faith was now planning her own applications for the following year and began to consider Barnard, NYU and CCNY, among other schools, so we could be close to each other. During her spring vacation, she and her mother came to New York so Faith could look at the colleges. Unfortunately, her vacation and mine didn't coincide, but I arranged for Ma and Joseph to take Faith and her mother to dinner which I was told went very well. When I returned from my vacation, we had been apart two weeks, the longest in the four months we had been going together.

The front door of her house had barely clicked shut when we swarmed each other, clinching and parting and clinching again like demented boxers forgetting to use their fists. After a moment I discovered that she wore no bra under her blouse, and I started to tear at the buttons.

"No Jack," she laughed. "Not here. Come, come."

She led me, not to the basement stairs, but to those going up to the second floor. I followed her into her bedroom, shaking with anticipation. Would we ...? She put a finger to her lips. "Don't say anything, Jack. Take off your clothes and get into the bed."

Believe me, I didn't question her but did as I was told, pausing only to remove the famous foil envelope from my wallet. The window shade was already pulled down, so when

Faith turned out the light I couldn't see her, but could hear the sound of fabric hitting the floor. The next moment she was with me, pulling the top sheet over us. I slid my arm under her back, pulled her to me and vibrated with pleasure wherever our bodied touched.

It was not a success. I tried to be gentle but was too eager. She grunted in pain at first, and I froze.

"Should I stop?"

"No, it's all right."

Only a few moments later I felt my climax coming and drove into her, which produced anther grunt. I immediately withdrew. I held her protectively mumbling incoherent endearments but felt the condom come off and scrambled out of bed. Faith turned on the lamp by the side of the bed and got up onto the floor holding the pillow in front of her.

I was frantic. "I'm so sorry. I hurt you. I'd never want to do that."

Faith shook her head slowly. "I'm all right, Jack. Let me get to the bathroom."

She picked up her clothes and slowly walked out of the room. I pulled back the top sheet. The bottom sheet was a mess, spotted with blood and my stuff. I took Kleenex from a box on the dresser and wiped myself and tried to do something with the sheet, but it was no use, so I got dressed. I had felt never so ashamed in my life.

After a couple of minutes, Faith came back into the room, looked at the bed and shook her head again. "I better put the sheets through the laundry before my parents get home."

Again, I started babbling apologies, but Faith put her hand to my lips. "Shh. I'll live. Gail warned me that the first time doesn't work so well. You'd better go. I'll call the dorm phone at nine."

She bundled the sheets, and we walked down the stairs together. At the front door she kissed me lightly. "Go home, tiger. Oh, Gail also told me it gets much better when you do it again—if you've got the right boy."

Thank God, I hadn't ruined everything.

A few days later, we did it again, and Gail was 100% right. I guess I was the right boy. I laid in a supply of condoms merely by asking the clerk at Cabot Drug and Pharmacy, who obviously had supplied them to many other Academy boys over the years. The effectiveness of our contraception became evident when Faith's period showed up one day just as we were getting ready to go at it again.

We had been so active at sex lately, that it took us a while to come up with something else to do. Then Faith said, "Why don't you teach me poker? My parents didn't want me to learn when I was younger, but now that I've become expert at other vices, it should be OK." She gave me a moment to grin at that then continued, "I can surprise Al when he comes home from Michigan."

I agreed and we went to the basement and hunted for cards but couldn't find any.

"Al keeps some in his room. Let me see if he left them here when he went away."

She ran upstairs and came down with two used decks, probably the same ones I had played with before, as they had the same sprawling vine pattern on the back. The basement refrigerator was out of soda, and while Faith went back up to the kitchen for Cokes, I started to shuffle the blue deck. Something caught my eye. Could the backs be different? I picked up one card and looked at it closely. There was a blue dot at the end of one of the white strands of the vine. I turned the card over. It was an ace. I spread out the deck. Some other cards had blue dots in the same or different places. All the aces and face cards were marked in matching ink! I quickly looked at the red deck. It was the same. Red dots which came off when I rubbed one with a wet finger. Al had been cheating everyone in the game and me in particular. Eighty or ninety dollars a year ago at Thanksgiving.

Rage flooded my mind, but I managed to hide it when Faith returned. Should I tell her? I was too angry to think clearly at the moment and needed time by myself. When Faith came back, I went through the motions of teaching her a little poker, then made an excuse and left.

She stopped me at the door. "Is something wrong, Jack? You're acting funny."

I assured her there was nothing wrong, kissed her vigorously and went home.

That smooth cocksucker. He wasn't a better player than I, he just knew what my hole cards were. No wonder he liked five-card stud with only one hole card. And he could usually see whether one of the marked cards was on the top of the deck to be dealt next. The bastard. In his own home, with his buddies. I had to do something, but what? I couldn't confront Al and demand my money back. He wouldn't return from Michigan until after my graduation. But I couldn't let him get away with it. If I told Bobo, he'd take Al apart, but he'd be leaving when I was and going home to upstate New York, a long way from Cabot.

I thought about it most of the time Sunday, picturing a scene where I told Al off, then, when a fight started, knocked him out. The trouble with that, was that Al, a football player, had three or four inches and forty pounds on me. I could tell Faith and show her the marks next time we were together.

That was tricky, though. Faith idolized her brother, probably would go into denial and never say anything to him, almost certainly wouldn't tell her parents. And what would that do to our relationship? Wouldn't she want to kill the messenger? But I had to do something.

I was supposed to call her Sunday evening, but still hadn't decided what to do. If I was going to tell her, I probably had to do it at the first opportunity. I couldn't figure a suitable conversation—she would tell something was wrong, so I didn't call. I didn't sleep much either.

Monday was no better. I still hadn't worked it out after going back and forth all day. My thinking was complicated because Al's crime brought back Jack Armstrong's, which I had gradually pushed out of my mind. Was I going to let Al go unpunished too? I was furious with myself when I realized I had abandoned my vow. I was in too much of a turmoil to call Faith and ran to the gym before supper, worked myself to exhaustion, too tired to eat more than a few bites, and dragged myself to bed.

Tuesday was much of the same. At baseball practice, we had an intra-squad game. I looked at third strikes twice and kicked three ground balls into right field. When I got back to my room after supper, there was a note under my door from Jim Jordan, whose room was near the pay phone. "Call Faith." I sat at my desk staring at the note, unable to move. What should I say? At nine o'clock, someone knocked on my door. It was Jim again. "Faith is on the phone, holding."

It was like I was bound to my chair and couldn't get up. "Tell her I can't talk to her." This was crazy, but my mind refused to function, and it was crucial that I get it right.

Wednesday morning classes were a complete blur. I think I got called on in English class, but can't remember for sure. I was back at my desk at two o'clock trying to read Hemingway's "The Undefeated." I couldn't have told you whether it was about bullfighting or chasing white whales. Suddenly, Bobo burst in the door.

"What's the matter with you, Jack? Faith is downstairs. She's almost hysterical. You have to talk to her."

I shook my head, frozen with indecision.

"What happened? Whatever it was, go down and talk to her. Go on."

I remember distinctly my reply, "I can't see her."

"You have to."

I looked down at the book and said nothing.

Bobo stepped toward me as if to pick me up and drag me downstairs but stopped. "You must be out of your fucking mind."

He went to the door and looked back at me, but I hadn't moved, so he left; the slammed door was a shotgun blast.

That woke me. I went over to the window. Faith stood in front of the dorm entrance, in her Cabot High jacket, her ponytail sticking out behind her baseball cap. Bobo came out of the entrance shaking his head and barely caught her as she collapsed. She leaned against him, and he put his arms around her shaking shoulders. Next to Bobo, she looked like a six-year-old. After thirty seconds or so, Bobo's arms loosened and Faith stepped back. She ran her sleeve across her face, turned and went slowly back to the road and down the hill to the Village. I watched her until the trees in their full spring foliage blotted her from my sight. A knife drove into my heart as I whispered after her, "That's for you, Al."

XVII

THE FIRST THING I DID when I came home after graduation from Cabot, was to call Isaac Horowitz, the donor of the scholarship that had sustained me for the past four years. The day before graduation I had received a brief letter, on stationery so thick you could have danced on it, requesting that I call him to make an appointment so that he might congratulate me in person. When I called, someone sounding just like Vanessa Redgrave informed me that Mr. Horowitz was engaged at the moment but that he would be pleased if I would come to his office two days hence at two o'clock.

I wore my good suit and was careful to arrive at ten minutes before two at the office of Horizon Realty and Construction, Inc., on the fifth floor of a twenty-story steel and glass building on Third Avenue. A small brass plate near the building entrance informed me that Horizon had built the building in 1970. How nice; we were the same age. An attractive receptionist took my name and reported my arrival via telephone. No, she wasn't Vanessa; that was the lady who came out to usher me into the inner sanctum.

Mr. Horowitz, a stout, bald gentleman in his sixties, wearing a three-piece suit that barely constrained his belly, did me the honor of getting up and trekking around the football field that served as his desk to shake my hand and show me to a chair. I declined his offer of coffee, tea or a soft drink. Probably not wishing to take up the time to make the return journey to his desk chair, he pulled up a second guest chair next to me. He waved aside my speech of gratitude and launched into a lengthy monologue congratulating me on my various achievements at Cabot, of which he had obviously been informed in detail, mixing in comparisons and contrasts with those of his late son, a picture of whom was prominent on his desk. He had clearly loved his son deeply and must have found that supporting me and those before me kept his own boy alive again at the happy age before the terrible illness struck him. This garrulous, slightly fussy man moved me; what would I not have given to have had a father like him?

He asked me whether I had thought beyond college. I said I hadn't. This triggered another monologue in which he extolled the benefits of a career in real estate, getting up at one point to walk around the room identifying the pictures on the walls of buildings he had built. He concluded by giving me his card and telling me to contact him if at any time I wanted a job either permanently or as a summer intern. This was a clear signal and I got up to leave. He opened the door of his office, walked with me through the reception area, opened the outside door for me and only then extended his hand in farewell. I must have looked puzzled, because he laughed and said, "Lesson one in courtesy, take your guest to the elevator. It shows him he is important."

My first year at Columbia was unsatisfying for a lot of reasons. As a day student, I didn't have the same feeling for the college campus life that is so appealing to most students. I had friends. Bobo had been lured by the opportunity to star on the traditionally weak Columbia football team; at Yale or Princeton he'd have struggled to make the squad. Mouth, whose grades weren't quite good enough for Harvard, roomed with him. Bobby was off at Stanford, but his best friend, Artie Doran, had come to Columbia. These were all good guys, but from rich families. Not having money meant less at Cabot where there was little to spend it on; in New York City, there was plenty, and I felt the difference, particularly when they planned entertainments I couldn't afford. Since they all liked poker, we soon had a game going at higher stakes than at Al's house. I overcame my reluctance to take money from my friends. They could obviously afford their losses, but it moved the relationship to a less comfortable level.

Working at the store on weekends and holidays was no longer comfortable, either. Luis had taken on more management as Joseph and Ma didn't want to work as hard as they had been. That made him my boss. We never had an argument, but it was awkward, particularly during periods when there was a full-time helper, usually a young relative of Luis, better suited to the role than an Ivy League student.

The classes were OK, but I couldn't seem to work up any enthusiasm for them. I had no idea what to major in and took stuff here and there without any purpose. Finally, there was Faith, or, more accurately, there wasn't Faith, only a bitter memory of what I had done.

I tried to fill the void by chasing every girl I saw north of 110th Street. Most of them were nice enough; several of them were sexually amenable. I tried to fall in love with each so I wouldn't think about Faith, like a penniless artist who paints new images on a used canvas. Other girls' faces, voices, bodies gradually obscured hers so only the faintest fragments of her original image remained. My other trick, when Faith came unbidden into my mind and I felt the guilt of what I had done to her and the pain of what I had done to myself, was to concentrate on Al, again invoking my anger and congratulating myself on my revenge. He would know. Faith wouldn't tell him everything, but at some point, she would mention that the last thing we did together was to play with the cards from his drawer. And he would realize that I had found him out and taken up the knife he had left me.

In the spring, I telephoned Mr. Horowitz and asked him about a summer internship in real estate. A couple of days later, I was called into the office of Minuit Realty, the firm that managed the Horizon buildings as well as many others. It took up a full floor in the same building as Horizon. A huge open area with many cubicles was surrounded by a number of windowed offices with glass walls separating them from the big room, commonly referred to as the "bullpen." At the opposite end from the elevators was a closed-in area which contained the mailroom, a conference and projection room, word processing equipment, a kitchen, a file room and restrooms.

Mrs. Elkan, the office manager, a trim, graying woman in a navy pants suit, seemed a bit chilly when she met me at the reception desk and brought me into her office. I understood that I was there as a favor to their major client, but this minor job couldn't be such a big imposition for what was obviously a very substantial operation. I got the answer from her first words after I sat down.

"Now, Jack, I'd like to make one thing clear. This will not be Real Estate 101. Almost everybody here is paid based upon performance. The brokers spend every minute pursuing prospects and have no time to stop and teach an intern who is only here for three months before going back to college. You'll be assembling and delivering sales materials, clipping ads and whatever scut work your asked to do. If you're a good observer and pay attention, you may learn something of how a real estate business is conducted. That will be up to you. If the job I described doesn't appeal to you, I suggest you go downstairs and tell Mr. Horowitz that you have changed your mind about working here. Feel free to repeat anything I've told you."

Since I had no preconceptions about the job, and since it sounded no more demeaning than what I had been doing for years at the store, I had no trouble in answering, "It sounds perfectly fine to me."

The chill melted immediately. "Very good, Jack. Unfortunately, I was not as forthcoming with the last candidate Mr. Horowitz sent us, and we had several uncomfortable weeks before he left. On his last day, he decided to stop for lunch before delivering contract documents for signature to a buyer about to leave town on vacation. Little mistakes can have big consequences."

The last item was my salary, which proved to be a little more than I had expected, considering I had no useful experience. Mrs. Elkan led me to a cubicle with a desk, telephone and file cabinet. "You are fair game for everybody who needs anything done. Oh, Sally. Come over, please."

A short black woman in her early 30s with a full Afro came out of a cubicle near Mrs. Elkan's office, walked to us and pulled off the biggest pair of glasses I had ever seen.

"Sally, this is Jack Stone who will be working at odd jobs this summer. Jack, Sally Morgan, my assistant, has been here twelve years and can answer most questions you'll have. Sally, assume Jack knows nothing about anything, and you'll get along just fine. If you have the time, give him the two-dollar tour."

Sally shrugged. "I don't have the time for more than fifty-cents worth, Daisy. Follow me, Jack." She led me through the bullpen to the back, into each of the rooms, occasionally identifying personnel in passing. Where her boss had been voluble, Sally was terse. "Maria's in charge of mail and packages. Joe's her assistant. Jack's a summer intern."

"Hello, Jack,"

"Hi, nice to meet you both."

"Nelson runs duplicating and supplies. He'll show you how to work the photocopiers. Jack's a summer intern."

"OK."

"Thank you."

"Elizabeth takes care of the kitchen. Jack's a summer intern."

"How ya' doin'?"

"Good, thank you."

And back to her cubicle all in less than five minutes. "You'll be helping all of them at one time or another, as well as whatever the brokers and property managers want you to do. I'll send everybody a message introducing you. Now, go to work."

I went to work and did what she had told me to do, and it all came out pretty well. People were friendly, but, generally, in too much of a hurry for more than a greeting in passing. The surprising exception was Sally. She brought her lunch from home as I did, and we often ate together at the table in the kitchen. She had graduated CCNY, but, with a weak job market and her skin color, had to settle for a secretarial position with Minuit while her husband got a master's degree. He was now teaching high school, but a child had arrived along with her promotion at Minuit, so her career path was now determined. Some day she would become an office manager somewhere; she would not be a university professor of literature.

In between talk about our favorite books, she clued me in on what was going on around me. I quickly learned the pecking order. The three partners had priority over everyone else. Brokers had priority over building management people, because making the deal was the most important result. If you screwed up, it was gone forever, while management mistakes could be patched over. Finally, loudmouths like Andy Grossman, a leasing broker, required attention above their station, preferable to getting yelled at in front of the whole bullpen.

I often proofed, duplicated and collated brochures, and would read what I was working on. I occasionally helped to carry plans and other materials to meetings and would ask the broker I was helping to explain the transaction. Sometimes, I went to look at buildings to see what the paperwork was all about. With all of that plus Sally's help I got a pretty good idea of the real estate business. I liked it. I could see a lot of money being made. It looked to be a lot better career than running a grocery store. With nothing to lose, I made a little extra effort in performing the few tasks the partners set me and was rewarded with smiles and praise when I said good-bye at the end of the summer.

XVIII

AFTER MY SUMMER OF WATCHING DEALS CLOSING and money being made, my second year at Columbia was unexciting, except for the weekly poker game in Bobo and Mouth's room. The first year's novelty of bevies of available girls had worn off, after doing its job of getting me over Faith. What finally soured me altogether was my failure to make the baseball squad in the spring. Like countless young stars before me, I was unable to hit the curve ball, which appeared at the college level, and my defensive skills were not enough to compensate.

Ma had developed something called "atrial fibrillation" that caused an irregular heartbeat. I was scared shitless at first, but the doctors put her on blood-thinning medication that stopped the palpitations and assured all three of us that it was not life-threatening. To cheer her up, Joseph persuaded her to travel to Italy with him. It would be a wonderful treat for someone who hadn't taken a vacation in twenty years. I supported him and volunteered, with more enthusiasm than I felt, to spend my spring break working in the store. Ma was moved by my sacrifice, but it wasn't like I was giving up the baseball team's Southern tour or a trip to Antigua with Bobo and Mouth. My first day, I took Luis aside and, after swearing him to secrecy, told him not to worry. I would not be making my future in the store but would encourage Joseph to let him have an interest in ownership and eventually take over when Joseph retired. From then on, I had no problem with Luis and ate Easter dinner at his house with his wife, brothers, sisters-in-law and several toddlers.

All right. I wasn't going to change "Joseph's Superette" to "Jack's Superette." What then? Real estate had looked good. They had liked me at Minuit Realty, and I might very well get a job there after college. What should I do to prepare for it? There were no courses at Columbia available to undergrads that would be helpful. Another two boring years? And maybe the people at Minuit would have forgotten me by then. Nah, go for it, Jack. I dismissed the idea of going back to Mr. Horowitz, who would, no doubt, have told me to finish college. Instead, I walked into Mrs. Elkan's office right after spring break.

Mrs. Elkan was pleased. "That's nice that you liked it here, Jack. And you were smart to come to me first. I've got the best handle on where you might fit in." She paused to think. "Ben Ullman, our new head of management, has brought in a group of buildings in the garment district. He needs a leg man to go around checking out the supers, handling complaints and so on. None of our existing employees wants the job; it will probably be a pain in the you-know-what, and Ullman is looking to hire. I don't think experience will be as important as having the right attitude; you showed us you have that. It would be a foot in the door for you. Should I talk to Ullman?"

I thanked her profusely. I hadn't had any expectations, and this job would tell me a lot about the nitty-gritty, which could be valuable later on. My interview with Ben Ullman went well. He wasn't thrilled at having to wait six weeks for me to start, but understood that I needed to finish out the college year. I offered to come in one afternoon a week on my own time before starting to get familiar with the buildings and the problems. That clinched the deal.

My interview with Ma that evening didn't go as well as the one with Ullman.

"You want to drop out of college?" She was incredulous.

"I'm not getting anything out of it. It's a waste of time and money."

"It may seem that way, but it's what you need to have the good careers, to become a doctor, lawyer, investment banker. Not just college, you need graduate school." She got up from the table and started to pace from one end of the kitchen to the other.

"Lots of people succeed in life without college. Look at Joseph." I didn't expect much from that argument, but thought I'd try it.

"So, what are you going to do, bag groceries for seventy hours a week?"

"No, I'm going to work in Real Estate. I've got a job back at Minuit."

She shook her head slowly. "Oh, you've already made up your mind without talking to me. Is that what you call growing up?"

I didn't have a good answer to that, so I fell back on the one that kids have given to their parents since our ancestor, as a young primate, decided to leave the Olduvai Gorge. "It's my life and I have to make my own decisions."

That drew a withering stare and, "Joseph, can you come here and talk some sense into the *boychik*?"

He couldn't and it was settled. She was right, of course, but right after the end of the semester I started work with a sort of promise to finish college sometime in the future.

My new job was every bit of the pain in the ass Mrs. Elkan had promised. These loft buildings were rabbit warrens of small manufacturers of clothing. The names constantly changed as one went out of business in this building and immediately reopened in that one. Air-conditioning and plumbing frequently broke down, each incident bringing a howling protest in one of a half-dozen languages. Hallways and fire exits were considered auxiliary storage spaces blocked with boxes of merchandise and an endless fleet of rolling coat racks. My job was to keep expenses down, putting off major repairs and replacements, using the cheapest contractors and hoping that the buildings wouldn't fall down until after I was no longer working on them. I had to learn on the fly how to deal with contractors and suppliers as well as tenants and supers. I didn't have much time for lunches with Sally.

I felt very good at bringing in a regular salary, although not a very substantial one. I could now pay all my personal expenses and even contribute something to the cost of rent and food at the family apartment, overcoming the protests of Ma and Joseph. It wasn't enough yet for a decent apartment of my own, since I couldn't count on my winnings from the Columbia poker game to which I was still made welcome. I was banking those winnings for a future apartment or other expenditures and still kept a few dollars in my pocket for entertainment or whatever.

One day in the fall, Mr. Ullman gave me a new assignment. A handful of people lived in the lofts they were renting in addition to conducting their businesses. Such occupancy was technically illegal, but a pull-out couch and refrigerator in a back room attracted no attention from building inspectors and could be palmed off as for occasional use only. One small loft, however, had been sublet without consent to a Delores Johnson, who was not only living there but, if rumor was correct, was conducting the business of prostitution rather than making and selling clothing. There had been complaints from neighbors, so, regretfully, since she was current in payment of pretty good rent, she had to be evicted. Ullman directed me to deliver the eviction notice in the company of Abe Wachtel, a retired policeman, sometimes referred to as "The Midnight Knocker" or just "The Knocker."

Abe had acquired that sobriquet some years before when he had been engaged to assist in vacating an old residential building so it could be demolished to clear the way for new construction. He would pound on an apartment door in the middle of the night until someone would come to answer. Then he would growl the latest offer in most alarming tones, although not making an explicit threat. The lock on the entrance to the building was repeatedly broken, allowing homeless men in to sleep in the lobby and on the stairs, which had to be used when the elevator broke down. The police were called but were slow to respond if they came at all. The holdouts brought harassment proceedings, but by the time they came up in court, the tenants had given up and accepted the buy-out offers.

Abe, now in his 60s, was over six feet tall and close to 300 pounds in weight. His face was furrowed and scarred, his hands the size of footballs and his shoulders as broad as those of an NFL lineman. Add a deep hoarse voice and I was scared of him even though we were on the same side. My job was to hand over the eviction notice and bargain for a vacate date while Abe would scowl and breathe heavily. In the cab going to the building he was as pleasant as one could wish for, called me "Jackie" and showed me pictures of his grandchildren.

When we rang the bell at the loft, the door was opened a crack, and an irritated voice said, "I said eleven-thirty, not eleven. Take a walk around the block." We were not whom she expected.

Abe pushed his way in and I followed, holding the notice.

A woman of indeterminate age wearing a loosely tied flowered bathrobe stumbled back from us, catching her balance on a table. "Who the fuck are you?" Her hair was in a tangle and she was dripping water onto the floor. We must have gotten her out of the shower.

I reached out the eviction notice. "I'm from the landlord's office, Miss Johnson. You're illegally occupying this space and must vacate. This is your eviction notice."

She took it and threw it on the floor. "Eviction?" Her voice rose, "I'm going nowhere, you cocksucker. Get out!" By then it was a full-throated scream, a rictus of anger on her face.

"We can give you some time, but you'll have to go."

"Get out," she screamed again, opened the top drawer of the table and pulled out a kitchen knife.

"I'll cut your nuts off, you little prick!" She charged me, the knife raised to stab. Her robe flew open; she was naked underneath it and her tits flopped as she charged.

I froze. Just before she reached me there was a loud bang. She stopped and turned. Abe had a gun in his hand. "Shit!" he yelled. "I shot myself." He staggered and blood came out of a hole in the seat of his pants. While the woman stood staring at Abe, I grabbed her knife hand with both of mine and twisted hard. She howled in pain and the knife fell. I picked it up before she could.

"Are you all right, Abe?" I asked.

"Fucking cunt," he yelled at the woman. "I was pulling the gun out of my pants and it went off and shot me in the ass. Hurts like a bastard."

"Should I call 911?"

"No. Let's get out of here. I've got a doctor nearby. Take the knife."

The woman looked as though she were going to attack us with her bare hands, but slumped and, realizing her robe was open, tied it. Her voice dropped. "Good, get out, you motherfuckers."

As we went through the door, I dropped a card on the floor. "Call me, Miss Johnson, if you want to discuss this calmly. Otherwise, get your ass out of here ASAP. I'll give the knife back when you move."

On the way to his doctor's office, in between cursing with pain, Abe thanked me for getting the knife away from her and made me promise to keep the incident secret. I have up to now.

I waited in the doctor's office while Abe was being attended to. Fortunately, the bullet had torn through and exited the fatty exterior missing all the muscles. When he emerged, a pain killer starting to work, he was principally annoyed that he would have to go home and miss his weekly poker game, leaving them short of players. Naturally, that caught my attention and I asked for details. The players were mostly men from the garment industry, a couple of whom were tenants in buildings I managed with an occasional policeman friend of Abe's. With some difficulty, I persuaded him to call the host to allow me to play in his place. I swore I knew what I was doing. If I could risk injury from a crazy woman with a knife I could risk losing a few dollars in a card game. On the way back to the office I stopped at my bank and withdrew three hundred dollars in cash, as no checks would be allowed.

The game was in the back room of one of our tenants, with folding chairs set up around a cutting table. They played fast with no chitchat. Cards were literally held "close to the vest." I played conservatively, folding early unless I had the goods, watching the players carefully.

I had some good cards to make up for all the times I dropped out and, when the game ended promptly at midnight, I had learned a lot and paid a mere $20 for the education. Everyone was pleasant to me and I was invited to play again the following week. The next morning, I called Abe to see how he was and to report on the game. He was pleased and we agreed to go together to the next week's game, after which I became a regular. I found I could read the other players, but Abe proved tough, because he would bet heavily with good hands, mediocre hands or outright bluffs; you never knew which. I bided my time until the night I checked a full house to him, and when he bet $50 with a straight I raised him. A shocked expression appeared on his face as he called and I raked in the chips. I was a little worried what his reaction would be, but he burst into laughter and clapped me on the back.

ALTHOUGH I WAS DOING WELL AT MINUIT, the future in management was limited, so I studied for and obtained a salesman's license. Mr. Ullman was not the hardest worker around and was only too happy for me to take over some of the leasing in the garment buildings, as long as I didn't cut into his share of the brokerage commissions. He was smart enough to recognize that he was getting credit for my good work and he got me a raise and a nice year-end bonus.

I was increasingly feeling oppressed by living with Ma and Joseph. Every time I came home late from a poker game, I feared that the closing of the front door, or a creaky board in the hall would wake them up. I had to tell Ma what I was doing out so late. She was very upset to hear I had become a regular gambler. That I was making money at it didn't help, and, although, after the initial discussion, she never brought the subject up again, I could feel her disapproval the morning after every game. I was welcome at meals, but had to let Ma know in the morning whether or not I would be home for dinner. Finally, I couldn't comfortably bring friends home—all right, make that girls. I needed to leave.

I couldn't afford much more than a closet in Staten Island, but started to look, hoping for a miracle. Then I got one. A Minuit client was planning to convert a building in Park Slope, Brooklyn, to cooperative ownership and wanted to obtain possession of apartments as tenants moved out for one reason or another (not the Knocker this time). Regulations prohibited keeping too many apartments vacant, a practice called "warehousing," and I was offered a one-bedroom apartment at a very cheap rent with the understanding that I would leave when the cooperative plan went effective and the apartment could legally be sold.

Ma and Joseph protested that I didn't have to leave, but, of course, they were delighted. Working at the store, keeping up the apartment, cooking for and otherwise taking care of Joseph was enough for Ma, maybe even already a little too much. She looked tired and had lost some weight. The day the three of us crammed into Joseph's van to go to the Atlantic Avenue antique (a euphemism for used) furniture stores for my new apartment, she had picked up a cold and was coughing the way she had years ago in Saugerties. I didn't want to spend all the little money I had on a home that I would soon be moving out of and, over Ma's protests, bought the minimum: a queen bed (in case of company), a night table, one dresser, a round kitchen table (in case of poker), six chairs to put around it, a two-seater couch, a table for the TV and a couple of lamps. To that I added the desk and TV from my old room and taped up my sports posters. I thought the old oak chairs went well with the marbled Formica table and the worn chocolate velour of the couch, although Ma shuddered when Joseph and I moved the last piece into place.

Shortly after I moved, a second miracle occurred. Every Friday, a memo was distributed describing all new sale or leasing listings the firm had received during the past week. I had, naturally, kept up with Bobby Miller, my former roommate, who was finishing his senior year at Stanford, and when I saw that Horizon Realty and Construction was selling a substantial shopping center in New Haven, it occurred to me that Bobby's father, who had other New England shopping centers, might be interested in buying it. I went in to Mr. Friedman, the senior partner, who was the listing broker, explained my connection to Harold Miller and was given permission to offer the center to him. Mr. Miller was interested and, under Mr. Friedman's direction, I prepared a package of descriptive materials, forwarded them to Mr. Miller and arranged to meet him at the center together with Horizon's on-site manager.

Mr. Miller seemed very pleased to see me and filled me in on his family. As I knew, Bobby was planning to go to the University of California business school in the fall. Mr. Miller was disappointed that Bobby wasn't coming back east, but hoped that he would join into his real estate business after business school. I didn't tell him Bobby had, after eight years, broken up with Roz and was seriously considering marriage to a girl from San Francisco. Bobby's younger brother, Danny, would be entering Amherst. Frank, the oldest brother, was working for a law firm in Chicago.

After the pleasantries, Mr. Miller became very business-like. His assistant, a Preppy looking guy in his late twenties, carried the offering materials and a clipboard, on which he made copious notes as Mr. Miller commented on what he was seeing.

"Can we get the blinking yellow light on Route 1 changed to a full red/green? There's too much backup waiting for the turn."

"The parking lots are crowded. Can we get cross parking with the movie complex next door that doesn't need all its parking during the day?"

"When does the coffee shop's lease expire? It's half empty. Maybe that's because it's dirty."

After going through the center, he got into his car and I followed him as he drove around the neighborhood, ending up at an Applebee's, where we went in for lunch. I kept my curiosity in check while we ate and made small talk. When we finished and stepped out to our cars, he shook my hand and said, "Thank you, Jack. I'll call Friedman tomorrow and make an offer." Six weeks later, the deal closed, Minuit was paid its brokerage commission and I deposited a check for more money than I had ever seen in my life.

But, before that closing, an unpleasant event occurred in my Columbia poker game. We were down to the last three hands of the night and I was sitting dead even. Not so bad, you might think, but this was the game where I expected to take home two or three hundred dollars each week except for the occasional night when I thought it politically advisable to be a loser.

I wasn't giving away anything last night, but I had lost a couple of big hands when someone hit pay dirt on his last card. This hand, seven card high/low, I had a club flush in the first five cards, with the queen high showing and the ace in the hole. Mouth showed the king and another heart and probably held two more in the hole. Artie Doran showed four beautiful low cards, and he and I were taking all three raises every round, with Mouth stupidly hanging in there with his four-flush.

We got our last cards down and Artie bet, and I raised, and Mouth called, which almost surely meant he had hit his flush, and when Artie took the second raise, I just called, and Mouth said, "Then *I'll* take the last raise." That clinched it. He must have pulled the ace of hearts on the last card and didn't have to worry if I had the ace of clubs in the hole. There was much too much money in the pot to consider folding so I tossed in the last twenty and we all picked up chips to declare: none for low, one for high, two for both.

Now, in my Thursday night "Garment Game," the players don't consider themselves gentlemen, and peeking or anything else goes that's not downright cheating. I was furious that Mouth had pulled the one card that beat me, and I forgot where I was. Artie was sitting next to me and, when I glanced down over the edge of the table into his lap, I saw his right hand close around a chip. Artie was going high! He must have a full house out of those low cards, or he wouldn't be going against my obvious flush.

"Whatcha looking at, Jack?" Mouth had noticed.

The table froze.

"What are you talking about?"

"You were looking to see how Artie was declaring."

There was nothing I could do but bluff him out. "You're full of shit, Mouth. I don't know where you got the idea from, but you can go fuck yourself."

Thank God for good-natured Bobo. "Come on, Mouth. Jack wouldn't do that. Finish the hand."

And for Artie, "Let's go boys, dee-clare."

Of course, I had to put out a chip for high and look astonished when Artie went high, and I even had to call his bet after the declaration.

Nobody said anything more about the incident, but it was unusually quiet in the elevator after the game. When the other guys hailed their cabs, I said I wanted to walk a few blocks for exercise and headed south to the subway. It wasn't to save the usual twenty-dollar cab fare to Brooklyn, but to punish myself for my stupidity. I had halfway decided to declare low on that hand even before I had seen what Artie was doing. I knew Mouth's flush had mine beat, and maybe Artie's low cards on board had paired those he had in the hole and my lousy ten low would beat him. Now, I had to hope that the event would be forgotten.

I also had a small financial problem. The check I had just written would clear—I had enough in the account to cover it as well as the checks I had mailed that morning for rent and to pay other bills. But not much more. I had gotten a little sporty lately in anticipation of what I would get when Miller closed on the shopping center. Minuit Realty paid on the fifteenth of the month, and today was only the fourth.

I didn't like doing it, but I went to Mrs. Elkan with a sob story and begged an advance. She knew about my recent coup and, after lecturing me, authorized the payment. I was a winner, Thursday night, so had plenty in reserve when Monday came around. Then Bobo called me and told me that the game was canceled that week and probably for the rest of the college year.

"Graduation is only two months away and most of us are too busy getting ready for life in the real world." He sounded as though reading from a prepared speech, which wasn't at all like easy-going Bobo.

"What busy? We've all been playing no matter what happens, even during exams." Well, their exams.

There was no answer. I didn't want to give up. "Does this have anything to do with me? Tell me the truth, Bobo. We've been friends for too long."

After another long pause he answered slowly. "OK, it does. A couple of the guys feel you're too good a player for the rest of us. I'd rather not say who."

"You mean they think I'm a hustler?" He didn't have to point out that I couldn't play at those stakes if I weren't a hustler.

"Nobody thinks you cheat. You're just too good a player and they wanted you out of the game. I said if that was the case, I wouldn't play in it anymore either. So, we closed it down. I'm sorry."

What could I say? "OK, thanks for sticking up for me."

"You're my friend, and this doesn't change that." That came out with feeling. Good old, loyal, Bobo. Of course, after he thought about it a little more, he'd realize the truth, which would change everything. Well he'd be at Harvard next year taking graduate courses in architecture and we weren't going to be seeing much of each other again anyway. I felt funny, though. When I got home that evening, I recognized the feeling as the way I had felt when Joseph had caught me smoking with Luis in the stock room. It wasn't nice to hustle guys who were ostensibly my friends—and, once caught, I couldn't deny it to myself. And these had been my only friends. The brokers at Minuit were my competitors and the clients of the firm were pigeons to be plucked just like those in the poker games. I missed the companionship of Harry Gelles and Bobby Miller.

On a more practical level, I was going to miss the fairly steady income from the game. I would have liked to find another, but had no good idea where to look. The next weekend, I took the special bus to Atlantic City to try the casinos. Starting at low stakes, I found that I had the same advantage there as in my other games, paid for my trip and hotel and pocketed a couple of hundred dollars. I planned to try the next level up at some time, but didn't like what it did to my life rhythm. I was used to walking out of a game at a fixed hour, even though a late one. I needed less sleep than most people and might be a little tired the next day, but otherwise I could function well. In the casino, the game went on forever. I started

Friday night, played until six the next morning, caught a few hours of sleep, then went back to the table for a long session Saturday night and played again Sunday. By the time I got on the bus Sunday night, I was a zombie, and was absolutely useless at my job on Monday. I couldn't do this often, unless I were to be good enough to become a full-time player with no other occupation. I wasn't ready for that yet, and doubted if I ever would be.

TO CELEBRATE MY SUCCESS in making the Horizon/Miller deal, I insisted on taking Ma and Joseph to dinner at the Four Seasons Restaurant and, well in advance, made a reservation in the famous Pool Room. Joseph looked very distinguished in a pinstriped, charcoal gray suit, off-white shirt and Nicole Miller tie. Ma wore the Chanel suit she had found at Loehmanns in the Bronx some years ago. She looked beautiful to me, but, maybe too thin. She still had the cough I had heard a couple of weeks ago.

When we were seated next to the bubbling pool, I suggested, "You should go south for a few days, Ma, and get rid of that cold. I'll treat you."

She shook her head. "Summer is coming. The warm weather will take care of it. But don't talk about me. You have to tell us all about the deal. How was Mr. Miller?"

I answered her and dropped the subject of her health until the evening ended, when I made her promise to see her doctor. The next afternoon she called me and asked me to come to their apartment that evening. She wouldn't say why. I had to work late and had a sandwich at my desk and arrived after their dinner. Although I still had a key, I rang the doorbell. Joseph opened the door, and I involuntarily stepped back when I saw he was wearing a white surgical mask.

"What the fuck?" I blurted. "Excuse me, Joseph. What's going on?"

"Come in and sit down, Jack. Your mother gonna explain everything. You put this on." He handed me a mask. I put it on and followed him into the living room where Ma was seated.

I rushed over to her, but she put her hand up. "Sit down, Jack, and don't say anything until I've finished."

I sat down and kept my mouth tightly shut. What could this be?

She began in the careful, methodical way she always used when explaining things. You couldn't rush her. "Remember when Ezra died, he had been coughing for a long time but was too cheap to see a doctor?"

"I remember." I didn't want to, but I did.

"He may have died from a sudden case of pneumonia, but he must have been coughing all that time from tuberculosis."

Stop now, please. I don't want to hear more. If you don't say it, it won't be so.

She continued, "And I started coughing, too."

My head started pounding and I was close to throwing up. I was going to lose Ma, the only really good thing in my life of meaningless victories.

The "cold" she had been coughing from the past two months was like I remembered from back then. I must have shown recognition on my face, because she cut the explanation short. "Yes, I must have had it, too. I got over it, but it's come back. I didn't want to spoil our dinner last night and didn't get the final test results until this morning, but that's what it is."

I started to get up to go to her, but she held up her hand. "Stay away from me for a few weeks. It'll be all right. I'll go into the hospital tomorrow, and they'll start the antibiotics, and I'll come home after two weeks and won't be contagious, and I should be completely cured in seven or eight months. It's not what it used to be. And I'll have to stop my blood thinner for a few weeks." She had to stop to cough. "And you have to be tested as soon as possible."

"Why? I don't have any symptoms."

"You were exposed to Ezra ten years ago and could have T.B. without symptoms. And you've been a little exposed to me. Thank God, Joseph hasn't caught it."

I couldn't believe how matter of fact she was. I was terrified. Those horrible sanatoriums and everything. I didn't know until Ma told me that they could cure it now, but a doctor I knew confirmed it. It was still a very bad thing; look what it had done to Ma already. Last night, when she had been dressed up, wearing makeup and in the flickering light from the Four Seasons pool, I couldn't see how drawn and flushed her face was. When she had hit forty last year and still looked terrific, she had joked about the gray hairs she had begun to color and the beginning traces of lines around her eyes. But now her youth was totally gone. That stingy son-of-a-bitch Ezra had done it to her. My fear turned to rage. Here was a big reason to kill Jack Armstrong. I hadn't even thought about him for months. If only I could find him.

All this went racing through my mind in the seconds I sat dumbly, shaking my head back and forth in futile denial.

"It's all right, Jakey. I'll be fine." She blew me a kiss. It was all too much, and I got up without saying anything, and fled the room. Joseph caught me at the front door and handed me a slip of paper.

"This the doctor, Jack. You call him tomorrow."

I took the slip and left. I don't know what I did with it and had to call Joseph the next morning to get the name and number. I called, had my tests and was told that I had not picked up the disease. Good news though that was, I was so focused on Ma, that I paid it little attention. She was hospitalized to begin her treatment, and, although she could have had visitors under careful conditions, she firmly barred me from coming to see her until she was discharged. In the meantime, I was limited to daily telephone calls. She tried to be cheerful, but I knew her too well to be fooled. I don't think it was just the disease that depressed her or being hospitalized. I believe she found herself back in Saugerties, working like a dog and constantly being beaten down by Ezra. My phone calls and visits from Joseph weren't enough to counteract that depression.

It didn't lift when she came home. Physically, she was better. The cough was gone as were the flushed face and the fevers. She had put a little weight back on, but seemed to have no interest in food and forced herself to eat. Joseph watched her closely and made sure she took her medication as scheduled. He told me she didn't argue about it, but if he was late in reminding her, she wouldn't take it on her own. I couldn't get more than a weak smile from her no matter what silly present I brought or what anecdote from work I told her. When given assurances that after nine months maximum she'd be completely cured, she would merely say, "We'll see," as though she didn't believe it. She insisted on going back to work at the store; it was the only activity in which she showed an interest. She had to do it.

After a few weeks, I began to get used to this new Ma. At first, I made sure to see her every day, even if only for a few minutes while she was working at the store. Getting back and forth to my apartment in Brooklyn wasn't easy, and several nights I slept on their couch to do that. She had made Joseph move into my old room until the treatments were completed. Since my being there didn't seem to make any difference to her, I gradually cut back on my visits until I only came about once a week. And I stopped tearing myself up with worry. She would be well soon and, when she saw she was, she would return to the old Ma. In the meantime, there was nothing I could do about it.

Building on the good-will arising from the Miller sale, I asked if I could work on other brokerage transactions. They gave me the worst assignment in the book: cold-calling property owners to persuade them to list their properties for sale with Minuit. If I could get an owner on the phone, I would tell him that I had a customer who was interested and ask for information. Of course, I had no such customer, but in the extremely rare instance where an owner had been considering putting his property on the market and told me to go ahead, I could always get one of the firm's contacts interested if the price was low enough. The calls themselves were a pain in the ass, but I learned some of the tricks of salesmanship and actually succeeded in getting interest from a couple of owners. At that point I was told to turn them over to the experienced brokers who took over to negotiate a listing agreement and hunt down the mythical buyer. And, lo and behold, one of the deals actually made, and I got a small bonus and a little more credit in the organization.

I was doing well at the Thursday night poker game, but missed the additional action and income I had enjoyed from the Columbia game. I decided to try Atlantic City again, but with better discipline. I played from eight until midnight Friday evening, worked out in the exercise room of the hotel and swam in the pool Saturday morning, went back to the table at noon after brunch and played until five. Then I took a walk on the Boardwalk, until the chill drove me inside and had dinner, played until midnight, had a drink in the lounge and went to bed. Sunday, I worked out, swam, checked out, leaving my suitcase in storage, played another three hours and was on the six o'clock bus and home at nine. I had no trouble getting up and to work Monday morning, after making a nice deposit in my bank.

On the bus coming back, I sat across the aisle from two attractive women in their twenties. I got into a conversation with the one nearest to me, a lively brunette with an engaging smile, while her companion slept. Linda worked for as a ticket agent at Kennedy Airport. She and her friend, Betsy, went to Atlantic City every few weeks to see a show and play blackjack. I was going to ask for her number when she disclosed that she lived in Far Rockaway, too far for a relationship. However, when she told me she would be returning to Atlantic City in three weeks, we arranged to meet at her hotel for dinner.

I wasn't happy when that evening arrived and the elevator in her hotel opened and two young ladies stepped out into the lobby. "Jack, you didn't get to meet Betsy on the bus. She's going to join us for dinner." Her eyebrows arched, pleading for forgiveness.

What could I say? I held out my hand to the intruder. "Jack Stone, Betsy. Nice to meet you." Now if you think that was an easy line to deliver, you are not in synch with the subtleties of sex in the nineties. I needed to be cheerful to show Linda I was a good sport and not angry with her. But I couldn't be enthusiastic lest she think that I was transferring my interest from her to her friend. A true master of the art could accomplish that distinction while conveying a subliminal message that he wouldn't be averse to climbing into bed with both of them. I was not at that level, although I wouldn't have rejected Betsy, a lush blonde reminiscent of Janet Hoving, my anti-Semitic first girlfriend, either alone or together with Linda.

Linda's smile told me I had accomplished my limited objective, and we had a reasonably pleasant dinner and floor-show, although I would rather have gone back to the poker table, since it was clear I wasn't going to split Linda off from Betsy. After the show, Betsy went to the ladies' room. Linda walked around the table to my chair, leaned over and gave me a brief kiss, just a bit more than a polite thank you. "That was very nice, Jack. You understand that I couldn't dump Betsy. We'll get together another time. Give me your number." We exchanged telephone numbers and, when Betsy returned, went off to our separate games.

A couple of weeks later, Linda called me. "Have you ever been to Puerto Rico?"

"No, why?"

"As part of my Christmas bonus they gave me a free trip. Would you like to come down with me?"

Considering the January weather, I would welcome the suggestion coming from anyone. And the prospect of the activities reasonably implied from her invitation made it a no-brainer. Except that Ma was starting the last month of her treatments. I couldn't leave town for three or four days until she was cleared.

"I'd love to, but could we put it off a couple of months? I've got a family problem to deal with."

She paused, then asked delicately, "It doesn't involve a wife, does it?"

I couldn't resist teasing her and responded slowly, "Well, I wouldn't want to go under false pretenses. The truth is that ...

I have never been married or engaged to be married or seriously considered marrying anybody."

She took it well. "Please, I'm not interested in your ancient history; just checking your present status. A girl can't be too careful, these days, and the lack of a groove in your ring finger doesn't prove anything."

I promised to call her within a month. Ma's interim reports had been good and I was increasingly confident she'd be OK, but you never could tell. She was coming out of her depression and was planning a vacation with Joseph and coming up with arguments why I should return to college. I was happy to be nagged. Her course of antibiotics finished in mid-February, her tests were negative and she was cleared to go back to her normal life. I was on the phone with Linda the same evening. She was owed some vacation time and agreed to a Friday to Tuesday trip over the Passover weekend. I reserved a room at the La Concha Hotel and Resort, which, of course, had a casino, and we each got our plane ticket.

An unusual April snowstorm delayed our flight and we didn't get to our hotel room until after midnight. We were both too tired for more than a friendly good night hug, but there would be plenty of time for more serious activities. I woke the next morning to see Linda stepping into a bikini bottom. She picked up the skimpy top and snapped it in my face. "What are you staring at, Sleepyhead?"

"You know Goddamn well," I answered and grabbed for her.

She stepped back. "Not now, we have to go to the beach before the sun gets too hot."

I groaned a complaint, but put on my trunks and we took our robes and sandals and went down to the beach. I got an instant erection when she took off the robe, lost it when we went into the water, and got it back in spades when I rubbed the sun tan lotion all over her back. After a half hour, we quit so as not to get burned and returned to the room. Linda took the first shower; then I rushed through mine and came back to the bedroom to find her stretched out on her bed wearing nothing but a thin gold chain around her neck.

"I think now would be a good time," she said in a matter of fact tone.

It was a good time, a very good time. What I remember most was how comfortable she was throughout the act. She did the things she liked to do, responded to what I did and made the noises she felt like without any hesitation or embarrassment. I found following her lead to be most rewarding and we finished together with great satisfaction. Afterwards, while she was in the bathroom, it occurred to me that Linda was probably so comfortable now because she had been with other men before. How brave Faith had been to bring me up to her bedroom that first time. The thought of Faith and what I had done to her brought my mood down with a bang, but then Linda emerged from the bathroom and paraded over to my bed.

"Again?" she asked in that matter of fact tone.

After we dressed and ate, we went down to the casino. I made the gesture of accompanying her to the blackjack table, although I don't like the game. You will ultimately lose if you play long enough. The best anyone can do is to play mechanically, following the odds perfectly to keep the house edge to the absolute minimum of about two tenths of a percent. In poker, you are matching your skills against those of the other players and can, like me, be a winner in the long run even after the house cut.

I sat next to Linda for fifteen or twenty minutes. She was good, knew many of the odds and was disciplined. She was ahead about thirty dollars when I excused myself and went to the poker room. We agreed to meet back at the room no later than seven.

The game was weak. Most of the players were obviously tourists happy to lose a couple of hundred dollars for the fun of it. Unfortunately, it was one of those days when bad luck overcame skill. I was down two hundred dollars at quarter to seven and didn't want to quit, but I would be back tomorrow and, in the meantime, lovely, lubricious Linda was waiting. We had a good dinner, went to the nightclub and danced for an hour, then went back to the room and proved that our successful first mating was no fluke.

I was shaken awake the next morning at ... seven thirty? Sex at this hour? What the fuck?

"Up, Jack. The bus leaves at nine and we need breakfast."

"Bus? What bus? Oh shit." In a moment of weakness, I had agreed to sign up for an all-day trip to the El Junque rain forest. "Not today, Linda. I have to go back and get even."

She shook me some more. "You can play after dinner tonight."

I groaned, "Let me go back to sleep. Maybe we can go tomorrow."

"Tomorrow we have tennis lessons. C'mon Jack. Rise and shine."

I sat up. "I'm sorry. I'm really not up for a bunch of monkeys and parrots today. Let's go for a swim, have breakfast and let me go back to the table."

Her voice chilled. "And what am I supposed to do?"

I got sloppy. I said "Play blackjack," but it sounded like "I don't give a fuck."

"I played for five hours yesterday. That's plenty for a weekend. And you played just as much poker." Then, with a touch of real concern, "You're not an addict, are you?"

All she was wearing was a pair of panties and her delightful breasts were only inches from my face. Early as it was, I was turned on again and murmured, "I'm only addicted to you." I pushed myself forward, succeeded in brushing a nipple with my lips, but, when she took a step back, I lost my balance and fell onto the floor.

She spun around and headed for the bathroom. "Do what you want, Jack. I'm going on the trip."

I climbed back into bed and pretended to go back to sleep as she banged around the room getting dressed and left for breakfast in the dining room. We had no further conversation. After she left, I fell asleep again until ten o'clock. I threw on some clothes, snatched a cup of coffee and a roll at the breakfast bar and was back at the table at ten-thirty. About one o'clock, the player sitting next to me poked me in the ribs.

"Isn't that you?" he asked.

I looked in the direction he pointed. A hotel bellman was walking around the room carrying a sign with my name on it printed in Magic Marker. When I stopped him, he told me to go to the concierge desk in the hotel. It was urgent. I stuffed my chips in my pockets and rushed back to the hotel.

The concierge asked me to identify myself and then read awkwardly from a note pad. Someone named Joseph had called the hotel. He paused. "Ruth?"

"Yes, Ruth, my mother."

"Ruth ... uh ... died this morning."

The machine called "Jack Stone" shut down. I had no thought, no feelings, no physical sensation. There was just nothingness; you could call it death. Looking back, today, I realize that Ma had given me life, figuratively as well as literally. And it was gone. But the organism doesn't easily give up. Someone must have put me in a chair and I was greedily gulping air, and the concierge was standing over me.

"Are you all right, Mr. Stone? I'm terribly sorry."

I moved my head in a circle, then flexed my fingers before speaking, "I'm OK." Thought returned. "Did he say what happened?"

"No, but the funeral will be tomorrow at noon. He should be home later today by four o'clock."

I started to work things out. First, I should cash in my chips. Then, change my ticket and get on a plane to New York. Pack, pay my bill and get to the airport. Was that everything? Oh, shit. Linda was out there in the jungle, not due back until five. I got the concierge to work on plane reservations and went back to the casino to cash in my chips. What I had won that morning was just a little more than what I had lost the day before. So what?

The concierge was apologetic when I returned. The snow storm that had delayed our flight on Friday had caused cancellation of a number of flights into New York, spilling their passengers onto succeeding flights for the next couple of days. Many colleges were ending their spring breaks, and the net result was that all flights were full the rest of Sunday and Monday morning. I'd have to get out to the airport and wait on standby. A single seat would probably open. Two was anybody's guess.

Moving fast, I could standby any flight from three o'clock on. If I waited for Linda, the best we could do was one of the few flights leaving after seven. There was no question. I had a quick conversation at the checkout desk. They would charge my credit card with the room and meals through our scheduled departure, Tuesday. I went up to the room, packed, wrote Linda an explanatory note larded with apologies, sat on the bed and let my grief and guilt roll over me in long, wrenching waves.

Although I didn't yet know how, my absence from New York must have had something to do with her death. I hadn't paid enough attention to her illness, had accepted whatever she told me about her test results and her doctors' findings, had left her care completely in Joseph's hands, had made do too often with telephone calls instead of visiting in person. Instead of being at her side to say good-bye, I had been wrapped up in my own pleasures, gambling, sex, food and drink. It was my fault, along with the fault of Ezra and of him whose real name I might never even know. I knew I couldn't sit in that room for long, though, if I were to get back in time for the funeral, so I wiped my face on the bedspread, picked up my suitcase and left.

When I called the apartment from the San Juan Airport, Joseph had not yet returned home, so I left a message that I was on my way. When he opened the door, we stood for a moment, looking at each other, as though deciding whether to fight or to embrace. Then he stepped aside and I walked through into the living room and sat down, leaning forward, my hands on my knees.

Joseph sat across from me and began without preliminaries. "Thursday, Ruth come home from the store and say she's tired. Friday morning, she don't feel so good so I make her stay home. Friday night, she cough some, says it's just a little cold, takes some Robitussin. I go sleep in your room. Saturday she still cough. I say to call the doctor. She say he's gone for the weekend; she'll call Monday if not better. I hear her Saturday night; I try but she won't go to the emergency room. You know how bad that place is. She was sleeping when I went to the store this morning. I telephone at ten; no answer, so I come home. She's gone. I call 911, but it's no use. At the hospital they say she had a hemorrhage that wouldn't stop because of the blood thinner she was back on. I should have made her go to the hospital. I shouldn't have left her alone."

He dropped his head. He was right—he should have made her go, and I should have been here, and so on and so on. All Ma's life, men failed her, even those who loved her like her father, her son and Joseph, who never intentionally did a thing to hurt her.

"And the funeral?" I asked.

He raised his head. "When she got sick last year, she join the synagogue around the corner, you know it. Didn't go often, but paid her dues and got the rabbi to promise to give her a Jewish funeral. Tuesday is the first day of Passover, so she has to be buried tomorrow. Thank God you're home or I wouldn't know what to do. That's everything."

After that we sat silently for a long time. Then one of us said something and then the other and the clock of life started ticking again. It was a short service. Luis and his wife, Millie, from the restaurant and one or two others came. The casket was closed, but I looked into it before the ceremony. It wasn't Ma, who was always in motion planning and executing, taking care of things and people, never resting, driven. This pale, motionless woman had found the peace that had always eluded Ma. Now, the only thing I could do for her was to fulfill my vow, but I was no closer to finding Jack Armstrong than I had been the day twelve years earlier when I had first heard his name.

XXI

ANDY GROSSMAN, THE ASSHOLE, was on the phone pitching some space, as usual, even though we should have left for our eleven o'clock showing ten minutes ago. I sat down in the chair next to his desk so I would be no more than a second or two behind him when he finally slammed down the phone and shot out of his chair. Otherwise, he would blame me that we were late. I wouldn't get any points staring at him. He was scribbling notes on a yellow pad—which might seem a strange activity since he was doing all the talking. But Andy needed notes so he could remember what he said to this prospective tenant about the space on this call, because he might say something totally different to another tenant on another call. Neither would be the truth, the whole truth and nothing but the truth, but, as Andy often reminded me, he wasn't under oath. I might not care for Andy's morals, but, since becoming his assistant six months ago, I had participated in big commissions he had pulled in on three deals.

To make the point that I wasn't eavesdropping, I picked up a *New York Post* from his desk. It was opened to an inside page featuring a photo of the latest bimbo stepping out with Donald Trump. I was about to read the fascinating details of her biography when a one-column headline next to the photo caught my eye. "Last Weatherman Surrenders." Jeffrey David Powell had just turned himself in to the court in Illinois. He had made a deal where he pleaded guilty to a misdemeanor for his participation in the 1969 "Days of Rage" demonstrations, paid a small fine, and that was that. Of course, I jumped at the thought he might be Jack Armstrong, but the article didn't have enough detail for me to tell.

"Move it, Jack," said Andy, halfway to the elevator, before I pulled my attention from the newspaper.

I jumped to follow him. It would have been awkward to take his newspaper with me, so I bought another one at lunchtime. That evening I pulled out my files and went looking for any mention of Powell. I found him in an old article photographed with several comrades. He looked nothing like the man in my mother's picture nor was there anything in that article or in the current newspaper article tying him to the Fort Drum bombing. The article was worth zilch. It was just a bitter reminder of my failure to fulfill my vow. I put the newspaper with all the other material back in the closet, and took off for that night's game.

Later, however, during the forty-five minutes or so it usually took me to get my misplaced hands out of my head so I could go to sleep, that newspaper article inserted itself in their place. The fucking thing bothered me, like I had missed something in the three times I had read it over. Cursing loudly, I turned on the light, retrieved the article from the closet and read it through again. Yes, it had already occurred to me that Jack Armstrong might have turned himself in for a similar deal, but when and where? I could hardly go to the FBI to ask. They would want to know who I was and why was I asking. In the unlikely event that someone was able to dig out the information and pass it on to me, he might remember the unusual request when the discovered individual turned up murdered.

I had already bothered the archivist at the *New York Times* with some cock and bull story, but the only references to Jack Armstrong she could find related to the radio hero.

Now, at four in the morning, my brain woke up. I had no idea when he might have turned himself in, but the article told me that, most likely, the "where" would be the place he committed the crime for which he was wanted. In Powell's case, that was Chicago. Jack Armstrong's bomb was set off at Fort Drum, just outside of Watertown, New York, and that's where he would have gone. Could I call the administration at Fort Drum and ask if anyone had ever been brought in for that old bombing? Chances were that the Army would be no more cooperative than the FBI. But if he had turned himself in, even if the *New York Times* didn't pick up the story, it would have been hot news for the *Watertown Herald Tribune Citizen Sun* or whatever the local rag was called. If I was lucky, it would be a weekly that had been put on microfilm. I might be able to skim the front page of all possible issues in a week while remaining completely anonymous. It was a reasonable long shot.

The next day I found that the *Watertown Daily Times* had always been a daily paper. They had put out almost 8,000 issues since the bombing. I couldn't put in two months on the long shot; I didn't bet on inside straights. What could I do to shorten the odds? Let's say I was right about the where— could I learn anything about the when? If the *Daily Times* maintained a subject matter index and the library had an updated copy someone could just look up "Fort Drum-Bombing." I called the library. Yes, they had back issues on microfilm, but no, they had no index. Next, I called the *Daily Times* and was delighted to hear that they did in fact maintain such an index. I was not so delighted, however, to be told that it was not available to the public, as it would be in a library, but that someone would search the index upon written request accompanied by a one-dollar search fee plus fifty cents per copy of each article requested. Were I to make such a request by mail, I would have to give a return address and could not remain completely anonymous, which was essential. I decided that I would have to go to Watertown and assess the possibilities when I was on the spot.

I had been considering ways to spend my new pleasingly plump bank account, thanks to Andy and a pretty good run at the poker table. I had thought of an apartment in Manhattan, although long-term financial commitments were dangerous for both brokers and hustlers. I had gone through a couple of dry spells and didn't care for the thought of seeing a nice reserve drain away in rent for a fancy apartment I would rarely use except to sleep. Now it came to me—a car would be great. Not just to go to Watertown, of course. Having the mobility of a car would cut down the negative of living in Brooklyn. The cost of cabs from the late games was a major expense, and, then, there were the Long Island beaches in the approaching summer and girls all over the place. Unfortunately, though, not in Far Rockaway. Linda had been sympathetic on my loss, when I called her, but was not interested in picking up where we left off. To clinch it, there was a garage in my apartment house with assigned slots for self-parking, and I could get Minuit Realty to give me one at a discount or maybe even for nothing.

I researched cars and ended up with a nice, clean two-year old Mazda. Without a family, I could keep the back seat down and have lots of cargo space. Regretfully, I passed up an adorable red one in favor of a less memorable black. But it still looked good to me after it easily fit into its slot in the garage.

This was going to be it. I knew it. I wasn't a kid anymore, concocting elaborate oaths while lacking the faintest idea of how to fulfill them. I started to plan scenarios and make lists of what I might need to buy and do when I found Jack Armstrong. The car was the first step. Next, a weapon, one I could be sure of without having to be an expert in its use. Knives were tricky, and pistols and rifles required knowledge and practice. I had none of the former and neither the time nor the inclination for the latter. The logical weapon appeared to be a shotgun. Although I knew no more about shotguns than I did about pistols or rifles, I was pretty sure that the spread of the pellets would forgive mistakes in aiming. I also knew, from my reading of crime novels, that most of the barrel could be sawed off so that the weapon could be easily carried without being visible. One of the paperbacks piled in my closet described the process. It was illegal to carry a sawed-off shotgun in New York, but, what the hell, it was illegal to murder your father by any means.

If there was any place where I could find plenty of shotguns, it would be in the middle of the north woods near Fort Drum where there was a large population of current and retired military personnel. They would also be cheaper than at Abercrombie and Fitch in Manhattan, and a short drive from wherever I bought one should take me to some isolated place where I could try it out.

Binoculars would be good. I'd probably have to do some observing at a distance. I found a good pair cheap in a pawn shop. I should have an instant camera so I could study carefully what I observed. The family Polaroid would do—I picked it up from Joseph. That was a mistake. It reminded me of how much Ma had loved snapping pictures on any occasion. There was a whole box of them gradually fading away in Joseph's closet. Thin surgical gloves would be good to avoid leaving fingerprints, but I could pick some up at any drugstore if needed together with hats, sunglasses and other stuff to hamper recognition.

Recognition was a major concern. There was only so much I could do about my appearance, if observed, but I needed to make sure that there would be no apparent connection between the killer and a man named either "Jack Stone" or "Jacob Gluckstein." Such a connection could be made with anyone who exhibited interest in "Jack Armstrong" or the Fort Drum bombing. I shouldn't use either name up in Watertown. By good luck, I had another identity available: one that couldn't be better for the purpose.

Back in the eighth grade, my school, like many others, had sponsored "Career Day" during which they brought in members of various trades and professions to give us some sort of idea of possible futures. It was a bunch of bullshit. All the speakers portrayed their careers as fascinating paths to fame and fortune requiring nothing more than a modicum of work and a ready smile. The real estate broker, for example, never mentioned the hundreds of cold calls trying to get a listing, the ass-kissing, wining and dining, the hours spent dragging prospective customers through properties you know they're never going to buy, or, after, miraculously, the deal closes, the throat cutting over the commission among brokers within the same company. You get the idea.

One speaker was a newspaper reporter named Jack Tomlinson, who worked for the *Village Voice*. At the end of his spiel, he passed out his business cards so that any of us who had a "hot scoop" would call him with it and share in the credit. Most of them ended up on the floor of the auditorium; I picked up a bunch, for no particular reason, and kept them in my box of memorabilia. I called the *Village Voice* and was told that Tomlinson no longer worked full time for them but they still occasionally bought articles from him. It was not likely that anyone in Watertown was going to challenge my use of his identity, but if the paper were called, he would be authenticated but not available on the premises. I couldn't do better.

I read up a bit on Fort Drum looking for a good subject for Jack Tomlinson's investigations. It had been a small facility up to World War II, since then greatly expanded. Ahah! It was a major training facility for New York National Guard units. Something in that could interest the *Village Voice*. The National Guard is composed of volunteers. How about an article on volunteers during the controversial period of the Vietnam War? That would be a subject that could easily include the bomb set off by Jack Armstrong. And I already had read a lot about the protest movement and could appear knowledgeable if necessary. Done.

I got Andy's grudging OK for a week's vacation, made a reservation at a motel near Fort Drum, stocked my car and acquired road maps. A bottle of Irish whiskey for courage, and I was ready to go. But one thing, first. On the way north, I detoured to the cemetery and stood before the temporary marker at Ma's grave. Joseph had ordered the permanent stone, which would be installed in a few months on the anniversary of her death. Jack Armstrong was the one who had put her there—his abandonment, Ezra, Ackerman Street, years of drudgery and finally the tuberculosis that killed her. The son of a bitch had caused it all and was probably still walking the earth under which she lay. But, now, maybe, it wouldn't be for long.

The drive up exhausted me. With stops for gas, food and a much-needed nap, it took a good eight hours, much longer than I had ever tried to go on my own. But I was up early the next morning, ate breakfast, and, carrying a notebook, appeared at the office of the *Watertown Times* at ten o'clock. The receptionist was most regretful that Mrs. Pettijohn, who maintained the "morgue," was out sick that day and that nobody else could run my search while I waited, but I could leave a request with the appropriate fee and my address. Or, I could come back tomorrow and maybe Elsie would be recovered from whatever it was. Since the former course of action put me right back in New York facing the same problems I had already decided to avoid, I smiled and said I would hope for Elsie's speedy recovery and return the next day.

Annoyed but not discouraged, I decided to poke around Fort Drum. Fortunately, it was an "open post" and the soldier at the gate cheerfully directed me to the information office without the slightest interest in my identity. The information office was a large room in the front portion of a long one-story building. The walls were covered with recruiting posters, photographs of groups of soldiers and old regimental flags. Several round tables waited for visitors to occupy the chairs around them and study the magazines neatly placed in racks around the room. In the back, an open door led to what appeared to be a library filled with bookshelves. The door was bracketed by formal photographs, President Clinton to the left and a much-medaled general to the right. A young woman in army fatigue uniform sat at a desk under each photograph. Clinton's desk had a sign proclaiming "Information"; the general had to settle for "Library." As I walked in, the two women raised their heads from their magazines and spoke, almost in unison. "Can I help you?"

I headed for Information and was rewarded with a big smile and a wave of the hand toward a chair in front of the desk. Could be that this hadn't been a very exciting day in the old OI (Army speak for Office of Information). A 3-D sign on her desk identified the smiler as "Sergeant Martos" just in case the chevrons on her shoulder and her name on the strip sewn over her left tit failed to adequately convey the information.

"Good morning, Sergeant. My name is Jack Tomlinson." I handed her one of my cards.

"Good morning." She studied the card for a moment, then straightened up in her chair and reached to smooth her curly, black hair. "What brings you all the way up to the Fort, sir?"

I gave her the prepared story. She followed closely and nodded her understanding at a few points. When I finished, she frowned slightly and contemplated the ceiling, giving me a good view of a smooth, creamy neck below a nicely rounded chin and a broad, full-lipped smile. "Come. I think I can find you something helpful." She got up and led me through the door between the desks. Was there an invitation in the roll of her hips? Hard to tell, under the baggy Army fatigues. At the end of rows of shelving was an area with a small table, two chairs, and several file cabinets. She pointed to one. "This contains all the back issues of *Drum Rolls*, our monthly magazine, going back to the early 60s. You can browse through them, but please put them back in order. Let me know if you need anything else."

I thanked her and got to work. The printing and binding were cheap, but most issues were pretty long, some close to 100 pages. I first pulled out some issues from 1969 and 1970, to support my story if the Sergeant happened to come back, and came upon a long article on the bomb explosion. The fence between the motor pool and a back road had been cut and the bomb exploded at 2 AM. Two vehicles were destroyed, but nobody was there to be injured. Right after the explosion, a witness saw a car, which proved to be stolen, speed toward the St. Lawrence River. Police found the car abandoned at a marina from which a motorboat had been pilfered. The boat turned up across the river in Canada, where the trail ended. For several months after, the magazine followed the fruitless search. An arrest would surely have been reported. I continued to pull the issues that followed, eagerly turning each cover page, patiently returning the discarded issues to their proper place, as ordered.

I hadn't gotten far when I heard footsteps, so I went back to the bombing article. "I'm going for coffee, Mr. Tomlinson. Would you like some?"

How nice could she be? "I'd love a black coffee. And please call me Jack."

Another lovely smile. "A doughnut with it, Jack?"

Go for it, kid. "Terrific. Jelly, if they have them. Here …" I reached for my wallet.

"No, that's OK. They don't charge us. We save magazines for them." And off she went.

I had gotten up to 1980, when my coffee and doughnut were delivered. Sergeant Martos sat down at the table with me and we made a little conversation while we ate and drank, but I must have shown my impatience, for she soon left saying, "I'd better get back to my desk. Throw your empty cup in the basket over there. Don't stay too long; we close at 4."

Well, this wasn't a social visit. I went back to my job. Frustration built with each issue inspected. Twelve in 1981, no dice. Twelve more in 1982, nope. 1983, the same. Shit, he had to have come in. I had to find him. But not in 1984 or 1985 or 1986. I slowed my pace as I approached the end. 1987, ugh. 1988, also ... YES! There it was in the table of contents for the December, 1988 issue. "1970 BOMBER ARRESTED. PLEADS GUILTY."

I eagerly turned to the article. Ralph Hill, of Waterville, Maine, had been arrested, brought before the Federal District Court in Watertown, pleaded guilty to various charges and been sentenced to six months in prison and a fine of $10,000. A picture—let me see a picture! I turned the page, and, wonderful, there was a picture of a man being handed into a snow-covered police car by two officers. But, the snow coming down blurred the details and he was wearing a mackinaw with a hood that covered most of his face and all of his hair. I so wanted it to be Jack Armstrong, but it was impossible to tell if it was.

I reread the article carefully. It didn't mention any alias. Was this man Jack Armstrong? He could be the other man Ma had met at Woodstock, the man who called himself "Terry Lee." It was puzzling that this article only mentioned one man. The witness to the getaway in 1970 had seen two.

I quickly went through the next year's issues, finding no further mention of the bombing or the bomber. Ah, but maybe there was something when he was released after serving his term, so I continued my search over the next six months. No dice. I might be no closer to the man I hunted than I had been before I had read that Jeffrey Powers had turned himself in. Or, I might only be a few hundred miles away.

I put away the magazines, dropped the coffee cup into the wastebasket, and brushed the doughnut crumbs off the table. Sergeant Martos was at her post when I came out of the stacks.

"Did you find what you were looking for?" A little cool.

"I did. You were very helpful. I really appreciate it."

I gave her my best smile, and she thawed.

"How long are you staying up here, Jack?"

It was tempting, but I didn't want to be remembered, even for a one-night stand, and so made my departure.

Ralph Hill came from Waterville, Maine. Not exactly a suburb of New York City, but he could have been living in Arizona or even Europe. Wait a minute, he may have been living there six years ago, but might not have gone back after his jail term.

Back at the motel I dialed information for Waterville. Yes, there was a Ralph Hill, and, tellingly, his number was "withheld at the customer's request." Aha! His wife got crank calls after he was arrested and changed their phone to an unlisted number. His term was only six months—he had probably come back home and was still there. Another telephone call informed me that the Waterville newspaper was called *The Morning Sentinel,* and, when I reached them I was told that they published daily (my informant was offended that I might think it was a weekly) and that back issues were kept on microfilm both at the newspaper office and the Waterville library. That was fine—unlike my previous search I knew the date of arrest and could pretty well estimate his release date, so a couple of hours at the library should get me what I needed to know.

I'd have to take another long drive to find him. Even if he had been Terry Lee, he might know where Jack Armstrong was. At least he would know his real name. Talking to him could endanger me, but this might be my only chance. And, of course, if Ralph Hill was Jack Armstrong, I'd have to be prepared to act, as I might only get one opportunity.

I looked at my road maps. Watertown to Waterville was more than four hundred miles, much of it on piddling two- and three-lane roads cutting across New York, Vermont, New Hampshire and Maine. I'd have to allow two days for the drive. If I went straight there and it took more than a day or two to find him and work out a plan, I'd go beyond the one week "vacation" I had arranged at Minuit Realty. A plan, yes, I would need a plan. I hadn't thought of one yet. It had been just find him and zappo, he would lay dead at my feet. It would take a lot of thinking, and a grueling drive wasn't the best time to think. I leashed my impatience and decided to drive back to New York and put Waterville off.

There was no hurry. I had booked the room for two nights, not knowing how long it would take me to search the infor- mation. And there was something useful I could do while I was up in the North Country.

The Yellow Pages sent me out on Route 11 to H. R. Penn's Hunting and Camping Gear, where I was delighted to find a wall covered with second-hand rifles and shotguns.

A teenager with a scraggly mini-beard sat on a stool behind the counter, eating a sandwich and watching a war movie on a small TV set. He paid no attention to me as I walked up to the counter.

"Afternoon," I said, to open the proceedings.

He sighed, put down the sandwich, took a slug from a can of beer that had been sitting next to the TV, put the can down, and turned his head just far enough to be able to see me with one eye. "Yeah?"

"I'd like to buy a second-hand shotgun."

He burped. "Burdeer?"

"Huh?" What the fuck was that?

He turned his head to look at me with both eyes. "Whatcher shootin'?"

"Oh, deer."

His face contorted with the effort to make a decision, then he came off the stool and, still looking back at the screen, sidled down the counter and took a shotgun off the wall and laid it on the counter. I came down to him, picked up the gun and pretended to look at it critically. It was what I vaguely remembered was called a "side-by-side," with two thoroughly scratched, parallel steel barrels. The wooden stock was worn and had been sloppily restained. "It's not in such good condition," I said, preparing to haggle.

"Wingmaster 870. They last forever. A hunnert' fifty."

I put it back on the counter. "A hundred twenty-five."

He looked back to check the movie again, then picked up the gun and turned to replace it.

"Oh, OK, I'll take it. And a box of shells."

He brought the gun back around and put it on the counter. "What kind?"

"Whatever's good for deer."

He reached under the counter and brought up a box, then went back under for a cleaning rod, a box of patches and cans of solvent and oil, put them next to the gun and shells, and cocked his head at me.

"Good idea," I said. "And do you have a manual or something about the gun?" I was admitting I didn't know jackshit about shotguns, but he must have realized that already.

"A manual?" Again, his face contorted. "Never seen one. But Harvey's got lots'a crap back in the office." He went to the end of the counter and through a door, leaving me all alone with the shotgun, the cash register and a shitload of valuable merchandise. A couple of minutes later he came back waving a couple of sheets of Xerox paper over his head. "Goddam, look a' this. Here ya go."

I scanned the sheets. It wasn't a manual—just a few directions on use and maintenance, but it would do. He added up the sale and then scribbled on a pad. "Name?"

He wasn't asking for ID so I gave him Tomlinson's name, paid him and walked off with the shotgun and a bag of the other stuff as the kid returned to his movie. I looked at the bill of sale. The writing was illegible; I could have been anybody.

About a mile back toward Watertown I had noticed a dirt road with a sign reading "Adirondack Park—Johnson Woods." Next to it, another sign said "Dead End—No Thru Traffic." I turned down the road, plowed snow banked on either side between thick stands of pine and hemlock surrounding occasional oaks and maples. I drove slowly in consideration of the low-slung Mazda and also so as not to miss a good stopping place. I saw a couple of wooden posts with signs on top indicating trail heads, but kept going about three miles until I reached the dead end with another trailhead and a turn-around that afforded room for two or three cars. There was nobody there at the moment, and it seemed unlikely that someone would show up to start a hike when the sun was going down.

I pulled out the gun and the directions. As instructed, I set the safety, broke open the gun, and looked down the barrels as I should have done before I bought the gun, but I was lucky. Someone had cleaned and oiled the barrels and, as best as I could tell squinting down them, there was very little pitting of the smooth bores. It should work. I loaded both barrels and walked over packed snow down the trail about a quarter-mile. I aimed at a big oak tree about fifty feet away and pulled a trigger. Nothing. What was wrong with the fucking gun? I tried the other trigger. Same thing. I peered at the instructions in the fading light and found the problem. I hadn't released the safety. For one moment I was about to drop the whole thing. This wasn't Mission Impossible; it was an impossible mission for a schmuck like me to accomplish.

But, I steadied myself, released the safety, took aim at that big tree and pulled the trigger. The blow to my shoulder knocked me on my ass. I looked up expecting to see the tree, riddled with pellets, toppling over. Nope. The trunk looked unharmed, although, when I approached it, I saw twigs on the ground underneath the far end of a broken branch. The trees further out past the branch had suffered damage. I went back to where I had been and tried again. Same result, on the other side. At least, prepared for the blow to my shoulder, I had remained standing. I would have to get closer than that to Jack Armstrong. But, a personal confrontation was called for, not just a long distance shot from an unknown assailant.

Dusk was descending and light dimming in the forest. I had no wish to get lost for the night and had accomplished my purpose. The gun would function, if I took off the safety. I returned to the trail, remembered to turn to the right, not the left, and was soon back at the car. A good thing, too, as it had already grown pretty dark. Back at the motel, I opened the package of cleaning supplies and, following the instructions, cleaned and oiled both barrels. It was a good start.

WHEN I RETURNED TO NEW YORK, Andy was happy to see me, although he'd never admit it. He had wangled the representation of a British company looking for 30,000 square feet of office space in a prime Manhattan building and promised me, in writing, a decent piece of his commission if I would help him make the deal. For the next month, I was on the job 24/7. Andy hadn't obtained enough information from the client as to their needs. He was more concerned with the size of the commission each landlord would pay and how it would be split between Minuit Realty, representing the tenant, and whichever company was the rental agent for the building.

He had already tipped me off to what had made him successful. I had once questioned why he was showing a client a partial floor in a large building when they had stated a preference for a full floor in a smaller one. "Schmuck. Don't worry about finding them what they think they want. Find out what's available and talk them into wanting it. Give them the attractive details—skip the negatives. That's how you make deals. Sometimes they're even good ones." A wolfish grin had appeared on his usually porcine face.

I red tagged a space elegantly built out, but the individual offices were so big that the client would have to repartition to fit in the number of people projected. Another was on sublease with only seven years remaining, which I would have passed up, but Andy approved. "We'll tell 'em they'll be able to get a direct lease from the landlord when the sublease expires."

"Will they?" I asked naively.

"What do you think? This is the second floor. United Communications has the third through the seventh and computer companies are taking off. If they want the space in seven years, who's the landlord going to give it to?"

I stared at him open-mouthed.

"Stick with me, Jack, and you'll be farting through silk." And he grinned again.

Fortunately, for what little conscience I had remaining, the client decided to go for a more reasonable space, and we entered the second stage—negotiating the deal. This stage allowed me to see Andy at his finest. Back and forth between the parties he went, nudging them together, threatening first one and then the other that this position or that point would break the deal and preventing any meeting where the parties might actually do so. Throughout the process, I swore my soul away backing up Andy's prevarications, and, when the lease was signed, he was so happy with it and with me, that his attempt to renegotiate our agreement was only perfunctory. While he was in that generous mood I obtained permission for another week's vacation. This would be it—I was sure.

I loaded up the car carefully, including everything I thought I might need. I would have everything in order for my cover (nice word) as a hunter. Except the license, of course. I wouldn't need one since I had no intention of going out into the woods. I would have liked to saw off the barrels of the shotgun before I left, but what if I got into an auto accident or had a flat tire and had to open the trunk? I bought the necessary hacksaw and extra blades, wrapped clothing around them, and packed them in my suitcase.

It was another long, exhausting drive, progress marked by spinning the dial of the radio as stations faded away. I cheered myself by stocking up on fudge at the Hebert Candy Mansion just before the Massachusetts Turnpike. At the first rest stop in Maine, I pulled into the parking lot, shut my eyes for a short break and slept for over an hour. It was another two-hour haul to Waterville, some of it with the heat on, some of it in the cold to stay awake. I sang a lot as loud as I could—that helped. And the thought that I might fail in my vow by falling asleep at the wheel kept me awake.

The next morning, I picked up a map of the city at the desk of the Holiday Inn and located the Library. I might have learned more in less time at the office of the *Morning Sentinel*, but I'd prefer to avoid the curious eyes of the press. I found the microfilm section and started with the issue the same day in 1987 as Hill's arrest had been reported in *Drum Rolls*. There it was—a front page article "WATERVILLE RESIDENT ARRESTED FOR BOMBING." There were a number of helpful details. Right off the bat, his address—"Ralph Hill, of 27 Preston Street, was arrested yesterday and charged with setting off a bomb at Fort Drum, Watertown, New York, in 1970." I learned that he had moved to Waterville in 1979, married the same year to Ann Reynaud, daughter of Armand and Marie Reynaud of Waterville, had two sons, and worked at Cole Fibers, the big manufacturer of paper plates and cups. Unfortunately, the picture accompanying the article was the same obscured photo I had already seen in Watertown.

A follow-up article two days later reported that he had waived extradition and pleaded guilty and been sentenced to six months in prison and fined $10,000. His wife and in-laws had refused to talk to reporters. The people at Cole Fibers had no comment. A couple of neighbors had spoken to the reporter. One said he had always been suspicious of Hill, who seemed "shifty." The other said that he was astonished, because Hill had always been a good neighbor and patriot who raised an American flag in front of his house every Memorial Day. I spent the rest of the day in a useless search forward, for news of his release from prison and backwards for news of his wedding. The former didn't make the paper and the latter produced only a short article with a picture of a happy white-clad bride with a big nose.

Sometime during his years in Waterville, Ralph Hill's picture had probably appeared in the *Morning Sentinel*, whether as a spectator at a high school baseball game, a participant in a charity fund drive or a proud father at his son's first communion. Going through seven years of issues in the hope of finding that picture with his name shown beneath it didn't appeal to me. I took out my little map and located Preston Street, a couple of blocks away from the Kennebec River. It was only a few minutes' drive from the Library. I slowed down as I came up to No. 27, but couldn't make out the name on the mailbox as I drove past. Shit! I wasn't going to turn around, pull up to the mailbox and look. Not at five-thirty in the afternoon, with people just coming home from work. There was a church on the next block and I pulled into the parking lot. It was a good spot. I could see the house clearly, two stories needing a paint job tucked into a narrow lot, a small motorcycle standing in the driveway next to the garage door. If my eyes were stronger I could have read the name on the mailbox from where I sat, but ... "You stupid, fucking idiot," I said to myself, got out of the car, opened the trunk, opened my tennis bag and removed my binoculars. There it was, "Hill," painted in black under the street number.

The hairs on the back of my neck stood up and I shivered. Even now, he might be inside that house, a block away from me. No more fantasizing, staring at the faded Polaroid, renewing my vow as though I were a knight searching for the Holy Grail, my mother's scarf fluttering at the visor of my helmet. I was going to have to face a real person who, by now, wouldn't look exactly like that photo. If he was Jack Armstrong, I would have to stop him, talk to him, and, finally, pull the triggers on my shotgun and blow him away.

First, though, I had to find out if he was the one. The dingy house and leaf-strewn yard told me whoever lived there didn't care to keep it up, but that was no help. I couldn't see whether there was a car in the garage. He might be still at work, or might have already come home. The motorcycle could be his or could belong to one of his sons, who would now be teenagers. For that matter, the former Ann Reynaud could have divorced him and sent him packing to God knows where. Well, I could give it an hour or so to see what might develop. There were a couple of other cars in the lot, and as I sat thinking, another one drove up and parked, the driver paying me no attention as he got out of the car and went into the church. I let the seat back and got myself comfortable.

About twenty minutes later, an old Ford slowed down at 27 Preston and pulled into the driveway. I hastily picked up the binoculars as the passenger door opened. A woman in a red down jacket emerged and opened the garage door. She looked like an older version of the girl in the Hill wedding picture. The car entered the garage, the woman followed, and the door came down. I never saw the driver. After a few minutes, it was obvious that they had gone into the house directly from the garage. It was frustrating. I wasn't going to sit there for hours on the chance they would go out for an evening stroll. Five minutes in case he might come out to walk a dog. That would be it. Then what? Wait until dark and peer in the window? If one of them or their sons or a neighbor saw me, all hell would break loose and I would have no control of what would happen. I decided to call it a day and come back in the morning, maybe get a good look, maybe follow him to work, maybe get a better handle on the situation.

I had a quiet dinner in the motel restaurant, and, after an early call the next morning, I was back in the church parking lot at seven o'clock, with a black coffee and a muffin to sustain me. There were plenty of other cars there for early mass. A chilly overcast obscured the dawn, and the worshippers walked quickly from their cars into the church, paying no attention to me. Number 27 was dark.

A few minutes after I arrived, lights came on in the upstairs bedrooms. At 7:45, the front door opened, and two figures emerged, shut the door and walked over to the motorcycle and took off. The binoculars made it clear that they were too young for either to be Jack Armstrong and were probably the sons referred to in the newspaper article I had read the day before. At 8:10, the garage door opened and the Ford drove out. The woman in the red jacket got out of the passenger seat, pulled down the garage door and got back into the car, which then began to back out of the driveway. I could not get a look at the driver.

I started the Mazda and brought it to the edge of the curb, waiting to see which way the Ford would turn out of the driveway. It went away from me and I pulled out to follow it down Preston Street. At Silver Street, it turned right and I followed it onto Elm. There were several cars between us, but, fortunately, none were black, so I saw it turn into the big municipal parking lot. At the far side of the lot, the Ford stopped and the woman got out and went into Delia's Beauty Salon. I drove closer to see whether the driver would get out also, but, instead he started up, crossed the lot and turned up Main Street.

I had assumed he was driving to work, but, as he continued out Main Street out of town and approached the highway, I began to worry that he might be off on a trip to God knows where. I was so frustrated that I almost sped up to bang into him. That would at least give me a chance to get a good look as we stood around waiting for the cops to come and ticket me. Before I did anything desperate, he drove under the highway, and a half-mile further on he pulled into a big lot identified by a sign saying "Waterville Transit Company." A fair number of green buses and other cars occupied the lot, so I felt pretty comfortable in driving in, but maneuvered far enough away from the Ford not to attract his attention. By the time I was parked it was too late to catch more than a glimpse of the driver as he entered the main building. He was wearing a red, wool ski cap, so I couldn't see his hair color.

Almost immediately a green bus drove into the lot and up to a platform in front of the building, where it discharged several passengers. The driver, a bulky man wearing a green uniform and a green officer's hat with a black visor, went into the building. A few minutes later another man in a similar uniform came out of the building and started up the bus. He was the same size as Ralph Hill, but I couldn't get a good enough look at his face for a positive ID, and another "flying saucer" covered his hair. He drove the bus over to the fuel pumps, put in gas, drove back to the platform, came out of the bus, looked at his watch, then lit a cigarette. Maybe—maybe not. Fuck it.

My cool analytical planning left behind in the Mazda, I walked rapidly to the platform, my eyes fixed on the ground before me, my heart pounding. As I got there, I saw a pair of well-shined black shoes, then green trousers and a green Eisenhower jacket with a nameplate saying "Hill" over a breast pocket. "Now," I told myself and lifted my eyes to his face.

He wasn't Jack Armstrong. No doubt about it. Even twenty-five years later. The eyes were too far apart behind the wire-rimmed glasses: The nose was too big; the complexion dark. I could even see black hair, mixed with gray, escaping under his hat. This was Terry Lee, as best as I could remember from the Polaroid, considering that I hadn't stared at *his* face a thousand times in the last twelve years.

"Can I help you, sir?" He sounded puzzled, but who wouldn't. I stood speechless, like some total moron. Frustration, disappointment ... relief?

"Sir? Do you want to get on the bus?"

My brain started up again. After all, I had prepared for this possibility. "Mr. Hill?"

"Yes?"

"My name is Jack Tomlinson." I fumbled a card out of my wallet.

He looked at it, frowned, and thrust the card back at me. "I don't talk to reporters. I'm sorry you had to come all the way from New York to find that out." He shot his cigarette away, turned and climbed back into the bus.

I put one foot on the lowest step and leaned in toward him. "Let me explain why I think you should talk to me. It could be very good for you." I climbed into the bus and stood next to the driver's seat. He started to get out of his seat, probably to throw me out of the bus. He looked strong enough and angry enough to do it. "Just give me a minute." I had rehearsed this line several times and sounded very sincere.

He shook his head slowly and sat back down. "All right, but make it quick. I have to start my run in ..." looking at his watch, "four minutes."

"My newspaper is planning a series on the anti-war underground movement, focusing on what's happened to various participants, how they were treated and what's been the effect on their lives. Not the ones who killed people for questionable motives, but those whose worst offenses were destruction of property. In particular we're interested in the stories of those who came in years after the war ended. Like you. People are interested in those years and what coming back was like."

"How do you know about me?"

"We've done our research and found that you pleaded guilty in 1988 to setting off a bomb at Fort Drum in 1970. You came here in 1979, got married, have two boys and have lived here since. We don't know what you did from 1970 to 1979."

"And raking this up again is going to do me good, when I'm trying to get people to forget about it? You're out of your fucking mind."

"I'm just coming to that. We've found that many members of the underground received only taps on the wrist when they came out of hiding. You and a few others were put in prison. Bill Ayers, who himself set off a number of bombs besides urging on countless more, wasn't put in prison at all and is now a college professor. Many others were given free passes. This has been raised with President Clinton. He has informally been considering pardoning people like yourself, who were disproportionately punished, but he needs more information. It can't give you back your time in prison, but you'd get back the right to vote and the ability to hope for a better job than driving a bus."

"What's wrong with driving a bus?" He had to say that, but his heart wasn't in it.

"What were you doing before, at Cole Fibers?"

"Head of sales for the Northeast. I don't know …" He reached inside his jacket and replaced his regular glasses with sunglasses. "OK. Sit up front, here. I have to start now, but we can talk quietly."

I sat down across the aisle from him and took out my little notebook.

"Here, you'll have to put that away when passengers get on." He closed the doors, started the bus and drove out to the street. "What do you want to know?"

"How did you start in the underground?"

"Like everyone else with a conscience. We were ignoring all kinds of bad things in society and pushing that fucking war. I grew up in Milwaukee and went to college at Marquette, but spent a lot of time in Ann Arbor, got involved in the Movement and dropped out in '69 after my junior year. I was with a group based in Milwaukee for most of the next year. We didn't do a lot, worked at odd jobs, ran a soup kitchen, organized study groups, passed out leaflets, picketed, that sort of thing. A couple of times I got hauled in to the station by the police, but never even got charged. Then, in the spring, a bunch of us stole a bulldozer and pulled down a statue of a soldier at a World War II memorial. It was my first recorded offense, so they gave me a suspended sentence and probation on condition that I get the Hell out of Milwaukee."

We arrived at the first bus stop. A couple of people got on, exchanged greetings with Hill and moved to seats in the rear.

He continued in a lower voice. "I moved to Chicago. The country wasn't getting any better. I met people who were into more serious action than pulling down a statue, and I learned something about making and placing bombs to cause damage but not to kill people. I was looking for a chance to do that when I met the son-of-a-bitch who ruined me. He came from upstate New York and was familiar with Fort Drum, near Watertown, and was looking for someone to go with him to set off a bomb there. Well, I thought he was a stand-up guy, so I went along with him and we did it. There wasn't a lot of damage, nobody got hurt and we got away across the St. Lawrence to Canada."

So, Jack Armstrong *was* involved in the bombing, as I thought. But how come the articles never mentioned a second person besides Hill? I was close to finding his name, but needed to be careful about it. Another stop—more passengers.

"How long were you in Canada?"

"Five years. I worked at different jobs where they didn't pay much attention to identification, although I got papers in my underground name, Terry Lee. From the comic strip, 'Terry and the Pirates?'"

"Sure. Who was your colleague?"

"Jack Armstrong, the all-American boy. From the radio character. The all-American prick, he is."

Here was my chance. "What did he do to you?"

The answer was delayed, whether through hesitancy or Hill's need to concentrate on his driving as he maneuvered the bus through a minor traffic jam to another stop where quite a few passengers got on.

"How are you, Ralph?" chirped a white-haired lady with steel-rimmed glasses, as she put her coins in the fare box.

"Just fine, Estelle," he replied curtly.

"And Ann and the boys?" I had spread my legs out over the double seat to discourage anybody from sitting next to me, but nothing could deter Estelle who loomed over me. "Excuse me, sir, I'd like to sit there," she said, and if I hadn't moved she'd have roosted on my lap.

Hill sighed. "They're fine, too. How's Henry's back?"

That triggered a lengthy disquisition on back pains and the treatment thereof, with particular attention to the short-comings of the Waterville Osteopathic Hospital. I managed to stay calm and restrain myself from throwing her off the bus at the next stop. Hill, too, seemed upset. The muscles in his face were tense and the tone of his monosyllabic reposes to Estelle was colder than Maine winters. Fortunately, she left the bus two stops later. I was afraid I would lose the important information he had been about to disclose, but he picked up on it right away.

"All right, I'll make it quick. I came back to Milwaukee in 1977 after Carter pardoned the draft dodgers. Although I didn't want to call attention to myself by applying for the pardon, by then the FBI's cases had been thrown out of court and they weren't looking for the ordinary members of the Movement except for a few who had committed serious crimes. My probation for the statue thing was over and there was nothing against me anywhere under my real name. I was able to get back into Marquette for my senior year, met my wife and a year later came to Waterville. I got a good job, had two boys and was perfectly happy until the day they came and arrested me."

"How did that happen?"

"My fucking buddy, 'Jack Armstrong,' heard that the guy in Canada who had first taken us in and gotten us papers had written a book about all the Americans he had helped and naming names. And he knew our real names. They can get you forever for destroying government property. Jack got a lawyer who made a deal with the Government that for coming in voluntarily and ratting on me he would plead guilty to a lesser charge and get a suspended sentence with no publicity, which might hurt his auto dealership."

"But why didn't they just ask you to come in voluntarily and give you the same treatment?"

"That wouldn't have been the same feather in their cap as finding me and arresting me. Besides, the bombing happened while I was still on probation for the statue thing. My lawyer told me I'd better suck it up and take it. I just got off probation for the bombing last year. If I were still on I couldn't be talking to you. So that's the story. I thought about going down to Westchester and punching his lights out, but I'd probably end up in more trouble. The best thing I can do is to try to forget it. Unless you can do something for me."

"What's this guy's name, anyway?" I asked casually.

"Jayson, Jimmy Jayson. That's the cocksucker. If you meet him, give him one in the nuts for me."

"I'll do my best. Let's finish off with some more information about your life here. Tell me about your old job and activities and what's happened to you since you got out of jail."

I didn't give a damn about any of that but wanted to carry out what I was supposedly doing. I was glad to find out my father had behaved like shit to someone besides Ma. He was a bastard in 1970 and just as bad eighteen years later. If he had turned out to be a wonderful man later, it might have weakened my resolve. This conversation had strengthened it.

I rode back to the bus depot with Hill. He was in a hurry to get to the bathroom, giving me time to get the Mazda out of the lot before he saw it with the New York license plate. I was pretty sure my alias would work. I also sensed that if he were ever to hear that Jimmy Jayson had been murdered, he would not be inclined to help in the hunt for the killer. I could barely wait to get back to the Holiday Inn and call Information. Yes, there was a James Jayson listed on Adams Road in Larchmont and a Jayson Motors on Route 1 in Mamaroneck. I had to walk out of my room and walk around for a half-hour away from telephones to keep myself from calling one or both numbers on the chance of hearing his voice. To make sure, when I came back to the Holiday Inn, I went straight to the restaurant for lunch and carefully read the story of how a bunch of Irish rebels in the 19th Century, who, through some miracle of mercy, were exiled instead of hung, became generals, judges and governors in Australia and America. I ordered a double Bushmills on the strength of that information and got over my impulse to do anything crazy or unplanned. I would hear his voice before I killed him—I'd make sure of that.

ON THE WAY BACK TO BROOKLYN, I allowed myself the frisson of excitement of briefly exiting the New England Thruway and driving past Jayson Motors, just to orient myself, of course. It looked like any Toyota dealership, new cars ranged inside of a glassed-in showroom, used cars on the north side running back to the service area in the rear. The dealership was flanked by a furniture store to the north and a 24-hour McDonald's to the south. I pulled into the McDonald's lot, drove past the Drive-Thru window, bought a Big Mac, fries and a Coke and parked in front of the restaurant with a good view of Jayson Motors.

A low fence separated the building from the McDonald's, with just enough room for vehicles coming out of the service part of the building to get to the street. Through the glass, I could see the twenty foot showroom occupying the front to a partition running back to the service area. From where I was parked, it appeared that the partition created two rooms, but the angle was too acute for me to see into them. Although I didn't hope for much, I got out of the car and went into the McDonald's. Whaddya know, the men's room was conveniently placed in the back on the north side with a small window in the entrance for ventilation. I had a perfect view of the two rooms. One was an office with a desk and filing cabinets. The other was a small conference and break room with a round table, chairs and vending machines. Nobody was in the office, but there were two men at the round table with sandwiches and coffees in front of them. The one with his back to me had thinning blonde hair.

I stumbled into a stall and sat down holding on to the paper dispenser. There he was, Jack Armstrong. My father. The man I had sworn to kill. He had been only thirty feet away, possibly close enough that I could have shot him through the two windows. Or would the glass of the second window have stopped the pellets at that distance? I pondered that question until my faculties returned to something like normal. First, I had to make totally sure that this was the right man, so I went back to the window. The two men had finished their lunch. They got up from the table, threw their trash into a wastebasket and left the room by a door at the far end. Shit! He never showed me his face in the process. But a sudden motion at the periphery of my vision made me turn my head to see him walk into the showroom. Someone must have spoken to him, for he turned in my direction, said something briefly, put on a pair of glasses, then walked out the door and got into a red Lexus with a vanity license plate reading "JJ CARS."

This time I saw his face clearly. He was the one: narrow face, closely set eyes, sharp nose, still slim. Blood did not call to blood, as I had feared. My resolution stayed firm, maybe even strengthened, as sight of the prey excites the hunter. It was enough for the day. I was tired and I needed to go home before I did something stupid.

During the week that followed, I thought through my project while leading prospective tenants around a vacant factory building in Queens, waiting for hands I had dropped out of to finish during the Thursday night game and even when I was up at Yankee Stadium during my once-a-season baseball game with Joseph. He had started taking me after he and Ma had gotten married and he was trying to overcome my hostility. At first, I went because Ma would have killed me if I had refused, but the second year it was OK between us and by the third, I was looking forward to it. He hadn't known the first thing about the game, and I got a kick about teaching him, the reverse of our usual pattern. He knew everything about the grocery business; he also taught me how to box and introduced me to the music of Bach. Teaching him the infield fly rule didn't exactly make us even, but he seemed happy to learn it.

After Ma died, I thought that we were done with the custom, but when he called to invite me, I couldn't turn him down. We had gone to dinner only two or three times since her death. They had been silent affairs, which I tried to fill with Andy Grossman stories, but there were only so many of them. I knew that, besides the store, he was giving boxing lessons at a Y and working at a soup kitchen for the homeless, but he had little to say about those activities or anything else for that matter. He said nothing about Ma and their brief time together except when we parted after the first dinner. He took my hands in between his big paws and said, "I'm so sorry, Jack, I should have done something."

It was the sound of raw misery, and when I said, "No, Joseph, you did everything you possibly could," he just shook his head slowly, dropped my hands and turned away. It was better at the game, but he mostly watched the action with a stone face and in silence, except, when Paul O'Neil was intentionally walked in the eighth inning, he smiled and said, "You once tried to explain intentional walks. When I couldn't understand you were so mad you dropped your ice cream."

After the game, we took the subway downtown, toward Brooklyn. As Joseph got off at 86th Street, he leaned over me. "Next month, the 17th, is one year. They'll put up the stone. You'll come with me?"

It was the last thing I wanted, but what could I say, except "I'll come." That decided it. That would be my deadline. I had four weeks to do it.

On the Saturday, I drove back up to Mamaroneck and walked into the showroom. As a last test of my resolve, I needed to see him up close and hear his voice.

"Can I help you, sir? I'm Mel," said an eager salesman in striped suspenders and matching bow tie, a little pad in one hand.

I was standing next to a new Camry, so I pointed to it. "I'm considering one of these."

"Very good. It's a great car. And your name, sir?" He held out his hand.

That caught me by surprise. I hadn't expected to be asked that. "Jack Tomlinson." That was all I could think of. He made a note on his pad and launched into a spiel extolling the virtues of the fucking car I had no interest in. My luck was running. He had barely started when the bathroom door opened and Jayson came out and walked toward me.

"Jimmy," said the salesman, "this is Jack Tomlinson. He's interested in a Camry. Jimmy Jayson, Jack, my boss."

"You couldn't do better," said the dead man. He flashed a grin and breezed past without stopping, without noticing how the acid gushed into my throat and choked me. Even in that brief glimpse of his face, I saw cruelty, greed, selfishness, very different from the faded Polaroid of the boy in his early twenties, standing with his arm around Ma.

Mel slapped my back, offered to get me a glass of water and, when I declined, continued his pitch. After another minute, I stopped him, took a brochure and his card, and left promising to return with my wife.

There was a telephone booth in the McDonald's lot. I called Jayson's home number. It rang six times before the answering machine picked up. Perfect. I got back in my car and found my way to the address in Larchmont on Adams Road maybe a quarter-mile east of Van Buren Road. It was a nice two-story house with a cathedral peaked roof and a stucco and wood front. A big oak spread its branches over most of the front yard and tall hedges separated the property from the neighbors on either side. The oak hid a detached garage from the street. I risked driving into the driveway and sneaking a peak into the garage. One side was empty; the other had enough furniture in it to make it clear that the owner had only one car, so I could assume there was no current Mrs. Jack Armstrong. At 11 in the morning, it was not likely that he would be leaving the dealership soon, so I quickly made a circuit of the house, finding no signs of life. The hedges that flanked the front of the house giving it privacy continued to the back yard, which ended on some woods. There was a break in the center of the tree line. When I came close I could see a narrow path going into the woods. Interesting, but I couldn't follow it in without pushing my luck too far.

I backed out of the driveway and drove back to Van Buren Road, and turned to the left, to see what else was in the neighborhood. After a couple of hundred yards, I took another perpendicular left onto Jefferson Road and drove along parallel to Adams Road. Jefferson Road was not completely residential, and I was not particularly surprised to find a restaurant about the same distance from Van Buren Road as Jayson's house was along Adams Road. The restaurant, called "Fiesole," was in what must originally have been a private house, sprawling back from the road, painted white with green shutters, screened porch and gabled roof. I followed the "Parking in the Rear" sign to a paved lot that ran behind the strip. There were a half-dozen cars parked in the lot, probably for staff as it was a little early for lunch. Behind the parking lot, guess what? Right the first time, woods with a little opening onto another narrow path. I wasn't going to check it out at midday, but the odds were that the two paths connected. I did go into the restaurant for a menu and discovered that it stayed open until ten o'clock most nights and one A.M. Friday and Saturday. I then drove the rest of the way down Jefferson, turned left onto Buchanan, left again on Adams past the empty house and right on Van Buren back to Route 1, the Thruway and home.

So far, so good. I knew what he looked like, where he worked and where he lived. I was pretty sure he lived alone. And best of all, I had a place to park my car unremarked while waiting for him to come home. Now, the decision—when to do it. First, I needed to check that path. Fortunately, my recent successes with Andy had gotten me a couple of leads of my own, not very good ones, of course, but enough so that nobody was keeping careful track of where I was. Monday afternoon, as the sky was darkening and Fiesole was setting up for the early evening diners, I pulled into the parking lot and casually let the car roll to a spot in the back where it partially obstructed the view of the opening in the woods from the back door of the restaurant. Enough daylight still leaked through the trees for me to see the bushes and branches through which I eased my way, careful not to leave any skin or fabric behind.

It took a little over a hundred yards and four minutes before it opened up into his back yard. I recognized the configuration of the rear of his house from when I had made my circuit of the property.

Figuring thirty seconds to cross the yard and get around the house and into position behind the oak tree in the front, I would have about five minutes after parking. The timing was important, because I wanted to meet him, in darkness, as he came home. I really didn't want to sit under the oak tree from six o'clock on getting more and more nervous. What if he had a late date and maybe even got lucky? Following him from the dealership into the driveway was out of the question. It would alert him with no way of telling what he might do, and, besides, the neighbors across the street might see and remember my car. I needed to know when he was leaving the dealership and heading home, and, if I could get enough of a head start, I could be there to greet him. I went back on the path to the edge of the parking lot, checked that nobody was looking, and took the course again. Two minutes and a few seconds, this time. Much better.

I drove back to the McDonald's and parked in the lot a few minutes before six. The service area in the rear of the dealership was closed, but I could see people in the sales portion of the building, and the red Lexus was still parked on the side. The place gradually emptied over the next half-hour. Jayson was the last to leave. He stopped at the front door and fiddled with something, probably setting some kind of alarm, then exited and locked the door. The alarm didn't affect my plans. I wasn't going to do anything at the dealership.

When the Lexus pulled out onto Route 1, I followed after it, letting another car in between us so he wouldn't notice me.

When he turned at the light on Van Buren and the car between us continued on Route 1, I continued on as well. Although I was pretty sure he was headed to his home, I made a U-turn at the next light, went back to Van Buren, east to Adams and past his house where I saw a light come on. If I had brought the gun with me and gone through the path to his yard instead of to the dealership, I could have done him tonight. It could have been all over. My fingers tightened on the wheel, but I took a deep breath and calmed myself. I mustn't be impatient. One night, when everything was properly prepared, I would be there, waiting and ready. I had done enough for this night.

Wednesday, at 5 o'clock I was again in the McDonald's lot. The dealership closed down as it had before, with Jayson being the last to leave. I had the Mazda started and ready to go, when the Lexus pulled out of the lot and headed *away* from Van Buren Road. I was nervous about following him when I didn't know his destination, so took the opportunity to time the trip to Fiesole. It took eighteen minutes in a fair amount of traffic. Adding that time, plus a minute to park, plus five minutes to get into position at his house gave me twenty-four minutes from the McDonald's lot to the oak tree in his front yard. Now, if I could only get fifteen minutes warning, I'd have enough time. I didn't know how I could be sure of getting that warning, but I decided to watch a few more evenings to see.

Thursday night I took a vacation from Jack Armstrong to play in my Garment Game. I tried not to think about him, but nothing would chase him out of my thoughts, and I lost as I deserved. At work, I was blowing off tenants who wanted afternoon showings, which wasn't so good either. Friday afternoon, I was back at Jayson Motors. As usual, the showroom emptied out shortly after six, but no Jayson. The red Lexus stood in its usual spot; where was its driver? Then a BMW drove up to the dealership, parked, and two men in overcoats came to the front door and pushed something at the side. It must have been a doorbell, for Jayson came from the back of the showroom, opened the door and shook hands with the two men, who then walked back to the showroom. A minute later, a black Lexus arrived, and its driver was welcomed the same way, as were two more men in the next five minutes. There was obviously some kind of meeting going on. I went into the McDonald's and peered out the restroom window into Jayson's conference room. I could hardly believe my eyes. The men were seating themselves at chairs around the round table, which was covered by a dark cloth on which were stacks of poker chips. My father was a poker player like me! Was it in the genes? I should go home. It could be hours before they finished. But something stopped me. I never was the first one to leave a game. It was bad form for a winner, and I usually won. Well, I didn't have to sit watching the whole time, chewing on a Big Mac. I drove south on Route 1 and treated myself to a steak dinner at an Outback up the road.

When I came back around 8:30, there was a pizza delivery truck parked in front of the showroom. A few minutes later, the driver came out and drove away. That meant they weren't close to quitting, so I took a nap in the Mazda. The cars were all there when I woke and I had to piss, so I went back to the McDonald's men's room. After relieving myself, I peered out the window at the game. Jayson had the biggest pile of chips in front of him. I wondered how much the chips represented and if he cheated. It would be ironic if I could somehow get into the game and clean him out. Too bad—I'd have to settle for killing him.

Around eleven, the winner of the current hand swept his chips in, looked at his watch and stood up. The others started to count their chips. Some then reached into their pockets for their wallets, took out bills, and threw them into a pile in the middle of the table, while others plucked bills from the pile. Then they all got up from the table and shook each other's hands. A couple of them slapped Jayson on the back. They all took their coats from a coatrack near the door and exited to their cars. Jayson took the remaining bills from the table and counted them. He shook his head appreciatively as he stuffed them into his wallet. He put the cards and chips into the bottom drawer of the file cabinet, then went into the showroom and came back with a large wastebasket, which he took around the table clearing off paper pizza plates, empty soda cans and napkins. He took the wastebasket back toward the service area, returned with it empty, went into the men's room, got his coat from his office, set the alarm and came out to the Lexus. Time from the end of the last hand, twenty-three minutes.

If they had the game every Friday, I now had two choices. I could drive to the dealership a little after ten to check if the game was going on, then go leisurely to wait for him in his front yard. Alternatively, I could get to the McDonald's around 10:30, point the car in the right direction, and take off the second the game ended, while Jayson was cleaning up. The former, less rushed, was probably safer, but might make me a nervous wreck if the game ran late. I decided to put off the decision until the night I was going to do it. I had to wait until next Friday to see if it was a regular game. If it wasn't, I would need another plan entirely.

I was exhausted when I got home. It wasn't that late, before midnight actually, but the week of watching, waiting, calculating, remembering had drained the energy out of me. My resolve was still strong, but my body wasn't. I slept until past noon, in between tumultuous periods of semi-wakefulness during which I fought in vain to remember where Jayson lived or where I had hidden the shotgun or some other crucial bit of information. After breakfast, I spread out my notes on the two spaces I was charged with peddling and tried to put together coherent presentations. Two hours work and it was all still a muddle, so when I discovered I had mixed up the two electricity provisions and had to tear up my spreadsheets, I threw my coat on and spent the rest of the day going from movie to movie at the local multiplex. Sunday was better; I didn't try to be brilliant, but went into the office, cleaned up the pile of mail and unanswered messages on my desk, and carefully entered the correct material in the correct places so I would have proper spreadsheets to work with during the week to come. I left them on my desk and went to the gym for a long workout and a short swim, followed up with a sushi dinner, a "Masterpiece Mystery" on Channel 13 and early bed. I didn't need to call up memories of Saugerties or Ma in her coffin anymore. I was in full pursuit of my prey and nothing would stop me.

I had an uneventful week, did my work nicely like a good baby broker and, Thursday, played a run of bad cards very quietly so as to end up, to my surprise, slightly on the plus side for my game. I left early, and got a good night's sleep. As planned, I drove to Jayson Motors at 10:30, Friday evening. The game was on. I sat in the car watching the showroom through the glass front wall. 11:00 came and then 11:30, and they were still at it. I rotated from the car to the McDonald's counter to the men's room, first carrying, then drinking, then releasing many cups of black coffee. Just after midnight, the game finally broke up. It took Jayson the same amount of time to tidy up before he left for his house and I for my apartment. That settled my question. I wasn't going to be able to stand and wait for him in his front yard. I'd have to wait at McDonald's and hope that his routine held and unusual traffic didn't slow my dash for position when the game ended. It would be the next Friday, the day before Joseph and I went to the cemetery for the unveiling of Ma's headstone.

XXIV

I DIDN'T NEED TO LOOK AT THE CALENDAR over the kitchen sink to know that this was the day. I had completed all my preparations for his poker night with a new moon rising after midnight. In the whodunits, the little mistake in the details always trips up the killer. I would make no such mistake. For example, I debated over and over whether I should put the duffel bag in the trunk, so that it wouldn't be visible to a curious policeman if I were stopped for something like a defective tail light (of course I had the car fully serviced and checked several days before) or create a temptation to a burglar. But then I'd have to open the trunk when I reached my destination, possibly attracting notice from a potential witness. I wedged it on the floor between the back seat and the back of the passenger side front seat. Would my two-year-old, black Mazda attract less attention if it were dirty or if it were recently washed? I compromised on a little dirt.

The garage in my building had assigned spaces and was unattended. It wasn't important, but I was happy that none of the other tenants were in there to see me pull out. I had taken a set of license plates from an abandoned wreck weeks earlier to substitute for mine, but decided that being caught at that hypothetical traffic stop with plates different from my registration would be a disaster. I would just have to make sure that nobody had any reason to record my numbers. With that in mind, I exited the Brooklyn-Queens Expressway at Queens Boulevard, drove over the Queensboro Bridge to Manhattan, crossed the Willis Avenue Bridge to the Bronx and, from there, drove to Westchester, avoiding all bridges with tolls and automatic cameras.

I pulled into the McDonald's at 10:30. A sprinkle of rain had started. Perfect. There wouldn't be any late strollers on his street and any dog walkers wouldn't linger. The same five cars that had come to the game the last two weeks were still parked in front of the showroom. Through the window of the McDonald's men's room, I could see that everyone was still sitting at the table, so I bought a cup of coffee and came back to the car to wait. I turned on some music to calm myself, but it didn't help. My hand shook and some coffee spilled into my lap. I must have looked as though I had pissed myself. That'll be next, I thought.

The showroom door opened and the first player came out and got into his Lincoln. Post time. I started the car, racing the motor in my haste, but the guy didn't notice. I had at least a ten maybe fifteen-minute lead while Jayson put away the cards and chips, emptied the ash trays and went to the can. It was enough time, if I didn't do anything stupid like getting into an accident or running a light when a cop was looking. North on the Post Road to the first light. Green, thank God. Now to the second. Shit, it turned red. One chimpanzee, two chimpanzee, three chimpanzee. Come on, change, twelve fucking chimpanzees. OK, it's changing. Shit, it's the left turn green. Finally. Easy, don't speed. Now the third light is red too, but I can make the turn, if that car in front of me will do it first. Move, you cocksucker, move. Now the third street on the left. Not the driveway, asshole, the street for just a quarter mile.

OK, there's the restaurant—just ease in to the back of the lot, where there's not much light. Two other cars back here but no movement—people must be in the restaurant. Not to worry, I'll be out of here well before one o'clock when it closes.

Open the duffel, put the galoshes on, oversized so my footprints in the mud would be too big to match. Get the shotgun, open the door, look around. Into the gap in the bushes, now, now, NOW! Four steps and out of sight. Grab that tree and you won't fall down.

Breathe, once, twice, three times. Christ, it's cold for April. This field jacket isn't warm enough. Now just follow the little path two hundred feet and it's his back yard, and there are no lights and no sounds. Keep going around the house and what do you know, that nice big oak is still there next to the detached garage. The lights over the garage and over the front door of the house are on. He's not home yet.

There I was, just as planned. The tall hedge hid me from his neighbor; the oak hid me from the road. There was only one problem. Whether it was the tension or the coffee at McDonald's, I had to piss. I couldn't very well ask to use the bathroom after I shot him. Wait a minute. I unzipped and watered the oak. There you go, Jack Armstrong, piss on you and your tree, both.

I had barely finished when I heard a sudden grinding noise behind me. I almost climbed the tree before I realized that it was the garage door, opening in response to his remote. A moment later came the lights of his car, as he turned into the driveway and drove into the garage. The car door opened and shut. The machinery started again, and he ducked under the garage door, walked to the front door, reached into his pocket for the key and ...

"Hello, Jack." I stepped away from the tree into the light and raised the shotgun to point at him.

"What the fuck …" He recoiled, stumbled on the welcome mat, lost his balance and fell to his hands and one knee. His glasses fell off in front of him.

"Stay just like that, Jack. Don't try to get up."

He was breathing heavily. "OK, mister, OK. Whatever you say. But you've got the wrong guy. My name is Jimmy, Jimmy Jayson. Please, don't shoot. Take anything you want."

This was almost fun. He was frightened enough to do anything I wanted. Too bad that there was only one thing I wanted from him.

"Maybe you're Jimmy now, but weren't you called Jack Armstrong for a while?"

He peered up at me. "Who are you? How do you know that?"

"Oh, I know a lot about you. Some of it you don't even know yourself."

"OK, OK. Whatever you say. Let me get up; my knee is killing me." He was less afraid now, as though the fact that there was some kind of connection between us lessened his danger.

"Move slowly. Keep the key in your right hand. Get your glasses. Hold them in your left hand. Now get up, open the door with your right hand, step inside, turn the light on and stand still." I knew I was being stupid. I should just shoot him and get out. What difference would it make whether he knew who his killer was and why? But, no, I had decided I needed to go through the whole story. And I couldn't do it outside; the oak wouldn't hide us both from the street.

He did what I'd told him and I followed him into the foyer, reached behind me and closed the door. He squinted, trying to get a good look at me.

"Wait a minute. You came into my showroom last month."

"Nevermind that. Turn off the alarm. Fast." The keypad was right above the light switch, a tiny red light blinking, probably timed for thirty seconds, forty-five at most. He turned to it and paused for a moment.

"The right number, or I'll blow your head off now."

He quickly punched in three numbers. There was a click and the red light went off.

"Very good. Now you can put your glasses on. Is that the dining room on our left?"

"Yeah."

"Take off your jacket and drop it. Good. One at a time, slowly pull out the side pockets of your pants and let everything fall on the floor."

I didn't think he was carrying a weapon, but had to make sure. "Walk slowly into the dining room and turn on the light." I followed him in. He had a nice set—a long, thin table of some dark wood with eight chairs and a matching thingamabob with a mirror over it. "Now, take the chair over there in the middle, turn it around and sit down facing the table with your hands clasped in front of you. Very good. Now we can talk."

I pulled out a chair across the table from him and sat down, resting the shotgun on the table, my right hand still close to the triggers.

The words burst out of him. "Who the fuck are you? How do you know about Jack Armstrong?"

Here it was—the moment of confrontation. "I know because I'm your son."

I don't know what I expected—maybe a burst of light, a fanfare of trumpets and tears of welcome. He just shook his head in disbelief. "No, you're not. You've made a mistake, buddy. Put that thing away and take off and we can forget this ever happened."

"It's not a mistake, Jack. Remember Woodstock?"

He shook his head. "Not really. I was stoned for most of it. So what?"

The cocksucker didn't even remember. I almost pulled the triggers right then. "You don't remember a girl named Ruth Taub?"

His face displayed the process of his thinking. A frown showed the effort to recall, then his open mouth signaled success for just a moment before another frown of concentration appeared, as he desperately searched for the right response. The final resolution was a smile welcoming a pleasant memory. "Of course, I remember Ruth. But it's been, what, twenty-five years?" And, perfectly timed, his head dropped and his face screwed up in honest disbelief. "Are you trying to tell me … you really are my son? Well, put down the stupid gun, and let me take a good look at you." He unclasped his hands and started to push himself up.

The man was a great salesman. But I wasn't buying. "Sit down, Jack."

"What?" He resumed his position. "Come on, kid. Watcha want? You need some money?"

So now I was "kid." We were getting there. "No, I don't need any money."

Neither of us said anything for the next minute. Then he started to shake like someone with a sudden chill and the words rushed out of his mouth.

"You've got to understand. I mean, what could I do? I was on the run from the police. Didn't she tell you? I ran all over Canada for five years, and, when I came back, I still had to stay under the radar for another seven or eight until things cooled down. It wasn't until I made a deal five years ago that I was really safe. I mean what could we have done? Brought a baby on the run with me? She was better off without me. Let me talk to her. She'll tell you I'm right. Come on. We can call her right now. And I do want to hear everything about you both. Yes, this is great. I always wanted a son. I have two daughters who live with my ex-wife out in California and I never see. What's your name?"

That was more like it. It was getting through to him.

"Originally, Jacob Gluckstein. But I changed it, I'm Jack, too, now Jack Stone. They call me 'Lucky Jack.' That started because 'gluck' in Yiddish is 'luck' and 'stein' is 'stone.' Kind of cute, isn't it?"

He forced a laugh. "Very good, Jack. Why don't you call me 'Jimmy,' like everybody does? 'Jack Armstrong' is dead and gone. Uh ..." He stumbled. "Uh, tell me about your mother. She was a beautiful girl, and if they hadn't been after me, I sure would have come to her. I'd love to see her again." Selling—he was still selling, trying not to look at the shotgun. Just a happy reunion, wasn't it? "How about a drink, Jack? Or I could make us some coffee?"

"Ma's dead. And I don't want any coffee."

That mobile face instantly became sad, concerned. "I'm so sorry. I would have liked to ... maybe done something for her or at least see her again ..." His voice ran down, and we sat in silence for a while. He looked at the shotgun, then at me. When he spoke, it was all business. "I don't know how you found me, but it can't have been easy. What do you want, Jack?"

"First, I want you to know what you did." This was the easy part. I told him the whole story—what I had seen for myself, what Ma had told me and what I had figured out must have happened in the few gaps. I was careful not to leave anything out, but, also, not to exaggerate. I was adding each detail to one side of a scale that held a man's life in the other.

He listened. I could tell that, because he occasionally nodded to show understanding when I was trying to explain something, and he grinned and shook his head when I told him I had become a poker hustler. Other than that, though, he didn't react to the narrative. Most of the time he looked either at me or at his clasped hands, although on one occasion when I took my hands off the gun for a moment to blow my nose, I found him glancing at a heavy Steuben glass bowl in the center of the table, so I moved it out of his reach. I wasn't too worried. Sitting with his chair turned around, he would have a lot of difficulty getting over the table at me or turning it over onto me.

I finished the story and we sat and stared at each other. This was the point at which my rehearsals had ended. What was there left to say or do except the final act? But I wasn't quite ready. "What have you got to say, Jimmy?"

He had mastered his panic, by now, and shrugged and started to open his hands but stopped when I automatically jerked the shotgun. "She must have been a fine person, Jack. And she had some very bad breaks. I'm glad she had a few good years near the end. I don't know what else you want me to say. I'm sorry that my part in her life caused her trouble, but you can't blame me for everything."

"I believe I can."

"That's not fair. Maybe I should have tried to do something, but I was just a scared kid who had gotten in over his head. Then ten, twelve years later? I figured it was too late. What was done was done. Maybe that was wrong too. I'm sorry, I really am. But killing me isn't going to change anything. You'll just put yourself out on the run, and I can tell you that's no fun. Instead, let me try to make it up to you."

As he got into his spiel, his oh so reasonable spiel, recited in his oh so sympathetic, soft-selling voice, I could feel his confidence building. Wasn't I just another customer wanting to make the deal, ready for that last little throw-in, maybe the flashy chrome wheels or a stereo sound system?

"I've never had a son, Jack. This could be wonderful for us." There it was, the clincher.

"No sale, Jimmy."

I got to my feet and raised the shotgun ... Disbelief flashed across his face, and he started to get up from the chair ... I curled my index and middle fingers around the triggers to shoot—but they wouldn't contract. No! No! The safety? ... Who was I kidding? I had taken it off when he had gotten out of the garage. He collapsed back onto the chair and took several huge gulps of air.

I brought the butt of the shotgun down on the table as hard as I could sending splinters flying all over. "You fucking son of a bitch! You no-good fucking son of a bitch! Do it, do it, you've got to do it ..."

It didn't work. I had come as close as I was going to get. I wasn't going to be able to rouse myself up even to that point again. Maybe if I could trick him into going for the gun? Forget it. I was a worthless, cowardly son of a bitch whose sworn oath was nothing but a bunch of bullshit and this piece of crap across from me was going to sleep untouched in his bed tonight. He didn't move in his chair. Why should he? There was nothing to fear from my mouth, which was the only thing going off in the room.

Now what? Turn the gun on myself? Ridiculous. For years, while I lived the life of an asshole, I'd pretended that fulfilling my infantile oath would someday redeem me. I would just go on with that life, perfect it, be the biggest asshole around, beyond redemption of any kind. Yeah, I would be my father's son.

"You're a lucky bastard, Jimmy. You came close."

"You're better off this way, Jack. You're not a killer. I wasn't one either. I set off an explosion up at Fort Drum when there was nobody around to get hurt. I've always been glad of that. You'll be glad, too. I promise you. You're luckier than you realize now, Lucky Jack." He spoke slowly, probably choosing his words carefully so I would feel better, calmer.

"That's what I get out of tonight? I get to be glad I didn't shoot someone? I get that every night."

"Well, think about it. You've found your father. You've confronted him, and he's apologized. Who knows what this might lead to? Why don't you give me the gun? You're not going to use it."

For the first time he sold too hard. I had planned for every contingency I could think of, but not for the possibility that I would find him but leave him alive. I had to improvise; handing over the shotgun couldn't be a good idea. There was no reason to trust him.

"No, Jimmy. I'll take it with me and get rid of it somewhere."

"So long as you're not going to come back with it. Right?" He forced a laugh.

I broke the shotgun open, took out the shells and put them in my pocket. "You don't have to worry. This will never happen again."

I stood up, and he did, too, very slowly. He stretched his hands in the air and slowly turned back and forth. "Oh, that feels good. I'm stiff as a board." He rotated his neck. "There, that's better. What are you going to do, now, Jack?"

"I don't know. I guess I'll start by going home. What are you going to do when I leave?"

If he thought I was going to plead with him … he could go fuck himself. Let him put the police on me. Ironic, after he spent so much of his adult life running from them. At that moment, I didn't give a shit.

He put his head to one side then shook it slowly. "Whatever I may have done twenty-five years ago, what gives you the right to assume I'm such a shit today that I would put my own son in prison? G'wan, get out of here, you self-righteous little prick. I didn't need you in my life before tonight; I can do without you just as well from now on. If I want to remember you, I can look at the wreck you made of my table."

That was it. I walked out of the dining room to the front door and out into the night.

XXV

I couldn't open my eyes. Oh, I was awake, all right. Whatever the dream had been, it had disappeared like steam on the
bathroom mirror after you open the door. But I didn't want to
look into any mirrors, real or metaphorical, because I knew I
would see the face of a coward who had broken his oath. Twice
during the night, a police siren, a noise I usually barely noticed,
yanked me out of bed and halfway into my clothes until the
sound Dopplered away. Daylight felt strong through my eyelids,
making it well past dawn, time to get up, yes, time to get dressed,
catch a cup of coffee and a muffin at the kiosk in the subway
station, yes, time to hop the train to Manhattan and Joseph's
apartment, yes, and to climb into the limo and drive north to
the cemetery where the monument company would unveil the
stone over Ma's grave. Yes, it was that time, but I couldn't very
well do all that if I couldn't open my eyes, now could I?

The telephone rang. No, the police wouldn't call first. Of
course, it would be Joseph, the human alarm clock, making
sure I was ready like he had before my college exams and other
occasions as long as I could remember. I could let it ring and
tell him later that I had gone for an early breakfast, but, knowing me as well as he did, he'd keep calling, worried that I was
in an all-nighter, losing, time forgotten. I found the bedside
telephone with my eyes still closed.

"Jack Stone," I answered.

"Good morning, Jack, this is Joseph Baccalini."

How many Josephs did he think were calling me at 8 A.M. that he needed to add his last name? Did he think I wouldn't recognize his deep, hoarse voice with its involuntary pauses when the English word didn't come right away, and he had to think of the Italian word and translate it to English?

"Good morning, Joseph. It's OK, I'm up." A white lie.

"Of course, you are. I was just checking. Have some breakfast. I'll see you at 9:30."

I couldn't remember any of the elaborate excuses I had come up with to avoid going today, and all I could say was "See you then," before I hung up.

No police, yet. It looked as though the man—I couldn't think of him as my father after so many years as a blurred image in a Polaroid—was keeping his word. Thank God for that. I still had to deal with Joseph, however. How could I face him after my failure? It didn't matter that he had no idea of what I had planned to do. He would know from my face, or voice or body language that something bad had happened and armed with sympathy and intuition wouldn't leave me alone until he extracted the whole story. That would end any chance of winning his good opinion, already a tough job while I devoted my energies to hustling poker games instead of to building a career and a family.

And my mother? I had no belief in any form of afterlife except for the essence that remained in the memories of survivors. She was not looking down from Heaven or whatever. But when the workmen pulled the cloth off the headstone, I would see the pristine, white granite stained by my betrayal.

What did I do? What we all do when we have to, whether we are called to shame, to loss or even to death. We submit. We get out of bed, shave, get dressed and go down to the subway. Haven't you done it yourself? Submission is the one constant of life for the only animal that knows it must die. Once you've submitted, all right, there you are, maybe it won't be quite as bad as you expected. I paused to lay two ties against my navy suit jacket before choosing the orange one with the blue dots. It wasn't suitable for the occasion, but Ma had given it to me. At the stand in the subway, I chose the blueberry over the corn muffin. The little tangy berries were delicious among all that sugar. Since I was ten minutes early, I stopped for a shoeshine at the store next to Joseph's building.

Joseph answered the buzzer. "Is the limo downstairs, yet? No? Then come up for a minute, I want to show you something."

He met me at the door to the apartment, looked down at my shoes and smiled. In the living room, everything was in perfect order as always. The two leather club chairs were equidistant from the couch, small piles of magazines lay in a tic-tac-toe row on the coffee table on either side of the shiny Nambe-ware ashtray that hadn't been used in years.

"What?" I asked. "I don't see anything different."

He gestured toward the window. The blinds were raised in a uniform line allowing the sun to flood the room. And then I saw it on the sill: a glass filled with wax and a small flickering candle. It was so incongruous among the reproductions of Renaissance madonnas and the photographs of Roman ruins, that it took me a moment to realize that it was a *yahrzeit* candle, a Jewish memorial lit on the anniversary of a loved one's death.

"Is it all right, that I did this?" His usual resonant voice was subdued. He was actually asking for my approval. I couldn't remember when that had last happened, if ever.

Even at that hour I knew what to say. "It's a beautiful thought, Joseph. Ma would be very pleased."

"Ruth used to light one on the anniversary of her mother's death. By the time we married, neither of us was very religious, but she never forgot that she was Jewish."

I hadn't seen much of Joseph since Ma's death, and looked at him more carefully. He looked older and a little smaller. It was hard for me to remember that I had once found his battered face menacing, now that the bumps and lumps had softened and lines and wrinkles filled the spaces between them. The eyes questioned, no longer confident as just a couple of years ago. Ma's death must have been a particularly vicious blow, since he would have assumed that, twenty years older, he would have been the first to go. I would have to be more attentive, in the future—no, he wouldn't want anything to do with me if he learned about last night. I couldn't let him find out. Just keep your mouth shut, Jack. It's not like it's going to be in the newspapers or anything. I didn't know what to say or do, but was saved by the buzz of the house phone announcing that the limo was downstairs.

Renting a limousine had been Joseph's idea. I hadn't volunteered to take my car, because I had known I was going to use it last night and felt funny about taking it back up to Westchester so soon after. Like someone would recognize it miles across the county. Stupid, yeah, but it was part of my conviction that even the minutest detail of my plan was crucial. Joseph had told me he didn't want to drive because he was afraid he'd get lost, but I knew better. He would have felt ashamed driving into the cemetery in the old van with "Joseph's Superette" and the address and telephone number on the side.

When we came out of the building, the driver was already standing by the rear door of the limo. I paused to let Joseph in first, but he shook his head.

"Wait a minute. I'll be right back." He walked across the street to the florists. A minute later he emerged with a large bouquet of red, white and yellow roses. There must have been a dozen of each. The driver opened the trunk, made room, and Joseph carefully laid the bouquet in. He straightened up, put a hand on the lid of the trunk and looked at me with a worried expression. "Is it too much, you think?"

"They're beautiful, Joseph. Just beautiful."

He took his hand off and nodded to the driver, who closed the trunk and opened the rear door. Then we all got into the car and started off.

As the limo drove through Manhattan across the Willis Avenue Bridge and onto the Bruckner Expressway, Joseph leaned forward, making sure we didn't take a wrong turn, but once we were on the Bronx River Parkway, beyond his territory, he sat back in his seat. Fearful of conversation, I stared out of the window for the next forty-five minutes, as though fascinated by the lush, green trees and the patches of yellow forsythia until the driver pulled up to the gates of the cemetery. The road to the plot took us to the bottom of a little hill where a small pick-up truck stood, picks and shovels in the back. Two workmen sat on a stone bench next to it eating sandwiches. When we got out of the limo, one of them pointed with a can of Coca-Cola to something a little way up the hill sticking out of the ground like a giant tooth, wrapped in a dirty tarpaulin. I could sense Joseph shuddering at the sight. The driver opened the trunk, and Joseph took out the bouquet and pushed it at me.

"You take it, Jack." I had to accept it or it would have fallen. Of course, Ma should think it was her thoughtful son who had brought the flowers.

"OK, Joseph. Let's go." Ten minutes and it would be over. All I had to do was hold on for ten minutes, maybe only five.

We walked up the hill. The man with the Coca-Cola followed us.

"Tell me when you want me to pull it," he asked when we reached the grave.

Joseph looked at me and I nodded. "Go ahead," he said.

The workman untied a knot and yanked off the tarpaulin. The white stone glistened as flecks of quartz in the surface of the granite caught the sun. It was so bright that I had to step closer and shade my eyes to read the inscription.

RUTH TAUB BACCALINI

1952-1993

LOVING WIFE AND MOTHER

EVER BEAUTIFUL, EVER BRAVE

Joseph had, of course, asked for my approval before ordering the stone, but I hadn't really paid attention. What difference would one inscription or another make to Mary Henderson in the grave to the right or Alexander Thal on the left? Neither was going to bring bread and salt to this newcomer to the neighborhood. I wouldn't be visiting. I wanted to remember Ma—not a piece of rock. Joseph would be the only one to come, so it was only fair for him to put what he wanted on the stone. He pointed down the hill, and the workman bundled up the tarp and walked down to the truck. I bent over and laid the bouquet at the base of the stone then turned to go back to the limo, but Joseph put his hand out to stop me.

"Wait, Jack. We should say something."

I would have begged her forgiveness for the violation of my oath, but she wouldn't hear me, wouldn't know that I walked away from the hypocritical pig that had ruined her life and put her so early into the ground beneath that beautiful, useless stone. I shrugged—whatever Joseph wanted.

He reached into the breast pocket of his jacket and pulled out his reading glasses and a piece of paper that appeared to have been folded and refolded many times. He put on the glasses and unfolded the paper.

"My dear Ruth. It's Joseph here with Jack. It seems like only a day since you left us. I'm trying to go on, like you told me to. For weeks, when I sat in the living room, each time I heard the elevator door open, I put my book down and started to get up to let you in. I've learned to keep the television on, whether or not I'm watching, so now I don't hear the elevator. In December, when they had the winter coat drive, I gave them your coats from the hall closet. I think I may be able to empty out your dresser in another month or so, and, when this summer comes, I'm finally going to buy an air-conditioner for the bedroom. I try to remember the good things we had together, the trip to Italy, the cooking school we went to, even counting up the money in the register at the store at the end of the day. And when I'm with Jack, a part of you is there, too. But I can't help it if I miss you every morning when I wake up and every night when I go to bed and all the time in between. That's the best I can do."

He fumbled as he put the paper and his glasses back in his jacket and turned his back to me. I was stunned. I had thought that their marriage was one of convenience—something to do with taking care of the store. I mean they liked each other all right, and Joseph was always kind and considerate to Ma, but I had no idea he felt so deeply. I stepped over to him and put my arm around him. I could feel him shaking. For a moment he seemed to collapse against me, but almost immediately, his muscles tightened as he drew himself up. He took the hand I had put on his shoulder, half-turned and brought it to his lips, then lowered it.

"Now you, Jack."

But I couldn't speak. Joseph's gesture of love had opened the dam I had constructed against grief, and I staggered as the built-up flood hit me. I had lived off of Ma's love all my life, and now it was gone, and how could I stand without it? Then Joseph's arms encircled me and held me up, my head against his shoulder until my sobs ended.

He let me go, and, when I shook my head, he nodded. "OK, Jack, let's go home."

We were both silent during the ride back to the city. I wanted to go back to Brooklyn and hide, but Joseph insisted that I have lunch with him. I sat at the old kitchen table, picking at the spots where the white enamel had come off, while he took the sandwiches he had prepared that morning out of the refrigerator and started the percolator. Photos, lists and notes held in place with magnets covered the refrigerator door. Most of the notes were still in Ma's handwriting. One had a heading in red, "FOR JACK'S BIRTHDAY." Below it was a list of ingredients for the birthday cake she had planned for me just before her death but had been unable to bake. She had always made a cake for me, a different one each year, even back in the days when Ezra grumbled at the cost of a special ingredient such as kumquats or mascarpone cheese.

That was Ma. No matter what she was suffering, whether enduring the drudgery of that house in Saugerties or that final illness, she always had the energy to do something special for me. And, later, for Joseph, too, like the beaver hat she called all over the city for that last Christmas. I cried again after reading the note, while Joseph, his back turned, was busy with the lunch.

As we ate, we made light conversation, giving our emotions a rest. After we had each eaten two of the brownies Joseph had baked the night before and were sipping our second cups of coffee, there was a long, silence, which was fine by me. I was just about to get up and call it a day when Joseph spoke.

"Are you all right, Jack? This was a hard day for both of us."

I couldn't find my usual smart-ass response, but answered weakly, "I guess so. I'll be all right."

Joseph leaned forward and scrunched his eyes. "You don't look all right. There's something else, no?"

I knew it! He could always read my face, even when Ma couldn't. There was no point in denying it. I would have to tell him about last night. This was the last thing I needed—to tell the full, humiliating, agonizing story while the sympathy left his voice and his face hardened. But there was no way out of it, short of getting up, walking out of this apartment, the second bedroom with my clothes still in the closet and my posters on the walls, Ma's candle guttering on the window sill, the only place in the world I could feel safe, the man across the table from me, the only person in the world I could trust. I couldn't do that. I had to tell him everything, even if it finally destroyed his faith in me that had somehow survived the wasted years since boyhood ceased to be an excuse.

I told him the whole story: what he already knew about my conception and Ma's exile, and her subjugation to Ezra, and what we hadn't known until just before the end, that Ma's tuberculosis originated in Saugerties and might have been cured if Ezra hadn't refused to spend the few dollars it would have cost to see a doctor about their chronic coughs. When Joseph heard this last, he muttered something in Italian that, if it wasn't a curse, would do perfectly well instead of one.

"Why are you telling me all this, Jack? Ezra was a bad man, but he's long dead."

"Yes, Joseph, but the man who caused all this was the man called 'Jack Armstrong,' and he's not dead." And I went on to tell Joseph of my vow.

"*Dio mio!*" And he crossed himself, which I had only seen him do at Ma's funeral. "But you can't do that Jack—murder someone. And ... your own father?" He jumped up and started to walk around the room.

"Wait, Joseph. Sit down and listen." And I told him the rest of the story, how I had found him, met him, planned everything, driven to his house, confronted him, pulled out the gun, gone into the house with him, made him sit and listen to all that he had caused—and then walked away and left him. It took a long time; I told him every detail of my failure. And more. Somehow, other incidents were mixed up in it. I told him what I did to Faith, whom he had met and liked, and the lies I told as a broker and even about taking the page from Leonard MacInnes's test. Those were all bad things to do, sins, if you would have it, but they didn't matter, because fulfilling my oath was going to wipe them all away like finding the Holy Grail would have cleansed the shield of the most sinful knight.

Not anymore.

Sometimes crying, sometimes yelling, I went on and on until I had dragged up every failure that added up to the pathetic mess I had made of my life, redemption now as irretrievable as the shotgun at the bottom of the river. Through all of my rant, I kept my eyes fixed on my empty plate, occasionally pushing a crumb around with my finger. I was sure that if I once looked at Joseph I would break down and run out the door, and it was necessary that I finish because I would never be able to do it again.

Then, it was done, like someone pulled the arm off a record in the middle of a song, like there was more of the same to come, but it just hadn't happened yet. Exhausted, I bent over the table, crossed my arms and dropped my head. Later, I remembered—that was the position insisted on by my kindergarten teacher for the fifteen-minute nap that broke up each morning's frantic activity. The kitchen was as silent as our schoolroom had been. The only sounds I could hear were the drone of the refrigerator and my own labored breathing. There was nothing more for me to say or do. Lucky Jack Stone was tapped out.

Lots of the children would fall asleep during the nap period, but I never did. After a very few minutes, I would start to feel uncomfortable and want to get up, or at least raise my head, considered a breach of discipline almost as bad as hitting a classmate. Now, however, I was in no hurry to get up, and would have been only too happy to fall asleep. No such luck. Although it seemed much longer, I'm sure it was no more than a minute or two before Joseph spoke.

"Listen to me, Jack." It was his normal voice, but I shrank like a puppy caught peeing on the rug. "You loved your mother very much, didn't you?"

Did I? It didn't seem that way, when I'd go for weeks without taking the short subway ride to come and see her. Or when

I'd tell her to mind her own business when she would tell me to get a haircut or, God forbid, go back and finish college.

I must have shaken my head or something, for Joseph's next words were, "Oh yes you did, Jack, and Ruth knew it. Whenever I said you didn't call her enough, like a good son should, she'd laugh and say 'The telephone lines go both ways,' and she'd pick up the phone and call you. And one time you said something fresh, and after you left I said you weren't properly respectful. She answered, 'You need to understand something, Joseph. For a long time, Jack had to depend on me for everything. He's just trying to break loose and be independent. He's a good son and loves and respects me as much as I could wish for.' And she came over to me and gave me a big kiss. You know why she did that?"

This time I did shake my head.

"Because my little boy didn't have the chance to grow up to be a good son, and she knew how much that hurts me. That was our Ruth. She always understood. She understood me, and she understood you, better, I think, than you understand yourself. Here, pick your head up and pay attention."

I sat up, although I couldn't look at him.

"You ever tell her you swore to kill this man?"

"No, of course not."

"What do you think she would have said if you had told her?"

"She'd have been horrified. She hated any kind of violence."

"Even against this … this Jack Armstrong, or whoever he is?

I had, of course, known Ma would have done anything she could to have stopped me, if she had known what I was going to do. But if she hadn't known until afterward, wouldn't there have been satisfaction that the person who had ruined her life, or at least a good part of it, had been punished? And by her own son?

"I don't know. She would have said I shouldn't do it. She would have been afraid what might happen to me."

Joseph got up, went to the counter, brought back the percolator and refilled our cups. "You're right about that, at least."

I hedged. "But it was his fault that she lost her whole family and then had to spend those terrible years in Saugerties, and he never lifted a finger to help her or even to find out what happened to her. After the one time she told me the story she was so bitter that she wouldn't let me even mention his name again. I had to do it—but I didn't." I dropped my head again. It was just too much. Joseph was being kind, pretending maybe it was just as well I hadn't gone through with it, but I knew better.

He sat back down at the table. "You think she would have secretly applauded you if you had killed him and gotten away with it? No, Jack, she wouldn't have. She once told me that she had come to understand how this young man, not much more than a boy, a few years older than she was, could have really believed that this anti-war thing was more important than what might happen to her. After all, he was risking jail, maybe even his own life with the bombs and everything. Some people were actually killed when that house down on Eleventh or Twelfth Street blew up."

I was amazed. "Are you saying that she forgave him?"

Joseph paused. "Well, she didn't exactly say that, but after she came to New York with you and her life got better, she pretty much stopped thinking about that man. And the idea of you becoming a murderer? I doubt if she could even imagine it."

"No? Maybe not. Or maybe she could imagine me trying and making a mess of it, so she wouldn't want me to try. Well, she was right about that. I did make a mess of it. I'll be lucky if he keeps his word and doesn't go to the police."

"Yes, you will. Let's hope he's not willing to send his own son to jail. But, you didn't make a mess of it. You stopped just in time. You never really wanted to kill him."

That was too much. "Of course, I did."

"And why?"

"I told you all about it. Because of what he did to Ma."

"And you thought you would avenge that?"

"Yes, damn it! That's what I've been telling you."

He shook his head slowly. "No Jack, you don't understand yourself. I know about revenge killings. Where I grew up in Sicily, they were common. I knew a family that was almost wiped out by revenge. The father and one son were killed by another family. The oldest son went after the murderers, kill two of them, but they catch and hang him. The youngest brother, my friend, was eleven years old, when I move to New York. So young, every day he do something to prepare to go kill the remaining murderers. He study their movements, learned how to use weapons, practiced stalking at night. I'm sure he tried as soon as he was big enough. He was an avenger. You did nothing for years after you swore that oath. It wasn't until Ruth died that you started to do something. No, it wasn't a revenge killing you were attempting."

I couldn't believe what he was saying. "What was it, then?"

"Jack, Jack you should learn to understand yourself. Like I said, you always loved Ruth. When you were a little boy and saw how hard her life was, you were too small to help or do anything to Ezra. Then he died, so you couldn't ever do anything to him, but there was someone named Jack Armstrong to blame. How old were you then?"

"Twelve."

"OK, old enough to feel guilty about never having done anything to stop Ezra. Maybe, too, you thought that you being born is what caused her troubles."

This was ridiculous. "When did you become a psychiatrist, Joseph, or should I call you Dr. Baccalini?"

The wisecrack didn't faze him a bit. "Me? I'm just an old fighter and storekeeper. But, Ruth taught me how to think about people. You figure that killing this man someday would make up for all the things you felt guilty about. To a twelve-year-old, swearing you were going to do it was as good as actually doing it. That proved your love. *Capisce?*"

He was confusing me. It was like having done it would have been a bad thing, but swearing to do it had been a good thing. But, he hadn't thrown me out of the house. Let him finish. "Go ahead."

"Then you come to New York. You were getting to be old enough to help, but she was so strong and independent she didn't need your help. She wanted you to do well in school; that would be enough. You worked hard and did well, and that was fine; you didn't need to think about killing someone. And then we got together, and you were such a loving son that you were happy for her and not jealous. Going out to hunt this man, wasn't on your mind. You were making your own life, and, if it wasn't exactly what your mother wanted, well that's what kids do.

"But then she got sick, and you found out her illness was from those bad old days. The whole thing came back to you, and you couldn't do any more about it than when you were a little boy. The boy's oath came back into your head. And when ... she left ..." His voice broke momentarily, but quickly resumed, quiet but relentless, "it was too late for anybody to do anything about it. All I could do was order that piece of stone. And light a candle once a year. And, just possibly, talk some sense into the head of the son she loved more than anything in the world. What you can do for our Ruth, is to be thankful you never killed anyone, forget that twelve-year-old's oath and go make the good life like she wanted you."

I felt the net of guilt and shame about me start to untangle as he spoke, and when he finished I knew I could loosen the last few knots myself. I ventured to look at him for the first time since he had begun. He was sitting up straight, his arms crossed over his chest, his head thrust in front of him, his eyes narrowed and fixed on me. It was the old gangster's stare that had frightened me from the beginning. It didn't frighten me anymore. It was just his way of concentrating.

"I'll try," was all I could respond, and I put my hands on the table and slowly pushed myself up.

Joseph smiled, and the gangster became my battered old stepfather. "Good, Jack, I need a nap myself."

He walked me to the front door and we hugged briefly, as usual. As I pulled the door open, he asked, "Do you plan to go up and see your father again, Jack?"

"No," I answered. "My father is right here."

— THE END —

BOB BACHNER is a graduate of Harvard College and Harvard Law School. He practices real estate law in New York City where he lives with his wife, Barbara Bachner, a multi-media artist. His daughter, Suzanne Bachner, is a playwright and director. *Killing Jack Armstrong* is his third novel. It was a finalist in the 2020-2021 Faulkner/Wisdom Competition as was *Last Clear Chance* in 2015. Bob's stories have appeared in several magazines and two one-act plays have been produced.

Made in the USA
Columbia, SC
27 January 2022

54445554R00162